PRINCESS

HOLLY S ROBERTS

WICKED STORY TELLING

CONTENTS

THRILLERS BY HOLLY

Morgan Family Thrillers
Rabid
Long Pig
Willow
Carter Family Shark Thrillers
Breach
Churn
Depth
Detective Eve Bennet Crime Thrillers
Only Girl Alive
Lost Little Angels
Pray For Her
Marinah and the Apocalypse
Shadow
Warrior
Beast

Queen
Princess

PROLOGUE

Marinah

MY HEART RACED AND sweat dampened my skin as I tried to get my breathing under control. The hellhounds came from all directions. I blew the whistle that should have kept them back, but it made no sound in my overly sensitive ears.

Protect the child! rang inside my head louder than a fire alarm.

The baby. Mine and King's baby.

I heard his yell too: "Marinah, protect the baby!"

Where was King? I didn't see him.

A hellhound rose up on its hind legs and raked its claws down the front of my body. I'd never seen one attack this way. They normally used their razor-sharp teeth followed by their claws to hold you in place as they savaged you.

Hellhounds were deceiving. Their monstrous form looked like something straight from hell. They ran on four appendaged legs with wicked, curved claws at the end of each foot. Their faces looked doglike with giant, sharp teeth made for tearing. Their bodies were covered in a gray, leathered skin, and due to the lack of sex organs, it was impossible to tell a male from a female. But we knew they weren't hellhounds. They were human dead, bioengineered, accidentally or intentionally, through the use of genetically modified proteins found in formaldehyde. They killed everything that crossed their path, or at least tried to.

The ramifications of hellhounds had reverberated around the world. Their existence almost ended humanity. There were still so many damn unanswered questions. Why did electromagnetic pulses signal the rise of hellhounds, and why did electronics attract them? Why was there a small hint of intelligence in their beady eyes? Were they zombies or something else entirely? We didn't have these answers, but we needed them.

I screamed when a hellhound bit my arm then went for my stomach. Its hot, putrid breath puffed into my nostrils. What the hell was happening?

Where was Ms. Beast, my Shadow Warrior form? She was a bigger monster than any hellhound. She always took over when I called her, but I couldn't feel her inside me. I couldn't feel my nova form either. They deserted me. I felt like the old Marinah with no power.

The baby.

That's all that mattered. I had to protect him no matter the cost. Was he old enough to deliver safely? The gestation for Shadow Warrior babies was three months shorter than for humans, but that was when the mother was human and the father a warrior. I was the first shifting female in centuries. I mated with King, the leader of the Shadow Warriors. No, that wasn't right. I was their leader now.

King and I were having a baby.

I fell on my knees and more hellhounds attacked. They grabbed my shoulders and arms, their bites hitting bone. My hands went to my stomach, trying to protect the life within, but there was nothing I could do.

I screamed but no sound broke from my throat. No pain. There should be pain as they ripped my stomach open. Warmth spread through my body, and a voice I had never heard before sounded in my head. "It's okay, everything will be okay."

That was a lie. Nothing was okay.

CHAPTER ONE

Marinah

"IF YOU WAKE HER, I will cut off your head and place it on a pike directly outside this door," King whispered angrily, his voice a low growl that didn't conceal his irritation in the least. The dim light from the hallway barely illuminated his sharp, brooding features, but I could picture the murderous glint in his eyes.

"That woman is driving me insane, and she insists on speaking to Marinah," Missy whispered back, her words laced with the same frustration.

I groaned, snatched the nearest pillow, a thick, overstuffed thing that smelled faintly of lavender and King, and hurled it toward the sound of his voice.

The pillow hit with a satisfying thump against his back.

"I'm awake," I grumbled, my voice scratchy from sleep. And the nightmare.

My throat felt raw from screaming, but obviously I hadn't screamed, or King would have woken me. The nightmares started when the baby began moving in my stomach. The dreams didn't occur every night, but they were growing in intensity. The one I'd just had was the first time the hellhounds took me down and got to the baby. The rest of the dream, no King, no Ms. Beast, and no Nova, stayed the same. Too bad I couldn't figure out I was in a dream when it was happening.

King backed away from the door and pulled it open fully with a huff of pure exasperation. "Where's my sword?" he bellowed, his voice echoing down the hall. "Beck be damned, I will kill him too."

I pushed myself up onto my elbows, already regretting it as my lower back throbbed in protest like I had battled the hellhounds. "You will be nice to Missy," I snapped, trying to keep my voice level despite the deep-seated irritation rolling through me. "That woman is driving us all insane."

Callie, my cat, jumped onto the bed and purred as I rubbed her back. If King kept bellowing and wouldn't comfort me, she would. Unlike King, cats were simple creatures. Yes, Callie was spoiled and particular about giving affection, but she was calm when I needed it.

As for Missy's knock on our door to complain about our guest, I didn't even have to say the woman's name. Everyone on the island knew who was causing endless trouble.

Maylin, Nokita's mate, abandoned ship after six weeks. She fled to the farthest part of the island just to get away from the wicked witch of the west. Poor Missy, who currently stood at my door looking utterly fed up, was pregnant and due around the same time I was. She looked about one sleepless night away from making her own escape plan.

"I'm sorry I woke you," Missy said, the words entirely void of any real remorse.

I yawned and rubbed my face. "What does she want this time?"

"To drive us all mad." Missy's hands pressed against her lower back as she shifted uncomfortably. "You need to do something, anything, or a whole lot of people are going to start following Maylin's example."

I sighed, letting my head fall back against the pillow. "Give me twenty minutes, and I will put a stop to this madness."

Missy turned on her heel and waddled away, her heavy stomps letting us know where we stood. I scowled, envious of how much smaller her belly was compared to mine.

King wasted no time slamming the door behind her, his fingers flexing at his sides. "I can handle this for you," he said, his voice a dangerous purr, his eyes burning with a promise of violence.

I lifted my arms. "Come here."

He needed no other encouragement. With a swift movement, he planted a knee on the mattress and scooped me into his arms, rolling onto his back so that I was cradled against him, my swollen belly pointing upward, his warmth wrapping around me like a shield.

Callie gave a short howl of disgruntlement and hopped off the bed.

"How is our princess doing this morning?" King asked, his breath ruffling my hair as he exhaled softly.

I snorted, shifting uncomfortably. "Our *prince* is stepping on my bladder with one foot and kicking a kidney with the other."

We'd been arguing over "our" men versus "my" men for months when it came to the guard, and I'd finally conceded to "my." Now, a new debate had taken its place: prince versus princess. The argument had become its own kind of game, a small piece of happiness in the middle of a post-apocalyptic world's insanity.

And right now, I needed all the happiness I could get.

"I have no problem carrying you to the bathroom to help with at least one of those issues." King's smile was gentle, the kind that almost made me forget he was a Shadow Warrior capable of taking a man's head off with one bite. He fanned my hair from my face with a soft brush of his fingers.

I narrowed my eyes at him. "You will only carry me to the toilet over my very pregnant dead body," I challenged.

"Your wish is my command."

The words dripped with amusement, but I could hear the patience beneath them. He stepped softly around me, as if he was handling an explosive that might detonate at any second. I had half a mind to mimic him in a high-pitched, whiny voice, just to point out how he was pacifying me like an overly hormonal Shadow Warrior ready to claw his eyes out. But I bit back the urge to snap at him. He was doing everything in his power to keep me safe and comfortable, even if it meant indulging my moods.

I let out a slow breath. "I will, however, allow you to rest me on my feet so I don't have to do the undignified climb from the bed."

He was up in an instant, moving with that infuriating ease, and set me firmly on the floor. The moment my weight settled, I let out a quiet groan. Everything ached. Everything was swollen. Pregnancy was a complete scam created by men. No woman would ever dream of this torture.

I shuffled toward the closet, adjusting my balance to what seemed like twenty extra pounds in my belly since I fell asleep the night before. Reaching in, I pulled out some clothes. The pants had an expandable band in the front, and the shirt, tight but stretchy, would hug my frame without suffocating me. Each day was a mess of meetings to handle the problems of the citadel, our so-called home away from home. But no matter how busy or "fat" I got, I still insisted on training with my weapons.

That meant I needed clothes that hugged my expanding belly.

"I'll wait for you," King said, his tone far too casual.

I stilled, eyeing him suspiciously.

King had given the word "hover" an entirely new, borderline stalker definition. Usually, I didn't mind. But the larger I became, the touchier I got. I forced the brightest smile I could manage. If I'd been in beast form, my sharp teeth would have shone. Without a word, I shut the bathroom door in his face.

Relief came the moment I sat down, the pressure on my bladder finally easing. Whoever said pregnancy was fun deserved to be locked away in a mental asylum.

My hormones were a wreck, my belly stretched so far it looked like it was about to pop, and my feet, oh, my poor feet, were so swollen that I could barely squeeze them into shoes. Not that it mattered, because I couldn't bend over to lace my Doc Martens anyway. My stomach had taken over all visibility of my toes weeks ago.

And the heartburn, which was currently sitting in my chest like I'd swallowed a live coal, was a constant companion. Oh, and I couldn't possibly forget the gas, that lovely addition to the mix in a list of bullshit that just kept growing as big as my stomach.

I exhaled slowly, trying to remove the unproductive thoughts from my mind. My reflection showed in the mirror. My hair, which had been cut short when we broke into the Federation stronghold, had grown several inches since then. Not that it helped. The dark strands stuck up at angles that defied both gravity and decency. I reached up, half-heartedly smoothing it down even though it was a lost cause.

Pregnancy glow? Please. The only thing glowing about me was the fire in my gut from whatever the hell I'd eaten last night.

I washed my face, letting the cool water chase away the last traces of sleep, and reached for my toothbrush. The sharp scent of mint filled my nose as I scrubbed away the stale taste of the night. By the time I finished, my stomach let out a low, impatient growl, loud enough to make me sigh.

I pressed a hand against my belly, rubbing slow circles. "I'll feed you shortly, promise."

It took about five minutes to wrangle myself into my clothes. The pants stretched over my stomach, and I tugged the snug shirt down over them, making sure it wouldn't ride up at an inopportune moment. Then came the sandals. They were simple plastic ones that Missy had found for me. They weren't my style, but they were easy to slip on without having to bend over, and that alone made them priceless.

When I trained with weapons, I kicked them off, preferring to go barefoot. It was instinctual. In Beast form, I'm a nine-foot-plus killing machine where shoes have no place, not that we could find any that fit if I wanted them.

A low, familiar grumble vibrated through my core. *Protect.*

Ms. Beast, my ever-present, ever-watchful companion outside my nightmares, whispered the command into my soul, the word forming not in sound but in sensation. It was like a ripple of energy traveling through my bones, a silent pulse that formed words. Actually, the sensation was impossible to explain.

I rested my palm against my stomach again, feeling the tension coiled inside me. Nova, my other beast, remained quiet, lurking in the depths of my consciousness. Unlike Ms. Beast, who prowled just beneath the surface, Nova emerged when things turned truly brutal. When she came out, evil humans and hellhounds died.

Things had been peaceful lately. No, strike that. Lesley Barnes, the woman we had kidnapped, made our lives hell and frayed everyone's nerves. How could I even think "peaceful"? She was President Barnes' wife, and he was our sworn enemy. She'd been festering inside our walls for three months, dripping venom into every interaction. Just being near her made everyone's hands twitch toward their weapons. I wasn't immune to it, but I had refrained from breaking her other leg.

The first one I broke for information. It hadn't worked.

Now, she hobbled around with a cane, though most of the time, her limp was exaggerated for sympathy.

The biggest problem wasn't the injury; it was her ceaseless complaining.

We had kidnapped her from the new U.S. government, known as the Federation, as leverage to force their hand and uncover the truth behind their future plans. But President Barnes had done nothing since we took his wife. No ransom demands. No desperate negotiations. Not even a token plea for his wife's return.

If I had to guess, he was relieved to have her off his hands.

Lesley, sensing that her husband wasn't coming for her, had switched tactics. Her burning hatred for Shadow Warriors had been impossible to hide at first, but now? Now she played the role of the misunderstood victim, the poor, abused wife of the President, trapped in a war she never asked for.

It was the worst kind of bullshit.

But today, this would end.

I was putting my plan into action.

The wise thing to do was execute her, and I'd given it serious thought. Cold, rational, logical thought, but unfortunately, it wasn't going to happen. Killing to defend my people was one thing. Cold-blooded murder, another.

I hoped, reverently, that she would say the wrong thing while I was in Beast form, something that would flip the switch and strip away the thin reluctance holding me back. If wishes were reality, I'd be scraping her guts off the floor right now.

With that pleasant thought lingering in my mind, I opened the door.

King sat at the table we used for meals, his broad frame relaxed, but his sharp blue eyes locked onto me the second I stepped into the room. A full breakfast waited, the scent of eggs, fresh bread, and sizzling meat wrapping around me like a warm, taunting embrace. My stomach clenched in betrayal.

"I have five minutes to waddle to Mrs. Barnacle's cell," I muttered, trying not to inhale too deeply.

King picked up his fork and took a bite, savoring it, the jerk. "You have thirty minutes, starting now. I sent a message that you'd be late." He stabbed another piece of meat and popped it into his mouth. "You're not leaving this room until you eat." It was said casually after he chewed and swallowed. The glow in his eyes made it clear. This was not a battle I was going to win.

I scowled, shifting my weight, but my body had already chosen sides. Ms. Beast purred, a deep, satisfied hum vibrating through my chest, sealing my fate.

Traitor.

With a resigned huff, I shuffled toward the table and collapsed into the chair across from King. Our room was one of the larger ones. It had a table with chairs for quiet meals along with a couch that we could relax on. We'd removed the couch, and a baby's crib sat in its place. King had offered to have a wall removed to give us more room, but I didn't want more room. We had a real home on the other part of the island that we rarely visited. I wanted that to change, and making our quarters at the citadel more pleasing wouldn't help.

The second my ass hit the seat, my restraint over the food evaporated. There was no decorum, and no pretense. I tore into my meal like I hadn't eaten in days. I consumed double the calories now than I ever had before.

King watched me with an amused smirk, shoveling his own food into his mouth at a more civilized pace.

Axel, our Shadow Warrior doctor, was playing this whole pregnancy thing by ear. Shadow Warriors hadn't mated with each other for over two hundred years, and as far as he knew, it had never happened on Earth before now. My entire pregnancy was an experiment.

Missy was human, which meant her child was half-human, half-Warrior, and not a good comparison. From what Axel had seen, human females carrying a Warrior's child had a gestation period of about six months. The babies grew fast, much larger than human newborns, averaging fifteen pounds at birth.

Going by those standards, my child would arrive within the next six weeks.

I glanced down at my belly, which was already stretched beyond the limits of reason, and scowled. The good doctor didn't seem concerned. He sympathized, sure, but that was it.

I had asked him what would happen if I had a twenty-pound baby. He'd laughed and without a drip of concern in his voice, he told me I was Shadow Warrior and could handle it.

I grumbled inside my head as I stuffed another bite of food into my mouth.

I really wish men carried the babies.

The entire human race would have gone extinct centuries ago, and that thought made me smile.

Chapter Two

Marinah

After cleaning my plate, I reached for more. King, ever patient, rarely interrupted before I went for seconds.

"How are you feeling this morning?" he asked.

I chewed, swallowed, and shot him a flat look. "Grouchy."

King smirked but didn't press. Instead, he leaned back slightly, his gaze assessing as he speared a piece of food with his fork.

"Why do you think the Federation hasn't made contact concerning Lesley?" I asked.

His eyes darkened. "The only thing that makes sense is that she's an insignificant loss to them."

"I agree," I muttered, rubbing my temple. "She's our burden now."

King's expression went even darker. "She doesn't need to be. I have no problem putting her out of our misery."

He wasn't smiling because he wasn't joking.

King had a stark, black-and-white view of our post-apocalyptic world. You were either useful, someone in need of protection, or you were a threat. And threats? He eliminated them without hesitation. It was one of the many things that made him a dangerous, effective leader. I doubted he would ever change, even though I was now the boss.

His solution, oddly enough, made me smile again.

"You like the idea too," he said, a wicked gleam in his eyes.

My lips twitched. "No, I like that you like the idea. Big difference."

His brow furrowed slightly. "There's a huge difference," he muttered.

I reached across the table, placing my hand over his, feeling the warmth and strength beneath my fingers. "If my idea doesn't work, you may get your chance."

His usual frown returned. "Do I want to know what your idea is?"

I squeezed his hand and gave him a slow, knowing smile. "You'll see."

King's gaze narrowed. "Said the spider to the fly."

"My, how well-read you are, my mate," I teased.

His lips twitched, and instead of answering, he lifted my hand, pressing a lingering kiss to the backs of my fingers. The heat of his mouth sent a ripple of warmth through me, just like always.

"I read to our child every night," he murmured. "I'm becoming educated along with her."

That pulled a genuine laugh from me.

There was nothing wrong with King's education. He hadn't been raised in the traditional sense. He was pulled from public school before puberty because male Shadow Warriors started shifting young, and that kind of transformation wasn't something you could explain away in a human classroom. His mother had abandoned them the moment she realized what her husband and son truly were.

But his father hadn't neglected his education. If anything, he had been ruthless about it.

King rebelled hard against his Warrior side, wanting nothing more than to be an ordinary adolescent. His father brought his Uncle Greystone to set him straight. Greystone trained him for war and forged him into a weapon. But he also believed in books, in knowledge, in strategy beyond brute force. He made sure King's mind was just as sharp as his claws.

Both his father and Greystone were dead now.

As were my parents.

That left us.

King had led the Shadow Warriors for years. Then, I went Nova, an even bigger monster than my Beast, and the burden of leadership fell into my lap. It hadn't been easy, and I was still adjusting. But pregnancy had given me an unexpected advantage. My temper had become legendary, and very few people dared stand up to me now.

King had somehow become the calm one in our relationship.

Most importantly, he kept me from dismembering my friends.

I hadn't known I was a Shadow Warrior until I almost died from a hellhound bite. That bite had changed everything.

All Shadow Warrior and human bodies were burned after death until only ash remained. We didn't want to know what the GMO formaldehyde would do to Shadow Warriors. It was possible it would have no effect, but we couldn't be sure and couldn't take that chance.

The Federation had taken hellhound horror a step further. They were injecting living humans directly with the same modified protein that had caused all the problems. That left people with two options: fight for the Federation or become mindless killing machines. The Federation killed the men and women instantly if they made the wrong decision.

I exhaled and set my fork down, rubbing my belly absentmindedly.

"I'm full," I said with a sigh.

King pushed another plate toward me. "There's more if you want it."

I shook my head. "I swear, you want me fat," I grumbled.

His eyes softened. "There is no fat on you. Just a very round belly. Your body needs more calories than mine, and you know it."

I rolled my eyes but didn't argue. He wasn't wrong.

"Don't worry," I replied. "I'll eat another full meal in a few hours." I had put off the coming altercation long enough. "Do you want to enter the black widow's den with me?"

His expression changed to revulsion. "Not unless you need me, but I'll walk with you until we hear her screams," he said seriously.

"Wow, so magnanimous," I praised.

"That's me, your magnanimous king."

I laughed.

He stood quickly and took my hand to help me stand from the chair. I would swear our son already weighed fifty pounds.

Chapter Three

Marinah

Lesley Barnes was lucky, even if she didn't think so. For one, she wasn't dead. And considering her disposition, it was a miracle. Her original cell had also been upgraded, though I doubted she appreciated the improvement. She now occupied a ten-by-ten box of a room, with an added bathroom outside those dimensions. It wasn't luxury, but it was better than the dirt floor and iron bars she deserved.

She was monitored around the clock. A guard stood outside her door at all times, enduring her endless complaints through the locked barrier. That guard wasn't there to keep her from escaping. He was there to keep others from deciding that killing her might be entertaining. Not that I really thought my Warriors would go against orders, but I'd hoped Lesley was a valuable pawn and I wouldn't risk her safety. That hope had quickly dwindled.

Maylin, our doctor's assistant, and mate of a Shadow Warrior, had taken care of Lesley due to her broken leg for as long as she could tolerate the woman's relentless whining. Then, with no small amount of relief, she'd given birth to a new baby and handed the duty off to Missy, who had far less patience and even less sympathy. Maylin made it clear that birth was not her primary reason for running to the other side of the island. She was worried the guards would need to stop her from murder.

On a brighter note, Nokita and Maylin were now the parents of three children. Baby Two and Baby Three would grow to be Shadow Warriors. Che, who would be seven soon, was human, but he didn't act like it. He worshipped Nokita. Maylin was a tough customer, but she loved her children and Nokita after losing her first Shadow Warrior husband when he rescued Che from hellhounds. I missed Boot, the fallen Warrior. He turned into a good friend after a rough start. Baby Boot, his son, was almost two years old and looked so much like his father. Nokita didn't mind at all. He loved his children equally.

Missy, after Maylin's desertion, removed Lesley's cast, an event that had only escalated the hourly screams demanding an audience with me. Mostly, I ignored her. But not today.

The Warriors stationed outside her door never failed to look traumatized whenever I arrived in response to yet another complaint. This visit was no different.

"Good morning, Togg," I said as I approached.

Togg was a Shadow Warrior on the shorter side, not that anyone would dare call him small. What he lacked in height, he more than made up for in sheer bulk. His muscles were thick, his shoulders wide, and his neck was about as close to the size of a basketball as a human, or near-human, could get. Togg was a deadly fighter, and I valued his fighting ability more than his brains or lack thereof.

He was here as punishment because he'd been caught teasing one of the island women in Beast form. Not with maliciousness, he'd simply thought it was fun, and he liked her. Unfortunately, he chose the wrong way to go about relaying his intent. She was shaking when I'd come upon them. The worst punishment I could think of for his stupidity was to assign him as one of Lesley Barnes' watchdogs.

Now, as I stepped up to him, he looked skyward, his expression one of silent pleading. I wouldn't have been surprised if he crossed himself.

"Good morning, Queen," he said stiffly.

King was King's given name. Mine was Marinah, but I'd given up trying to convince the Shadow Warriors to use it. Queen was better than Mate of King, at least.

"I don't hear the usual screams."

"Beck's mate told her you would be down shortly. She's been silent since."

"Thank you. Please unlock the door." I would have told him Beck's mate had a name, but his thick skull wouldn't have understood. Any woman mated to a Shadow Warrior was on a pedestal, and the Warriors felt it such a great honor.

Togg did as I asked, and I stepped inside. Lesley immediately stood from her chair and grabbed her cane to look more pathetic. She was about five feet four inches tall with brown hair that now had gray in the roots since she no longer had access to a beautician. She had a thin, regal face with few signs of her age, which I assumed was late fifties. Her nose was a little too long, but it worked for her wicked witch persona. She was smart as a whip and a scientist like her husband. Not that we ever saw her brilliant side. Playing dumb might have been her greatest skill.

"It's about time," she said angrily. "Does anyone on this God-forsaken island have a clock?"

I ignored what she said. "I have good news for you. You have a work assignment. It took a week to arrange the room, but at least you won't need to stay here day and night. You even have a window, though it's high and you can't see directly from it, sunlight filters in."

She stared at me for a moment. "You expect me to work with my leg in this condition?" She pointed at said leg with an imperious finger.

"When you don't work on the island, you don't eat. Everyone has a job. We cooperate and make this a better home for the people. If you choose not to do your assigned task, I'll have meal delivery stopped." I kept my tone neutral.

"Again, what do you expect me to do with a crippled leg?"

"Work."

"I thought my husband and the men under his command were cruel," she bemoaned, her voice heavy with theatrical despair. "I never expected it from another, umm, another woman."

"You're more than welcome to say how you feel," I said coolly. "Would 'monster' be more appropriate? I have no problem being a monster." I let the words settle before adding, "And on that note, Missy will no longer be helping you. You can help yourself or do without. I'll check on you once a week if I have time. Otherwise, you'll be locked in this room or in the workroom we've set up for you."

A single tear slid down her cheek.

I had no idea how she managed to cry on cue, but she did it flawlessly every time. The woman was a backstabbing viper, and I was done wasting energy on her. She was too dangerous to allow free roam of the citadel. We couldn't afford for her to learn anything about us. Worse, she would have no problem stirring discord among the island's women. And I had just gotten them settled and made changes that gave them a sense of stability. I wasn't about to let this woman unravel my progress.

Lesley crossed her arms, her expression shifting from sorrow to pure defiance. Then, to drive home her so-called crippled state, she tapped the foot of her injured leg against the floor.

The sound was deliberate.

Annoying.

Calculated.

She wasn't fooling me. It had been a clean break, and Axel, our doctor, had set and immobilized it properly. He'd said it would be as good as new in a couple of months. Lesley had milked her injury for long enough. Her days of idleness were over.

"Come with me," I ordered, turning toward the door.

"I'm simply not up to it today," she whined.

"No problem," I said with a touch of glee. "Your food will be discontinued until you are."

Without another word, I marched to the door, opened it, stepped through, and shut it behind me just as the wailing began.

I turned to Togg. "Unfortunately—" I cut myself off as a bloodcurdling scream rattled the walls. I waited for her to take a breath before continuing, "—she'll be without food until she complies. If she doesn't, her screams should grow weaker within a day or two."

Togg straightened, his lips twitching with something dangerously close to amusement. "Yes, my Queen."

Somehow, I doubted he'd mind the screaming as much.

I went to the meeting with the household staff.

Four women sat with me at a table tucked off to the side of the main kitchen. They ranged in age from twenty to sixty, each with a distinct presence that radiated the quiet confidence of women who knew their worth.

"My meal this morning was excellent, thank you," I began.

"You are very welcome," Beatriz said with a warm nod. As head of the work staff, she oversaw everything from the kitchen to the team of workers who kept the citadel running smoothly. At five feet nothing, she didn't seem particularly imposing until she got angry. Then, she might as well have been a giant.

She was also bilingual and served as the spokesperson for the others. I was slowly learning Spanish, but I wasn't confident enough to hold a full conversation without butchering it and possibly causing an irreparable incident because I used the wrong words.

"How are things going in the kitchens?" I asked.

"Much improved," Beatriz answered. "Axel has asked us to add more fruit to your diet, and we received a nice shipment from the south island this morning. We have guava and mamey sapote for you. They will be included with your evening meal."

I had no idea what mamey sapote was, but at this point, food of any variety always sounded good. "Thank you," I said, offering a smile to everyone at the table.

Then I added, "Lesley will not require additional food today. She's been assigned work duty and has refused to comply. When she's hungry enough to work, her meals will resume."

The soft smiles around the table transformed into full-fledged grins after Beatriz translated.

"Do you have enough staff now, or do you need more?" I asked.

Beatriz leaned forward slightly, her expression shifting to something more serious. "*Por favor*, please do not place the evil señora on kitchen duty," she begged.

I couldn't help but chuckle. "You have nothing to fear. She will work in a solitary room where she has no chance to poison us."

"*Gracias*," she said with a relieved nod. Then, her expression brightened again. "We have much help now, and it is easier to feed the large beasts. They are also thanking us for the work we do."

That last part caught my attention. The *beasts*, as she referred to them, weren't known for showing gratitude, but if they were making an exception for the citadel's staff, it meant they were finally figuring out that a simple thank you went a long way and improved our living quality.

It was a small shift, but a telling one, and exactly what I needed to hear.

I'd made it crystal clear that if the Warriors didn't respect the people who kept them in food and comfort, I would start assigning them to the duties they didn't appreciate. The lack of respect had been one of the women's biggest complaints. The other had been the absence of a clear leader among them.

To fix that, I'd had them vote by private ballot. All but one chose Beatriz. I strongly suspected she had been the lone dissenting vote.

"Are your supplies up to the standards you need in case of a siege?" I asked next.

"We are prepared for anything," Beatriz said proudly, lifting her chin.

"Good." I nodded. "Is there anything else you'd like to discuss?"

Our weekly meetings were a chance for them to voice grievances and keep me informed of things they thought I should know. My mate was a brilliant commander when it came to his men, but he had no idea how to handle women. They had been too afraid of him to say anything. The responsibility of leading the Warriors and working out the problems with the women fell on my shoulders now.

It had been a steep learning curve. I was adjusting to life as a Shadow Warrior, commanding our Warriors, and being mate to King all at once. The new changes that I'd implemented with staff had only been in effect for a few months, and Beatriz had been invaluable in helping me gain the trust of the women.

Beatriz's eyes flicked toward Yamila, a pretty young woman who never quite met my gaze. Shy, I assumed.

"Señor Alden would like to court Yamila," Beatriz said.

Yamila's face turned crimson. Her English had improved enough to follow the conversation, and she clearly hadn't expected to be the topic of discussion.

I kept my tone careful. "Does that pose a problem?"

"Yamila's parents are dead, and I am acting as her guardian," Beatriz explained. "We would like to know more about this man."

I understood. "He is one of my personal guards," I said simply. "He wouldn't hold that position if I didn't trust him. And if he ever disrespected any woman on this island, I would personally ensure he regretted it."

Beatriz nodded, but the young woman still looked uncertain.

"Yamila is afraid of his beast side," Beatriz added.

I understood this too. "It is scary," I admitted honestly. "But this is Yamila's decision, and Alden will respect her wishes."

Before I knew I was a Shadow Warrior, they had terrified me too. Their beasts looked like something out of a nightmare. Think fictional werewolves on steroids: raw power, sharp edges, and barely contained violence. Add teeth and claws, and we were hairy and scary.

Yamila nodded slowly, then finally lifted her gaze to mine. "I like him," she said in English.

A small smile tugged at the corner of my lips. That had taken courage.

I turned to Beatriz. "They have my blessing, if you are willing to give yours. I hope it works out."

I had learned that the women preferred decisiveness. They didn't want hesitation or drawn-out discussions. As long as I was fair and honest with them, we were all happy. Taking care of the needs at the citadel was an endless job, and comfort would fall apart if it were left to the Shadow Warriors. It almost had.

The meeting wrapped up, and as I stood to leave, Beatriz handed me a small bowl of guava with a promise that a full meal would be waiting in my room when I finished my morning rounds.

I took the fruit with a nod of thanks, then made my way toward the practice area to see what King was up to.

CHAPTER FOUR

King

I STOOD ON THE wide training field, watching as Shadow Warriors and human islanders sparred side by side. Marinah had ordered us to integrate and train as a seamless unit, learning each other's strengths and weaknesses. We had done this in small, controlled groups before. Now it was entirely different.

It wasn't how I had done things, but the camaraderie was needed, and it worked.

Eventually, many of the Shadow Warriors would leave the island, turning its defenses over to the humans who lived here. Marinah wanted that day to come soon. Whether that was realistic or not, I wasn't sure.

To prepare for that future, we had a team working on a serum to protect humans from the toxin in hellhound bites and scratches. As it stood, any human who was wounded by a hellhound died. And worse, if the remains weren't burned, their body, though it would take years, would eventually come back as one of the monsters that had nearly wiped us out.

Shadow Warriors weren't immune to the toxins that killed humans, but we had an advantage. Our small science team had discovered a serum that kept our stronger bodies alive long enough to heal. We each carried an emergency injection that could save us most of the time. If we knew we'd be facing hellhounds in battle, we took the injection in advance, ensuring we wouldn't go down if teeth or claws made contact.

I scanned the field, my eyes landing on several men and women who had once been part of the Federation's attack against the island. That had been almost four months ago. We had interrogated them, studied their motives, and in the end, more than half had been given a choice to fight with us or become part of the island community.

President Barnes had turned his lowest-level troops into fodder, injecting them with the genetic modification that ensured, if they died, they would quickly rise again as hellhounds. The ones who had joined us had been given a promise that if they died, we wouldn't let them come back as monsters.

The humans who didn't want to fight were assigned tasks on the island.

One of them, Kenneth, had been a medical intern when the first hellhound war broke out. He now worked alongside Axel and his mate Garret, assisting in the medical units. Kenneth made a deal that if Axel continued training him, he would stay behind when the Warriors pulled out for good.

He was a puny human, awkward in movement and reliant on glasses to see. His first pair had been lost during the battle, but we had managed to find him another set. He wasn't a warrior, not by any means. But Axel and Garret liked him and said he was a great asset for the people.

In the end, people mattered most.

I spotted Amy across the training field, her stance tense as she fought with another human. She was young and determined but not fully healed. My mate, in Nova form, had broken Amy's wrists when she begged for mercy during the heat of battle. The bones had mended but left weakness that would take more physical therapy to completely heal.

I strode toward her and lifted my hand. The fighting halted immediately.

"The sword is too heavy for you," I said.

Amy's expression flickered with defeat, but before she could protest, I continued. "That might not be the case in a few months, but right now, you're still recovering. Anything you learn with a lighter sword will go into muscle memory. When you're ready for the heavier one, you'll be surprised how much you've improved."

She swallowed hard and nodded.

I turned to her practice partner. "Go with her and help find something that won't cause further damage to her wrists."

"Yes, sir," he replied quickly, already moving.

I hadn't wanted Amy on the field at all but Marinah insisted. Amy wanted to fight the Federation for what they had done to her. She had been one of the unneeded soldiers who wore a red stripe on her uniform, the ones sent in first, their deaths considered meaningless. She'd been injected with the poison so she would continue to kill after death.

Marinah saved her life. I wouldn't have hesitated to end her. This was only one of the reasons Marinah was exactly what we needed. The world was not "either or" the way Shadow Warriors saw it. Marinah was the Shadow Warrior who tempered our beastly natures.

After watching Amy train for two weeks, my opinion had shifted. She wasn't the strongest. She wasn't the fastest. But she never gave up. She had something to prove, and it showed in every movement, every strike, every stubborn refusal to quit.

Marinah had a knack for saving those who deserved it.

"You want in?"

I turned at the familiar voice. Beck stood a few paces away, grinning like a man who had just flattened someone and enjoyed it. The human soldier at his feet groaned, struggling to stand.

"You looking for someone to kick your ass, or do you want me to go easy on you?" I shot back, drawing my sword.

Beck's grin widened.

Within minutes, those on the field stopped sparring, their attention shifting toward us. Beck and I were *nearly* evenly matched, which meant our clashes were always worth watching.

The clang of steel rang out in the warm morning air.

I tightened my grip on the hilt; my focus locked onto Beck. He moved in a slow, deliberate circle, his stance loose and his eyes calculating.

"You planning to swing," he taunted, "or are you just going to stand there holding it like a staff?"

His smirk was as irritating as ever.

I smiled. "I was just giving you a head start," I shot back, lunging forward with a quick strike aimed at his shoulder.

Beck parried easily, the flat of his blade meeting mine with a deafening clang. The impact sent a jolt up my arm, but I adjusted, rolling my wrist to strike again. This time, I went lower, aiming for his side.

He anticipated the move.

Pivoting smoothly, he sidestepped just enough to evade my blade before countering with a strike toward my exposed flank.

I barely managed to block as our swords locked together with a metallic clang. He leaned in, pressing his strength against mine, giving a huff of warm breath with his determination.

"You're still too predictable," he murmured. "Your weight's all wrong."

"Maybe you're just old," I countered with a grin, shoving back to disengage.

Beck barked out a laugh. "Old? Or just better?"

His next attack was fast. He made a feint to the left, followed by a spinning arc aimed at my midsection. Instead of retreating, I stepped into the blow, catching his blade with mine and twisting hard.

The move knocked him slightly off balance, and I pressed the advantage, raining down strikes that forced him to backpedal.

"Better, King," he said, as if offering a training critique. "But I still know your openings."

To prove his point, he snapped a sudden kick to my knee. It wasn't hard enough to injure, but enough to send me stumbling sideways.

Before I could jump to my feet, the flat of his blade tapped against my ribs.

"Dead," he declared, smugly.

His victory was short-lived.

"Look down, old man."

We were the same damn age, but ever since Beck had mated with Missy, he'd developed something dangerously close to a sense of humor.

Beck's gaze dropped to where my knife, the one I always carried at my waist, rested dangerously against his junk.

He let out a low chuckle. "Missy would not like that."

I wiped the sweat from my brow and nodded. "Again?"

"Again," Beck said.

This time, there was no humor in his voice.

We went at it once more. I won in half the time. We were about to launch into round three when I caught movement in my periphery.

Marinah.

"Do you want to baby Beck's arrogance all day or are you ready for a real opponent?" she asked, her words laced with challenge.

Pregnancy hadn't stopped her from training, and I doubted anything could. I didn't like seeing her on the practice field while she was carrying our child, but it wasn't my call. At least if she was fighting me, I could make damn sure there were no accidents.

Beck stepped aside with a grin, and Marinah took his place, standing across from me, her sword at the ready. Her posture was too relaxed, but her eyes told another story. They gleamed with the quiet promise of violence.

Our blades met in a flurry of strikes and the sharp clang of steel filled the air.

"You're holding back," she growled, circling me like a predator. "I can feel it. And it's pissing me off."

"Don't be ridiculous," I replied, feigning a quick jab at her left shoulder.

It was slow. She dodged easily and countered with a sharp swing aimed at my midsection.

I blocked, but half-heartedly.

She saw it.

Her next strike came harder, and I barely countered in time. My grip tightened on the hilt.

"You think I can't handle you because of this?" she snapped, gesturing briefly to her stomach before stepping forward with a storm of rapid strikes. "You think I'm fragile now?"

I didn't answer. I just kept moving, deflecting each of her attacks. I gave her the smallest of grins.

It was worse than an answer.

"Stop it!" she hissed, her swings growing wilder. "Fight me, King. Like you mean it."

"I am," I said evenly, stepping back to dodge a blow aimed at my head. "You're faster than ever, Marinah. But I'm not going to hurt you or the baby."

Her face flushed hot with anger.

"I don't need your protection!" she roared, slamming her blade against mine so hard the impact echoed across the clearing. "I'm a Shadow Warrior, not some delicate flower!"

My frown deepened, and for just a fraction of a second, my sword lowered.

She didn't hesitate.

With a swift, brutal attack, she swept my legs out from under me.

I hit the ground hard, my sword skidding out of reach. Before I could react, she loomed over me, the blade pressed to my throat.

My chest rose and fell with heavy breaths, but the satisfaction I expected to see in her eyes wasn't there.

"Feel better?" I asked carefully, not quite understanding what had gotten into her.

"No," she snapped, throwing her sword to the ground and stepping away. "You're treating me like I'm weak. I've survived hellhounds, human battles, and the Federation's top forces. I don't need you to go easy on me."

I stood slowly, brushing dirt from my clothes. "And I've watched you risk everything, over and over. Forgive me if I want to keep you safe, even from me."

She spun to face me full on. "You don't get to decide what I can handle. That's my choice, not yours."

I was silent for a long moment. Then I picked up her sword and held it out to her. "Again," I said. "No holding back."

For a moment, she stared at me angrily. Finally, she grabbed the sword and stepped back into position.

This time, when our blades clashed, it was full force.

The speed of her strikes doubled. I'd never seen her move so fast. Maybe it was the hormones, but I wouldn't tell her that. She trained like everyone else, even when I complained about it. Sweat ran down my back as she parried my strikes and tried to slip past my defenses. She wasn't going to win, but this made her happy, so I would indulge.

Suddenly, she tripped over air, or so it seemed, and stumbled, rolling on her side. I dropped my sword and went to my knees.

"Sucker," she whispered with her knife at my throat.

"That's me," I said with a smile. "King of the suckers."

"I needed that," she said, no longer fighting her grin.

"Your confrontation with the barnacle went that bad?" I asked as I helped her to her feet.

"Not really. She won't be fed today, and we'll see if it improves her disposition, and she decides to follow my orders tomorrow. The meeting with the household staff went well. I left them in a great mood by telling them not to send food to her room until I returned her privileges."

"How long do you think she'll hold out?" I asked.

"Probably by dinner time, but she's out of luck until tomorrow."

Marinah had fooled me with her slip, and it took ten years off my life. But it felt good to see her happy.

She went to her toes and kissed me. "I'm sorry for that. I had another dream last night and no one came to save me from hellhounds. It shook me up and I needed to get it out of my head."

"I will always come to save you."

She kissed me again.

"Hungry?" I asked.

"Starving."

Chapter Five

Marinah

TOGG WAS BACK ON duty at Lesley's door the next morning.

"How's our gilded prisoner?" I asked as I approached.

He gave a rare smile. "Surprisingly quiet."

I raised a brow. "Not sure if that's good or bad, but I'm going in."

"Good luck."

I liked Togg, even if he could be an idiot at times. After his last bout of trouble, I had asked King about his childhood. King had just shrugged and said, "He never talks about it."

That alone told me plenty.

Unlike most of the Shadow Warriors, Togg didn't have farming skills or a formal education. But he was a quick learner, deadly with a sword, and most importantly, trustworthy. Keeping him busy was the best way to keep him out of trouble. I intended to take him off guard duty and end his punishment. I had something else lined up that would occupy his time.

He unlocked the door, and I stepped inside.

Lesley lay on the bed, watching me with silent, unreadable eyes.

"I'd like to show you your work assignment if you want to start today. The choice is yours." I kept my tone light because I knew I'd won.

She didn't answer right away. Instead, she stared at me for a long moment before speaking in the softest voice I had ever heard from her. "Why do you hate me so much?"

I considered ignoring the question. But the truth was easier.

"I was the one who captured you," I said evenly. "I'll never forget the contempt in your voice and hatred in your eyes. You're a good actress, maybe good enough to fool someone into believing you're just a poor, misused president's wife. I won't fall for it, and your act won't get you out of confinement. You are a danger to my people. Hatred like yours doesn't just float away. It festers." I let the words hang between us for a beat before continuing. "Now, back to my original question."

Lesley exhaled sharply, then swung her legs over the side of the bed. She faced me with a look of pure defiance.

"You're wrong about everything," she said stubbornly. "Especially me. And I'll prove it." She lifted her chin. "I need to eat, so I'll start this wretched work assignment you've decided can only be done by me."

Her speech had been almost convincing. Almost. But I saw through it. She still believed she was too good for work, a delusion that likely came from being the wife of President Barnes.

I remembered the way she had offered me the name of her manicurist before I kidnapped her, like that was the kind of information I needed. I had no doubt the manicurist had taken the job to avoid wearing a red stripe.

Mrs. Barnacle wasn't just a liar. She was privileged. She thought herself above everyone else.

"Will I be able to eat before beginning this job?" she asked, her tone clipped but edged with practiced innocence.

"Food will be delivered once you start working. I'll order it as soon as I go over the assignment. Follow me."

I stepped into the hallway and motioned for Togg to follow.

"Could you possibly slow down?" Lesley huffed, already breathless.

I could, and I did. My legs were longer than hers, and I was in far better shape even with my advanced pregnancy. I didn't mind giving a little.

When we reached the designated workroom, I unlocked the door and turned to Togg. "Put this on your keyring," I said, handing the key over. "Let the other guards know she will be here six hours a day." I ignored Lesley's sharp inhale.

We stepped inside, and the task ahead of her became immediately clear.

Lesley took one look around, her lips curling in revulsion, which grew as her nostrils picked up the smell of sweat and dirt. What could I say? Shadow Warriors worked hard, and sometimes their clothes stunk. We'd found a system that worked best for them. The Warriors didn't care if they wore each other's clean clothes as long as they fit.

"You expect me to do laundry?" she demanded.

"You'll be sorting laundry," I corrected. "Clothes come down the chute above and land in a pile. You'll check the size, sort them, and place them into the canvas bags marked with the correlating sizes. After you leave in the evening, the bags will be picked up.

Once you get the hang of this, I might add folding, but I'll need to set up a larger table for that."

I gestured to the side. "The small table is where you can eat. Through that door is a washroom. If you do your job, you will be provided food. Do you have questions?"

Lesley's eyes filled with pitiful tears, her hand trembling as she lifted them to her throat, the picture of practiced helplessness.

I felt nothing.

Neither did Togg, judging by the look of disgust on his face.

Protect baby, whispered Ms. Beast.

My Warrior side said this a lot when I was in Lesley's company. Ms. Beast didn't like her either.

Lesley crossed her arms, her expression turning venomous. "My husband will hear about this after I return home," she spit, allowing the real Mrs. Barnes to slip out. "He will come for me, and then he will kill you."

I didn't so much as blink.

We wanted him to come. It was far easier than tracking him down again.

"One more thing," I said, ignoring her threat. "Screaming and yelling will also remove your access to food. If you plan to start work without the temper tantrum, I'll stop by the kitchen and have a meal delivered."

If looks could kill, I'd be nothing but a blood smear on the floor.

Lesley huffed, turned her back on me, and limped dramatically to a small pile of clothes and leaned over it.

The universe had perfect timing. At that exact moment, another load came tumbling down the chute and buried her.

Togg snorted. I barely bit back a laugh. We slipped out of the room and shut the door behind us before we completely lost it.

"I know this assignment is supposed to be punishment," Togg said, grinning as he locked the door, "but I believe I'll enjoy it now."

"Good," I replied, still smirking. "Because your punishment ends tomorrow. Try staying out of trouble, Togg. Don't make me send you back here, even if you might enjoy it."

"Yes, my Queen," he said with a grin.

One disaster down.

Now to deal with a pint-sized one.

CHAPTER SIX

Marinah

I RECEIVED WORD LAST night that Ruth was back at the citadel. No doubt she had made Maylin's life hell, and Maylin had finally had enough. She had taken Ruth, a royal pain in my ass, with her so Che would have company on the southern end of the island. Ruth was Missy and Beck's daughter though Beck was still getting his feet wet over gaining a daughter due to his mating. Missy had shot Beck when he jumped from a plane in a parachute and Ruth wanted to kill him after he landed. He spoiled the girl rotten. My anger at the child was still in simmer mode. She insisted on endangering her own life along with Che's to kill hellhounds. They were both human and too fragile, even if they didn't think so.

This morning, I sent a message ordering Ruth to meet me in the gym where I usually trained her. I had no intention of arriving on time. Instead, I showed up twenty minutes after I told her to be there, expecting to find a sulking, petulant child waiting for me.

Instead, Ruth was warming up, stretching as if preparing for whatever I planned to throw at her today.

Interesting.

I had considered canceling her training, knowing full well that would hurt her most. Her reckless behavior had continued long enough. If I trusted Mrs. Barnacle, I might have assigned Ruth to laundry duty and locked the two of them in the same room together. I couldn't think of a worse punishment for either of them.

Ruth turned as soon as she heard me enter. Excitement flared in her eyes, only to vanish, replaced by something I never expected to see on her face.

Guilt.

Was she acting?

She stepped forward hesitantly, lifting her chin. "I owe you an apology," she began.

I folded my arms and waited.

"I acted irresponsibly," she said. "I'm sorry. I'm going to try harder if you'll still train me."

She kicked the floor with the toe of her boot, glancing up briefly before continuing.

"I'll even try if you don't want to train me."

I narrowed my eyes, studying her.

Was she coached? Did an alien take the real Ruth and replace her with a decoy?

I wasn't sure how to react, so I went with my gut.

"What brought on this sweet new child act?" I asked bluntly.

Ruth shifted uneasily. "Maylin had a long talk with me," she admitted. "She said I endangered Che, which means I can't be trusted around him."

Her voice changed. "He's my friend," she all but cried.

Ruth and Che had lost their human fathers to hellhounds. They wanted to cleanse the world of every last one. Great goal if they were older.

"You've been told this before, and it did no good," I challenged.

Ruth didn't shrink away. She met my gaze head-on.

"There's a girl where Maylin is staying," she said. "I like her, and she's my friend. I invited her to Maylin's place, and she taught me how to cook a meal she loves. Her mother came to check on her and took her away when she found out I was there. She didn't want me near her daughter."

Her face darkened, and for the first time, I recognized the emotion for what it was: embarrassment.

"Maylin translated," Ruth continued, voice quieter now. "She said the woman thought I was dangerous, and Maylin agreed." She swallowed. "I wasn't allowed to see my new friend again."

She took a deep breath, bracing herself. "I want to kill hellhounds," she continued. "But I also want to teach other kids the things you show me. Most humans my age don't know how to fight. Will you help me?"

There was something different about her. The way she held herself and the edge of real desperation in her voice.

I studied her, trying to find cracks in whatever act she might be performing. But Ruth wore her emotions on the outside, and right now, all I saw was sincerity.

"I can't personally help you train them," I said.

Her face fell before I continued.

I held up a hand. "However, I'll still train with you in the mornings when I have time. And I have someone in mind who can help you if children want to participate. The kids will need their parents' permission."

Ruth nodded quickly, hope flickering back to life.

I narrowed my eyes. "Listen to me, and listen like your life depends on it. If you ever endanger them with another one of your idiotic stunts, I will personally see that you're locked up when there's no one to watch you. Have I made myself clear?"

She didn't answer.

Instead, she launched herself across the three feet between us and threw her arms around me.

I hesitated, then wrapped mine around her in return.

"I really am sorry," she murmured against my stomach. "I promise I'll be good at this."

I leaned back just enough to meet her eyes. "You won't just be good at it, Ruth. You'll be the best." I let my voice soften. "I'm proud of you for doing this."

Tears welled in her eyes, and she quickly wiped them away, as if realizing what she had done.

If Ruth was actually sincere, I owed Maylin a huge thank you.

"Are you ready to train today?" I asked.

"You bet," she said eagerly. "Are we using weapons or just conditioning?"

I blinked.

She hated conditioning.

Yep. Aliens were the only explanation.

"Weapons," I said.

Forty minutes into our sparring session, Alden entered. I could tell by the look on his face that something bad happened.

"An outpost was attacked on the mainland," he said.

I lowered my weapon. "Have the guards meet me in the argument room in ten minutes."

"I ran into Cabel on my way here, and he's alerting them."

I nodded, turning back to Ruth. "Training is cut short. Tomorrow morning, I'll bring the person who can help you with your plan."

"I'll be ready," she said, eagerly.

I left the gym, my mind already shifting into battle mode. The attack didn't surprise me. It had been too quiet. The thought of casualties, though, scared me. We had Shadow Warriors stationed in half the human outposts on the mainland. The other half had refused our help.

I burst into the argument room, which was the name I'd dubbed our conference room. The new name was mostly because of Beck and his never-ending need to be difficult. I would think his contrary behavior just for me but he had been the same way with King.

My guards immediately rose from their seats. These were the men who led their own contingency of Shadow Warriors. My gaze swept the room, landing on Labyrinth's empty chair. A familiar ache tightened my chest. He should be here.

He'd taken too many Federation bullets during Lesley's capture. By the time we stopped running, he had lost too much blood. I would never see his unique eyes again. Never hear his laugh. It hurt so much.

His death would stay with me forever. It was somehow worse than Boot's.

Shoving the grief aside, I took my seat and turned to Beck. "What outpost?"

"The closest one north of Landan's. It's one of the outposts that refused our help."

A small, exhale of relief escaped me. At least it wasn't one of ours and I refused to feel guilty for thinking it.

"What are the casualties?" I asked.

Beck's mouth tightened. That wasn't a good sign.

"Originally, all but the young," he said.

A cold pit formed in my stomach.

"They injected the dead with hellhound serum, and after they transformed, they let them kill the children."

I shot to my feet. "What?"

"They left a message for you."

"For me?" My voice was sharp with disbelief. "Not King?"

Beck's jaw flexed. "Knet told them who's in charge now. They know it's you, and the message proved it."

My hands clenched into fists. "What do they want?"

"Your head on a pike," Beck said. "The president's wife returned unharmed. And every Shadow Warrior to turn themselves in."

"Or else?" Ms. Beast surged inside me, hunger curling like fire in my gut. *Teeth. Claws. Rip them apart.*

King's hand closed over mine. My lungs expanded as I sucked in oxygen. Ms. Beast retreated.

"They'll kill every man, woman, and child they come across," Beck said. Then, for the first time since this nightmare unfolded, his tone shifted. "I do have somewhat good news. Three additional outposts have requested our aid. They want to meet with the Shadow Warrior in charge."

His eyes met mine. "They're willing to meet at a place of your choice."

I turned to King. "What are your thoughts?"

"They come here," he said. "We supply the plane. There's a chance this is a trap. The outposts that refused our help have always kept their distance from Landan and his people. We have no way to vet them."

"I agree. What about the rest of you?" My eyes met each Warrior in turn.

"Agreed," Beck said.

"Axel?" I asked.

He exhaled sharply. "We have nothing to go on when it comes to your pregnancy, and you're safer here. Even if I went with you, that wouldn't change. I have the best labor and delivery unit here at the citadel. You need to stay close."

Before I responded, Cabel spoke.

"I have a better idea," he said. "You won't like it, but hear me out."

I folded my arms. "Go on."

"Let King take the lead while you stay in the background. Knet didn't know about your pregnancy, and the quieter we keep it, the better."

I considered his idea carefully.

This was hard. But he was right.

I turned to Beck. "Send them a message. Tell them King will arrange a plane. I also need you to offer the outposts we already protect another opportunity to relocate here. I know they probably won't take it, but suggest it again. If they're only willing to send their noncombatants and children, we will keep them safe."

Beck gave a firm nod. "Consider it done."

Chapter Seven

King

MARINAH HANDLED TAKING A back seat better than expected. It impressed me because I didn't know if I could have done it. The upcoming negotiation was important, and even I thought she would be better at it. My patience wasn't the best, especially since she became pregnant. My outward calm for her sake was getting harder to maintain. I wanted to wrap her in cotton, take her to the safest place I could find, and sit on her until our child was born.

I, fortunately, understood it wouldn't happen unless I wanted my head separated from my shoulders with a bloody mess to show for it.

We eventually heard back from Landan about our offer. His message had been short and to the point. His people weren't coming, and they wouldn't send their children either. I liked the man, but I didn't agree with him. He said he would reconsider if things got worse, or if we received intelligence that a large-scale takeover was imminent. For now, his people were well-protected, and the Shadow Warriors stationed among them were on high alert.

Marinah had spent most of the previous evening discussing how to handle the people arriving from the other outposts. I could see in her eyes that staying away was hard, but she knew the less information we gave President Barnes about our child, the better.

The outposts were sending four people total. We couldn't trust a single one of them.

I understood their desire to remain independent, but we didn't control Landan; we simply helped protect him and the outposts he'd aligned with. The ones who made foolhardy choices cost lives, and this wasn't the first time, but it might be the most horrific.

Unleashing newly created hellhounds to slaughter innocent children burned inside me like a blast furnace.

They said we were the monsters.
They were wrong.

We had spent months crafting the citadel as a multipurpose façade, carefully designing it to reveal only a limited picture of our resources. But Knet had changed everything.

His betrayal was almost impossible to fathom, and whenever I thought about it, rage burned deep. He had been one of my Shadow Warriors. A man I trusted.

He gave our secrets to President Barnes out of jealousy, and for that he would die. It would be a slow, painful death, and even that wasn't good enough for him. Marinah wanted the pleasure of killing him herself, but I wasn't sure I could hold back if I got to him first. I didn't think any of our guards could.

His death was imminent, and when it came, one of us would receive the gift of ending his miserable life.

In the meantime, Marinah made sweeping changes to our security.

Our strongholds on the southern end of the island had been altered, and anything that could be moved had been relocated. This included setting up some of the tunnels with explosives and not using them to hide our people. The changes were almost complete, but until they were finished, we weren't fully protected.

And that meant we were still vulnerable. Knet's knowledge of our security measures could be our downfall.

Losing Labyrinth hadn't just been painful; it had been a blow to our defenses too.

Beyond the loss of a friend, he had been vital to our operations. He was a man of many talents. Nokita was good with anything mechanical, but if Labyrinth needed to take over for him, he could. Same went for helping Axel in medical. Labyrinth couldn't perform complex surgery, but he could keep a man alive until help came. He had many talents, and I'd taken advantage of all of them. Now he was gone.

Marinah had to choose someone to take his place, even though it would be nearly impossible to find someone as good. She'd been dragging her feet because she was still struggling with his loss.

I needed to push her on it again.

And she wouldn't like it.

I turned a corner just as Beck came around from the opposite direction. We nearly collided.

"The plane is on schedule," he said. "They'll arrive within the hour."

"I'll find Marinah and let her know," I replied.

Beck gave a sharp nod before spinning on his heel and heading back the way he came.

I found my mate in the practice gym with Ruth and Togg?

That stopped me. I thought she had reassigned Togg to the southern part of the island.

"I'll leave the plans to both of you," Marinah said when she saw me. She turned to Ruth. "Togg is in charge. If he says you're endangering anyone, I'll pull the plug on this. Understood?"

"Yes, understood," Ruth nodded eagerly.

Had the hellion misled Marinah again? The child could turn on a dime. One minute she agreed to something, and the next, she was endangering the people around her. Marinah had more trust in her than I was willing to give.

And Togg?

I had thought his punishment was over. But if she had stuck him with Ruth, that meant he had done something else.

Yet, he didn't seem bothered.

In fact, he looked almost eager to get started on whatever Marinah had planned.

"One hour," I said when she approached.

"Good," she replied, her tone unreadable. Then, as if something had just clicked into place, her expression shifted. "I have an idea."

"I'm all ears."

That made her smile.

"I want to gag and bind Mrs. Barnacle and parade her in front of whoever exits that plane."

I blinked. "Is there a reason?"

She looped her arm through mine and led me from the gym. "Of course I have a reason," she said, just a hint of irritation slipping into her voice. "One, I want them to report that she's alive in case one or more of them is feeding information back to Barnes."

I raised a brow. "And the second reason?"

"I'm getting no enjoyment over the next few hours, and I like fucking with her and I could care less if it's petty," Marinah said, her voice laced with amusement. "She's doing a horrible job sorting the laundry, and she isn't getting lunch today. Combined with no food, making her visible to our visitors should take her down a peg or two. If the people coming in aren't reporting back to Barnes, they still need to know we have her and that we stole her from under the Federation's nose."

"Why gag her?"

"I don't want her telling them anything. No secret hand signals, no dramatic pleas, nothing."

I grinned. "I like it."

She stopped mid-step, turned, and kissed me.

"I thought you might," she murmured when she pulled back.

I wrapped an arm around her, pulling her as close as her growing stomach allowed. "I'll have to agree with you more often."

She smirked. "I like it when you agree, but I love it when you don't. There's something satisfying about dragging that stubborn streak out of you. Gives me the warm fuzzies."

I kissed her again, lingering just long enough to taste the smugness on her lips.

"I'm sorry you won't be there today," I said when we finally pulled apart.

"I'll be listening," she said, and the way she said it gave me pause.

"Through the vent," she clarified. "Nokita has been working on it. He'll stay with me, and if I need you to shift tactics, he'll interrupt."

I chuckled. Only a few months ago, she had been fighting the idea of being in charge. Now, there was no holding her back.

We continued walking, but before we rounded the next corner, a blood-curdling scream echoed down the hall.

I turned toward the sound ready to charge in that direction, but Marinah caught my arm.

"No worries," she said, completely unbothered. "The bitch has just been informed she's not getting lunch."

I snorted.

"I, however, am starving," she added. "Let's grab a quick meal before the performance starts with the outpost delegation."

At this point, everything Marinah did revolved around food. Axel had sworn she wasn't carrying twins, but I wasn't entirely convinced.

We picked up two meals and took them to our room. Marinah ate with gusto, but she looked tired.

"Lie with me for a minute," I said after we finished our meals.

She didn't argue. She lay next to me, and I slowly began massaging her shoulders. She moved to the side so I could reach her back. Our sex life had been interesting with her new shape, but it had slowed during the past two weeks due to how tired she was at the end of the. day. I hated to see her exhausted, and the last thing I would do was add to it. I didn't mind simply having her close. Touching her like this was also special.

She moaned when I hit a sore spot. I worked the kinks out of her muscles, and her hand slipped down and rubbed my crotch.

My hand slipped between her thighs, my palm pressing against her. Her hips thrust against me, and I kissed her. She moved faster and moaned again, adding pressure to my hardness. I wasn't a teenage boy in danger of coming in my pants, and it felt good, but giving her pleasure felt better.

She growled into my mouth, and a moment later, her back arched.

I pulled away slightly and simply watched her. When she finally opened her eyes, she gave me a soft smile.

"What about you?" she said.

"I can wait. If we keep our guests waiting, they might become aggravated."

"I don't care," she said, reaching her hand toward me again.

I stopped her pursuit. "Yes, you do. You're beautiful when you come. Thank you."

Her cheeks pinkened, and I repositioned her so she was lying with her back against me. My hand went to our child, and I gently rubbed her belly.

"I love you," she said.

"I love you both."

CHAPTER EIGHT

Marinah

I DIDN'T GET TO watch the complete degradation of Mrs. Barnes. The old me would never have found it pleasurable, but it was something war did to you. If President Barnes had me, I would be tortured and publicly executed. That's if I was lucky enough to escape the experiments they would perform on my Shadow Warrior body first.

A few minutes of shame for the president's wife wouldn't kill her. I would have King tell me all about it over dinner.

I stood in front of the citadel until one of the Warriors alerted me that the motorcade was only a few minutes out. I gave one last look at Lesley, trussed up, giving me the stink eye because of the gag. I'd been kind enough to have her tied to a chair so she was comfortable, but I doubted she appreciated it.

I walked to the closet beside the argument room. Okay, dammit, I waddled. On the training field, I had no problem getting into my fighting stance because it required my legs to be apart and my knees bent. Walking was another story, and unless I wanted to walk like I had wet underwear, I waddled.

Pen and paper were waiting for me in the closet. This would enable me to silently pass Nokita commands if they were needed. He was just as wound up as I was. Being away from Maylin and the new baby was hard on him. I planned to send word for Maylin to return and sweeten the deal by promising no Lesley duty.

Nokita and I waited impatiently for the meeting to begin. Finally, I heard the door open.

"Take a seat," King said.

King and Beck were the only Shadow Warriors in the room with the human group. Water and fruit were placed on the table. If things went well, we would provide a full meal before they left. If not, they could survive on what was in the conference room.

The scrape of chairs against the floor echoed as they settled.

Then, within seconds of sitting down, "What's your offer?" a deep voice demanded antagonistically.

Not a good way to start with King.

"I don't have an offer," King said evenly. "You either want our help with security and you work with the other outposts, or you don't. We don't need you. The other outposts would be safer with more people, but we have Warriors stationed with them. The rest of us are safe here, and we can sustain ourselves far longer than you can."

The man hesitated, then asked, "What happens if we don't accept your offer of protection?"

"More than likely," King said. "You die. The Federation is killing anyone who won't fight with them. Do you know that they're injecting humans with the protein that turns them into hellhounds?"

"We think it's bullshit," the man scoffed. "Lies being used to scare us into cooperating."

A woman's voice cut in before King responded, though I didn't miss his low growl.

"Dave," she said, firmly. "The information came from people we trust. We need the Shadow Warriors' help."

Silence.

Then the woman continued.

"Dave's brother lived at the outpost that was attacked. He escaped with his wife and their youngest. Their older son stayed behind to fight."

She swallowed audibly before finishing.

"The Federation killed him."

I clenched my jaw. Dave's brother should have sent his son with his wife and their other child. Inside me, Ms. Beast growled low with disapproval, agreeing fully.

King must have had the same thought I did. I could almost see his eyes gleam, because Dave immediately went on the defensive.

"Jack, my brother, lost his leg two years ago," he said, his voice edged with belligerence.

I didn't need to see King to know he gave a slight nod in acknowledgment.

The woman spoke again. "The Federation will systematically wipe us out. Our people are split fifty-fifty on taking your help. It's fear," she explained. "It's the history of our country. They fear what's different from them."

King's voice remained steady. "If we send Shadow Warriors, I need to know they won't be stabbed in the back."

"We will feed them and give them shelter," she assured him. "We are at war with the Federation, and we can't handle an attack from both sides." Then, after a brief pause, she asked, "Do you have the same poison that turns humans into hellhounds?"

I might actually like this woman.

"We don't," King said. "And we don't want it either. Once we get our hands on the stuff, we'll destroy everything we find along with the scientific data. We do, however, have a serum that keeps Shadow Warriors alive if we're bitten or scratched. We're working on the same for humans, but so far, we haven't produced it."

A chair scraped back abruptly, the legs screeching against the tile.

"So, you can save yourselves but not us?" Dave snapped.

King's tone didn't change. "Shadow Warriors heal faster than humans, which enables us to fight off the bites and scratches while the antidote gives us added time," he said. "If we develop a human antidote, it will be shared freely, with or without your willingness to accept our protection."

"Dave." This time, the woman's voice was sharper and more insistent. "You lost your nephew because of the Federation. They are the enemy, not this man," she said coldly. If you can't control yourself, step outside."

She held authority. And that surprised me.

"Dave is my husband," she continued, her voice settling into something quieter but no less commanding. "He's been angry for a long time, and it gets the best of him." There was a pause. "I am Carmen, the mayor of Tully, our outpost. It was named after Dave's father."

She gestured toward the others.

"Kevin is the mayor of Second Son, and Mason is the mayor of Territory Three. They also have questions."

If this was an act, I'd eat my plastic sandal.

A man cleared his throat. "I'm Mason," he said. "Landan mentioned you'd allow them to send their children here. Is that true?"

"Yes," King answered.

Mason hesitated. "Would you allow us to send ours?"

"You may send your children and anyone not capable of fighting with you."

"Why?"

I actually heard King inhale sharply.

"Shadow Warriors value children," he said, his voice laced with restraint. "We do not make war on them. Too many have died. Too many parents have died. We live in harmony with the humans on this island. We protect them, and in return, they fight alongside us and help in all aspects of our care. When the war with the Federation is settled, we will return the island to its people. We'll move to the mainland and find a home there."

"Is there an islander we could speak with?" Mason asked.

I was surprised King didn't lose his temper.

I quickly scribbled a name on my paper and handed it to Nokita. He left the room, and a moment later, I heard the door open again.

King's voice followed a moment later. "Fetch Beatriz."

A beat of silence.

"The woman in charge of the staff will be here shortly," King continued. "I am trying to hold onto my temper and accommodate you. I understand that you fear us. I still don't understand why."

The woman spoke again.

"We were fed lies," she admitted. "And no matter how stupid those lies are, and believe me, most of them don't even make sense, but once you've heard them enough times, they become hard to ignore. I worked for the Federation's development division," she added. "So did Dave. We escaped when I was ordered to report to the military as a red stripe."

Her voice dropped slightly. "Until then, we thought we were fighting you. The Federation made you out to be uncontrollable animals. We stayed away from the outposts that worked with you, but some of our people have relatives among them, and they noticed things were not what we thought."

The door creaked open.

"Yes, Señor?" Beatriz's voice came, a little shaky.

King didn't hesitate. "Take my seat."

A chair scraped against the floor as he stood.

"These people have questions for you," he said. "Answer honestly, even if you think it's something I might not want to hear."

I knew he had moved toward the wall by the vent because a second later, I heard two small knocks to let me know he was close.

"Please, ask your questions," Beatriz said, her voice stronger now.

A new voice spoke. A man's. It had to be Kevin, since I didn't recognize it.

"What's the worst thing you can think of to say about the Shadow Warriors?" he asked.

"They eat too much," she said without missing a beat. I could hear the smile in her reply. "They go through too many shoes, and we are forever trying to find more. It's hard when their feet are so big." She stopped speaking.

"That's it?" Kevin asked with obvious skepticism, after about ten seconds.

Beatriz let out a soft chuckle. "What do you want me to say?" She didn't wait for a response. "When they first came to the island, we were afraid, like you," she continued. "We attacked them, and they tried very hard to stop us without killing anyone. When we realized we could not win, we accepted our fate. And you know what? It ended up being good. We are safe. Our children are safe. And the only thing they demand is that everyone works for the good of the island. If we choose to fight, they train us. If we choose to work on the island, they find something we enjoy. They ask for our opinions. They respect our wishes."

She paused for a brief second before adding flatly, "You are stupid for not accepting their help."

Silence.

"Are there more questions?" she asked, unimpressed.

This was why Beatriz ran the citadel.

A different voice, Mason's this time, broke the silence.

"We heard there is a female Shadow Warrior?"

"There is."

"Where is she?"

Ire entered Beatriz's voice. "She has bigger concerns than you," she said bluntly. "If you have questions about the Señora, ask the Señor, her mate."

A chair scraped loudly against the floor, followed by the soft click of the door shutting.

A second later, King retook his seat.

"I think you made her angry," he said.

"For that, I am sorry," the woman replied. Then, she dropped a bombshell. "We have children who need care," she admitted. "We discovered twenty-six in an orphanage fending for themselves. We are struggling to feed them, but we will continue if it is our only option."

Shit.

It was hard enough for the outposts to care for their own families. Now, they were trying to keep orphaned children alive, too. My heart went out to the children and those trying to help.

My mind kicked into overdrive, and I began making plans. We had families who would help. And if it came down to it, more would step up.

"I have no problem taking the children," King said. "They can return on the plane after you go back. We have medical personnel. Will any of them need extra attention?"

"If you could send a few women, they won't be so afraid," the mayor replied. "A medical person would be helpful, but overall, they're in good shape."

She paused for a moment before glancing at the other leaders. "Kevin? Mason? Any more objections?"

"No," both men said in near unison.

"Dave?"

A beat of silence. "I'm sorry for my belligerence," Dave said, his tone less confrontational now. "I don't know what I expected by coming here, but it wasn't this. We have items for trade. My wife has a list. And," his voice steadied. "We need help. We promise your Warriors will not be stabbed in the back."

"If it's settled," King said, "help yourselves to some fruit to tide you over for the next hour. We'll provide a full meal before you return."

"Thank you," the woman said, though hesitation crept into her voice. "But we'll decline the full meal. The children already know they may be coming here, and they're nervous. Honestly, some are terrified. The sooner they meet their future, the better."

"I understand." King said. "The plane has been refueled. I'll have your meals delivered and food for the children put on board. I'm sending twenty-one Shadow Warriors as guards, seven per outpost if that works for you. If needed, we can send more in a week. They will report directly to the three of you. They are guards, not laborers. When they're off duty, they rest."

He laughed slightly. "Beatriz wasn't lying when she said we eat a lot, so we'll send extra food for them, too."

The woman exhaled, the relief in her voice unmistakable.

"Thank you."

CHAPTER NINE

Marinah

"WHAT WAS YOUR TAKE?" King asked me.

The plane left thirty minutes ago. My guard was gathered in the argument room.

"I couldn't see their faces or expressions," I said, "but that might have been a good thing. It forced me to listen and focus on their voices and tone." I tilted my head slightly, recalling the meeting. "There was fear and anger at the start, definitely. But it shifted. By the end, I heard sincerity."

King's lips curled into a small, knowing smile. "They pushed my buttons."

"And I'm so proud of you for not pushing back." I gave him a wink.

"Good call on Beatriz," he said.

I chuckled. "She rules the staff with a broom in one hand and a frying pan in the other." My gaze flicked to Nokita. "Did you tell her not to give information about me?"

He grinned, amusement dancing in his eyes. "No. I only told her they were afraid and hesitant to accept our help. Her back went up all on its own when they asked about you."

I let out a short laugh, shaking my head. "We should use her diplomatic relations abilities more often. She's got a better natural instinct for it than most."

My attention shifted back to King. "Do you think Landan will agree to trade with them after he gets your message?"

King exhaled, leaning back slightly. "Landan is stubborn, but he's not stupid. He knows they're stronger together, and their resources complement each other. I'm more worried about the mayors. Landan has three outposts who call him governor. These outposts won't want him stepping on their toes."

"Agreed." I nodded. "Thankfully, Landan can handle that himself without us getting involved." I straightened, changing course. "I spoke with Missy before she left." I turned to Beck. "Don't blame me about her flying while pregnant. That woman could win an argument with an angry bear." I continued when Beck didn't respond. "She'll help me assign homes." I turned my attention to Alden. "We'll send a group south to look for families who are willing to help. Those families will need Warrior escorts. You'll be in charge of coordinating it."

I shifted to Axel. "Garret was the perfect choice to send on the plane. Once we have his input, we'll have an easier time matching the children with the right families."

Axel's lips twitched in amusement. "It wasn't my choice," he admitted. "Like Missy, Garret insisted. I grumbled about it, but he wants our names on the list. We're willing to take in a child or two."

My guard was formed to iron out politics and strategy. But it was also about people and giving them better lives. Family was special to Warriors. Garret and Axel would be great parents.

"Do you have a preference? Gender, age?" I clarified.

Axel exhaled, considering. "I need Garret in the hospital and traveling to clinics. He's a huge help. With Maylin's new baby," he cut his eyes toward Nokita, "I'm shorthanded even though Maylin is as stubborn as Missy and working part-time at the southern clinic while she's there." Nokita shrugged, and Axel's gaze returned to me. "A baby would make things harder for me and Garret. We don't care if the child is a boy or girl. Above toddler age would be easiest for us. If that's not possible, we'll take an infant and adjust our schedules."

If I'd spoken to Carmen, I would have a better idea of the children's ages. But for now, all I could do was prepare for the unknown.

"We'll know more when they arrive, but please consider you and Garret at the top of the list." I shifted the conversation. "I need to bring something else up. Ruth—"

The second her name left my lips, the entire room tensed. Faces paled, even my mate's.

I sighed but continued. "Ruth and Togg are starting a training academy for any juvenile, seven and older, provided they have parental permission, who wants to learn to protect themselves."

Beck arched a brow; his voice laced with dry amusement. "Is that wise?"

"It keeps her from getting bored," I countered. "And it gives us leverage. She wants this badly, and if she pulls another one of her harebrained stunts, she'll be removed from the program and someone else assigned with Togg. It was her idea, and I agreed. The kids who join will feel safer if they know something about self-protection."

"Did you run this past Missy?"

"Not yet, but I doubt Ruth kept it from her."

Beck's lips twitched. "Missy will back anything that gives her more control over Ruth. Beating her isn't an option; otherwise, the child would be black and blue." He paused. "I don't speak for my mate, though. Run it past her when you get the chance. Every day she was around Lesley Barnes, she was thinking of ways to kill her without you figuring out who did it." His voice was lighter, but the truth behind it wasn't lost on me. "We appreciate you taking her off viper detail. Missy thinks highly of you right now."

"It was unfair to her, and for that, I apologize." I met his gaze. "But it did come in handy for Shadow Warrior punishments."

That got a reaction. The tension in the room cracked as smiles broke out.

When King was in charge, he had knocked heads when needed, but that wasn't how I handled things. The men much preferred head-knocking. Guard duty for Lesley Barnes was an undesired punishment.

"We'll reconvene tomorrow after we know more about the children," I said. "Tonight, I'm feeling antsy, so I plan to go after hellhounds around midnight." I glanced at King, already anticipating his reaction. Before he spoke, I held up a hand. "I know I'm pregnant. But sitting out the discussion with Carmen and the other mayors put me on edge." My gaze swept the room. "If anyone wants to join me, you're invited."

"I'm in," Alden said immediately, earning a sharp glare from King.

"Too busy," Axel replied, shaking his head.

"I'm heading south to Maylin," Nokita added.

Beck smirked and shot a wink at King. "Missy would kill me."

King folded his arms. "You will not be going without me."

I gave him a knowing look. "I didn't intend to."

With that, our meeting adjourned.

Seven hours later, just after sundown, the new children arrived.

I stood waiting with several women who had volunteered to help care for them. One woman, Maria, clutched her husband's hand. She had given birth to a stillborn child just months before, and now, she had hope in her eyes.

The first to step off the plane was a teenage boy, maybe fifteen, his defiant sneer a challenge to the world. Two Shadow Warriors followed him, their expressions unreadable.

Garrett came next, his usual calm presence reassuring. An island woman came after him, then the rest of the children began to descend, stepping cautiously into an entirely new world. Most looked between five and twelve years old, their faces worn with the kind of wariness that came from survival. I counted four older than seven or eight, including the first boy.

My biggest question was how they had managed to survive before the outposts took them in.

Finally, Missy emerged with the other two women we sent. Each cradled a toddler, their tiny arms curled around the women's necks. Vehicles stood ready to transport them to the citadel. Missy, smiling, made her way to me with her own waddle.

"This is Fred," she said, shifting the small boy in her arms who rested almost on top of her round belly. "He's a handful, but also a sweetie. The four oldest children have been looking after all of them. They're worried about being separated."

"We'll work something out." I met her gaze after peering at the child who appeared to be about ten months old. "Thank you for going in my stead."

Missy's grin widened. "Us fat bellies need to stick together."

I let out a small laugh, my hand instinctively resting on my stomach. "Want to trade?"

"Not on your life."

Our laughter faded, and I shifted gears. "Did Ruth mention her plan to train the children for self-protection?"

Missy exhaled, shaking her head with something close to amusement. "She did. I'm unsure what's changed in that child. I haven't had to reprimand her once since she got back from staying with Maylin." She paused, lips quirking. "I think Maylin beat her. If so, it worked, and I will adopt that strategy immediately."

Missy was in a good mood, which meant things had gone better than expected.

"Let's grab one of the cars and get these kids settled."

A piercing scream ripped through the night from twenty feet away.

Chapter Ten

Marinah

Hellhounds advanced from the road we'd driven in on. I stopped counting at ten. I hadn't seen this many together, other than the Federation's attack, for over a year.

The teenage boy who had stepped off the plane first reacted instantly, pulling a knife from his waist. The other three teens, two girls and another boy, rushed forward with him, weapons in hand.

The hellhounds' sharp claws and teeth gleamed in the dim light. Their forms were deceptive. The true horror emerged when you saw them strung up. King's men had captured two alive, and their elongated limbs stretched grotesquely, arms unfurling from too-broad shoulders with legs that extended downward in an unnatural way for canines. They were actually dead humans.

Their appearance wasn't the worst part, though. This group seemed different. It was like someone controlled them. They weren't behaving as erratically as what happened when the whistles were used to control them. These movements were almost orchestrated, and I'll admit it freaked me out. I had often wondered if a tiny bit of their humanity remained behind. If so, I hadn't seen it, yet. Actually, I didn't want to see it. So much easier to think their brains were mush and there was nothing left inside.

We weren't sure if older human corpses that turned into hellhounds were natural selection via the modified formaldehyde or if they all turned, and the newer corpses formed a different breed. Either way, they were our human dead, twisted into something monstrous. If you didn't know what they were, the signs were easy to miss. Until King told me what I was looking at, I didn't see the truth.

They were also hard to kill, and the only way to do it was to remove the head. They turned to ash shortly after death, as if the horror they embodied refused to leave a trace. It made studying their corpses impossible.

The humans, including the children, were in serious danger. I shifted to Ms. Beast mid-stride, my body flowing into Warrior form effortlessly with a strong burst of K-5, the hormones and chemicals that gave us the ability to shift. The nightmare I had this morning flashed through my mind, and I had to shake it away. I ran and leapt over the teens, clearing their heads by a foot. King stayed close beside me, his powerful muscles sending him even higher. My Warrior form incorporated the baby, and my stomach didn't stick out more than a few inches.

"Guard the children!" I commanded the Shadow Warriors who were moving toward the action. I glanced back at the teens. "Their bite won't harm us, but it will kill you. Stay back!"

A low, guttural snarl rolled through the darkness. Gleaming eyes locked onto me and King.

The stench of cloying rot thickened the air. My senses sharpened, and K-5 pounded through my veins. Growls vibrated deep inside my chest. Ms. Beast wanted blood.

Beside me, King's Warrior form was a thing of sheer power. His massive frame bristled with raw energy, his fur rippling like liquid fire under the tarmac lights.

The lead hound came at me, a blur of coiled muscle and jagged teeth. I pivoted to meet the attack, claws flashing as I raked them across its throat.

The sound of tearing flesh met my ears, and black blood splattered around me. The beast howled, its body convulsing violently before it collapsed. I quickly decapitated it with my claws.

Another sprang from the left, jaws snapping at my shoulder. I caught it mid-leap and sliced through its ribs, carving deep. It made a low guttural sound, twisted violently, and its claws raked across my side. Fire lanced through the wounds, but I didn't slow down. I drove forward, slamming my weight into its chest, sending it to the tarmac. My teeth found its throat and I tore at flesh, and with another brutal bite, its body went limp, and its half-severed head hung uselessly from shredded tendons.

I caught sight of King. A hellhound lunged at him, but he caught it mid-air, his jaws locking onto its neck. The beast thrashed, its body whipping like a ragdoll before he hurled it into two others. They tumbled, snarling, but King was already moving. His claws sank deep into another hound, carving deep furrows down its spine. The creature shrieked, its body spasming before it collapsed.

I caught a rush of movement slightly behind me. Too close.

I spun just in time to dodge teeth that barely missed my leg. Another hellhound struck from the other direction, and its claws raked across my back. Hot pain flared. I turned with a snarl, my teeth finding its throat. Then, I tore.

Flesh ripped apart.

More blood sprayed around me. The hellhound gave a strangled gurgle before it crumpled, lifeless. We killed two more. The remaining beasts hesitated now, hackles raised, their glowing eyes flickering between King and me. They were fucking calculating their next move.

Two lunged towards King at once. One clamped its jaws onto his shoulder, and King roared. His massive hands shot out, and his claws severed its spine. Then he crushed. The glorious snap echoed in my ears. He tore its head from its body, flinging it aside like discarded trash. I took out another and then another.

The last hellhound bolted straight toward the teenagers.

A thunderous growl tore from my throat. I sprinted across the tarmac, my muscles burning. I wouldn't make it in time. The hound leaped, fangs extended.

The lead male teen moved fast and jabbed his knife into its stomach. One of the girls followed, her knife slicing across its throat though she didn't sever it. They jumped back, and the other two teens moved in.

Stab. Dodge. Slice. Jump. They worked like a seamless unit.

The hellhound went down and stayed down in under ten seconds.

My breath came heavy as I scanned the nearly silent battlefield. Headless corpses littered the area, their black blood pooling in thick, inky puddles that would soon be dust. King stood over the last one, his chest heaved, his fur was covered in streaks of blood.

His blue eyes met mine.

A quiet understanding passed between us.

The battle was over.

For now.

I shifted back to human, still covered in blood. Intense body aches from the hellhound bites and scratches assailed me, and I tried not to show it. Warm blood trailed down my arms and legs in thin rivulets. The children stared, some wide-eyed with awe, others frozen in terror, their small bodies pressed together like a flock of startled birds.

I turned toward them, forcing my voice to stay calm. "You're safe now."

King stepped beside me and slowed his breathing. "Welcome to your new home."

That was King and I, communication specialists, not.

My gaze shifted to the four teens. "Have any of you been scratched or bitten?"

They exchanged quick glances then scanned each other for wounds. They understood that a single drop of hellhound saliva in a wound or even a minor scratch meant death.

"No," one of the girls confirmed.

I studied them. "I'm not sure why you're here," I said, not unkindly. "You can fight. Surely the outposts needed you?"

The boy who had sneered earlier lifted his chin, his grip tightening around his knife. He pointed it, not in threat, but in fierce protectiveness, toward the children huddled behind the Warriors.

"They are our family. And we aren't leaving them."

The sneer may have been gone from his face, but his voice still carried its edge.

I met his gaze. "I have no intention of separating those who want to stay together." I gave them a nod of respect. "Thank you for your help. Will you assure the children that they are safe and we mean them no harm?"

The boy didn't answer immediately. His eyes raked over me, as if weighing my sincerity. But before he spoke, the same girl who had answered my previous question replied.

"Yes, we will," she said.

The four teens turned and walked toward the younger children. They had the discipline of soldiers, and the wariness of survivors.

I glanced at King. "They can fight."

"I saw." His voice was contemplative. "With a little extra training, we can use them." A sardonic smile tugged at his lips. "Now, tell me, did this quench your thirst for hellhound blood, or are we still heading out tonight?"

I yawned, exhaustion tugging at my limbs. "It'll take hours to settle the kids. I'll wait to answer."

I stole another glance at the teens. "They aren't afraid of us."

King shifted to human. "That's an interesting turn of events."

His tone was thoughtful. "The mayors were."

I smirked. "I don't think Carmen was afraid of us. She was worried the men with her would do something stupid, and she wouldn't be able to fix it."

King grunted. "Said every woman everywhere."

I didn't agree or disagree. Some things were just true.

The children were guided into vehicles, their small, weary faces barely visible through the windows. King and I took up guard duty, riding alongside the vehicles on motorbikes, our senses on overdrive in case of another attack.

I'd had constant arguments with Axel about riding a motorcycle. It was getting to the point where I needed to listen to him. My stomach felt almost too heavy as I bent low and moved with the bike. King wisely kept his mouth shut about my mode of transportation. This would be my last ride until the birth. I could live with it.

Baby safe, Ms. Beast said.

Yes, baby safe, I assured her.

The roads remained quiet, and we didn't encounter additional hellhounds.

When we arrived at the citadel, the kids climbed out of the cars, disheveled and their movements sluggish from the long journey. Missy still carried the toddler. He was asleep in her arms.

We led them to the indoor training facility. It was large enough to hold them and had bathrooms. Long tables were set up in the corner with steaming trays of food for those hungry enough to eat. One of the older girls saw the food and led a group of the children toward the tables. Food overrode wariness.

Maria, the island woman who had lost her child, lingered near Missy, hovering, her hands clenched tightly together with an expression of longing. It was mixed with loss, and my heart physically hurt for her. I couldn't help placing my hand on my belly for a few seconds.

It took about thirty minutes for the children to settle. Some sat with plates balanced on their laps, eating mechanically. Others cradled plastic cups filled with water, staring blankly, unsure of what came next.

Axel examined me, his usual tight-lipped expression on full display as he cleaned my wounds with antiseptic. It burned like holy hell, but I didn't make a single whimper, or he would have complained more. I sustained some type of injury almost weekly, and he took it as a personal affront.

"How many hellhounds?" he asked.

"Eleven." I hesitated, trying to keep a hiss out of my next words. "There were twelve, but the four older teens took it down."

His brows lifted slightly. "Interesting."

He didn't say more, but I could practically hear the wheels turning inside his head. Four untrained adult humans would have trouble bringing down a hellhound and living to tell about it.

Axel moved to my stomach, pressing the stethoscope against my skin, listening intently.

"The baby appears no worse for wear." His lips quirked. "I'll have an entire medical textbook written by the time this child is delivered. I suppose you rode one of the damned motorbikes."

"Last ride until after the baby is born," I said.

"It's about time," he grumbled. "After the birth, we'll know more about hellhound toxins and how they interact during pregnancy."

He worried constantly about what a hellhound bite or scratch could do to the baby. At least we knew after several scratches and bites from earlier altercations, they didn't seem to have an effect. But he was right, and the definitive answer would come after the baby was born. Ms. Beast didn't worry about me shifting form and fighting. I trusted her to a point.

Axel's tone hardened. "Would you follow orders if I told you to stay in bed tomorrow?"

I simply stared at him with a 'what are you, dumb?' look.

He sighed. "I didn't think so."

I patted his arm. "Take care of King while I speak to the children."

Axel grumbled under his breath before muttering, "Yes, my Queen."

I shot him a glare, but he only smirked. He knew exactly how much that irritated me, especially coming from him.

I stepped toward the children. Their chatter died.

My gaze swept the group. "Hi, everyone. I'm Marinah." My voice carried through the training center. "I know you're tired, and you're worried about what happens next."

A flicker of unease rippled through them. Several clutched younger children, and their arms tightened.

"I'm aware that the teenagers have been caring for you, and you don't want to be separated." I let the statement hang, making sure they knew I understood. "It would help if you could break into groups with those you want to stay with. Please do that now."

Silence.

No one moved.

The four teens sat on the floor, positioned in front of the group, like a shield.

I directed my question to them. "Is there someone who speaks for you?"

The boy with the attitude stood.

"I do."

Of course he did.

I nodded. "Please call me Marinah. What should I call you?"

"Desmond," he said, belligerence laced into the two syllables.

Now that I could see him clearly, I took in the details. His wavy brown hair hung limply to his shoulders, damp from either sweat or the humid night air. He was tall, still growing into his frame, thin, but wiry rather than emaciated. A square jaw framed his face, his teeth clenched so tightly that the ever-present sneer seemed permanently etched there.

I ignored his attitude. "Is it possible for them to divide into groups?" I asked, keeping my tone even.

Desmond spread his arms wide. "This is our group."

Alrighty then.

"There are three babies," I pointed out. "Did everyone take care of them?"

He gave a single, firm nod.

I turned my attention to the younger children. "This is the citadel. It has enough beds for everyone, and we can arrange rooms to fit four of you together. You will all be in the same hall. The citadel won't work long-term," I continued, "but for a few days, you'll be fine. We have families on the island who want to help. Maybe if you take some time to think about it, you will see that being on the island will give you a better life."

Did the younger kids understand? I wasn't sure. I wasn't good at this. "You'll have the chance to meet the families to make your decisions easier. If you decide to stay grouped together at the citadel, we will find a way to make it work."

A few of the children exchanged glances with the teens, but their expressions remained filled with distrust.

"I do need to warn you," I went on, "some of the families I've told you about don't have an English speaker in the house. Does anyone speak Spanish?"

Silence. No hands went up.

I turned to Desmond. "Do they need your permission to answer?"

His expression darkened. "No," he said flatly. "They just don't want to."

I exhaled through my nose, keeping my expression neutral.

Hanging Desmond up by his thumbs probably wouldn't go over well.

CHAPTER ELEVEN

Marinah

"I NEED TO SPEAK to the four of you in private," I told Desmond and nodded at the other three teens.

"And if we say no?"

This kid. Sheesh. He and Ruth would get along famously.

"If you say no, I will honor it." I met his eyes, making sure he knew I wasn't here to force them into anything. "We help each other on the island. We work together. That's what I would like to talk to you about."

The girl beside Desmond raised her hand. Her hair was a shade lighter than his, a bit longer but similar in texture. Siblings, most likely. Her nose matched

Desmond's. It was her eyes that set her apart. While Desmond's were blue, hers were a vivid green, striking against the overhead lights in the gym. Shadow Warrior's almost always had blue eyes and with her green ones, she made me think of Labyrinth. He had one of each. My gut tightened.

I nodded to her. She shot a glance at Desmond, a silent conversation passing between them before she squared her shoulders and turned back to me. "My name is Julia. I want to hear what you have to say."

Desmond gently elbowed her, but she scowled, then shifted her gaze to the other two teens. "Come on. We're here, and there's nothing we can do about it. We might as well hear her out."

She took a step forward, her posture straight but not stiff, and after a brief hesitation, the other two followed, their expressions wary and slightly resigned.

"Shit," Desmond muttered before grudgingly stepping up as well.

"There's a small meeting room next door," I told them. "The children won't be taken from the gym. You have my word."

Desmond grumbled something under his breath, too low for me to catch even with my heightened hearing. I let it slide. No use getting into a pissing match with a teenager over his discourtesy.

I led them to the small office I had assigned to Ruth and Togg. Inside, the two of them were bent over a desk, papers spread between them. Their conversation stopped when we entered.

"I hate to ask," I said, "but we need to use your office for a few minutes. Would you mind helping in the gym?"

Ruth's gaze flicked over the teens, and interest sparked in her expression. For a second, I expected some kind of protest, but instead, the alien being that had possessed her body surfaced. "Come on, Togg."

Ruth moved past me without another word. I barely stopped myself from gaping at how easily she complied.

"My Queen," Togg murmured as he passed.

The door clicked shut behind them, sealing me in with the four wary teenagers.

"You're her," Julia said. "The female Shadow Warrior."

Desmond grumbled. "We saw her shift. Unless there's more than one, of course she's her."

Julia ignored him. They had to be siblings. She had that exasperated patience, like she'd been dealing with his foul moods for years.

"The mayor of Tully told us you had anti-venom for hellhound bites, but we didn't believe her. I saw a hound bite you, and you survived."

Desmond muttered something unintelligible again.

"Yes," I confirmed. "Our scientists are working on an antidote for humans. Bites and scratches are safe for us now and if we know we're going to encounter hellhounds, we take it hours before. We had planned to go hunting tonight, and were prepared. The bites and scratches still burn, but that's all they do to us now."

"That's so cool," the other girl said, her eyes wide in fascination.

I smiled at her. "It is rather cool, and it's helped us tremendously."

Desmond scoffed. "Are you going to keep chitchatting like the world hasn't ended, or can we get down to business?"

To hell with diplomacy. I turned and faced him. "Your attitude is about to get you into trouble," I said, my voice very low, which should have warned him. "I have been extremely patient, but you keep pushing. Do you expect me to toss you in a cell and throw away the key? Is that what you're after?"

"You and what army?"

He barely had time to blink before I moved.

In half a second, I had him pinned, his own blade pressed against his windpipe.

"This army," I said, even lower. "I'm a one-person wrecking ball. I'm also in command of the island,

and the last thing I want is to hurt any of you. But you're making that difficult."

I shoved him back toward his friends and flipped the knife in my palm, offering it to him hilt-first. His jaw clenched as he took it, slipping it back into his waistband without a word.

Julia smirked at him. I wouldn't have been the least bit surprised if she'd stuck out her tongue.

"We're worried about the kids," she said, her amusement fading into something more serious. "We're the only family they have."

"What did the outposts do when you arrived there?" I asked.

"They housed us in a large barn, and it was hard for the children." She shrugged, the motion tight with old frustration. "I know it's difficult because there are so many of us, but we lived alone for years. We only went to the outpost because a virus broke out, and everyone was sick."

"Do you know what the virus was?" I asked.

Julia nodded. "The nurse at Second Son said it was measles. One of our babies died, and that's what finally made us look for help. They provided food, but made us stay outside their walls until no one was sick. It took over a month. Most of them resented us."

I inhaled slowly, keeping my reaction measured. "We don't resent you. We asked the outposts to send their children here so they would be safe from the Federation. Your group is the first they agreed to send."

Desmond let out a bitter scoff. "They didn't want us, and didn't care if we lived or died."

"That's not true," Julia snapped, turning on him with barely restrained frustration. "They're struggling just like everyone else. They wanted to help, but didn't have the resources."

I lifted a hand, cutting through their rising anger. "We do have the resources. So instead of fighting about the past, let's focus on making this transition as smooth as possible. The children are exhausted, and if we keep arguing, they'll end up sleeping on a cold floor. If anyone has a solution, I'm all ears."

Julia clenched her fists, clearly holding back whatever sharp retort she had for Desmond. After a second, she exhaled and said, "I'm sorry." She met my gaze. "It would help if we knew the children were with families who wanted them."

I liked this girl. Practical. Protective. Smart.

"Okay," I said. "I'll work with that. It would also help if you sat in at our meetings concerning you and the children. The Federation sees the citadel as a threat, and it's not necessarily the safest place for kids, though we do have some who live here."

I turned to Desmond, holding his gaze. "I'd like both you and Julia to be part of the meetings. I know you don't like us, but we do want to help. More than that, we want to keep the trauma to the children as low as possible."

He didn't answer right away. His shoulders were still tense, but something in his posture shifted slightly. A hesitation rather than outright defiance. He gave a curt nod, the first real crack in his tough exterior. It wasn't much, but it was something.

Progress.

"I do have a favor to ask," I said carefully. "One of the islanders recently lost a child at birth. She's hoping to care for one of the toddlers. She's willing to stay here with you until we have everything sorted out. Would you be open to that?"

Julia glanced at Desmond, gauging his reaction. He didn't protest, just held his silence, which was as good as approval. She turned back to me. "Cade is the toddler Missy carried. He wants nothing more than to be held."

I allowed myself a small smile. "I think Maria would be thrilled to hold him all night if that's what he needs."

The tension in the room softened, just a little. Their exhaustion and uncertainty still hung thick in the air, but at least now we had a starting point.

"Let's get everyone settled," I said. "We'll start working out the details tomorrow."

Julia gave a small nod. "Thank you."

Chapter Twelve

King

WHILE MARINAH HANDLED THE children, I checked in with the Citadel's watch. The number of hellhounds that had attacked us at the airport gnawed at me. It had worried Marinah too. Before she headed to the training facility, I told her my plans, and she agreed that we needed to understand the battle we'd just had.

I climbed our highest tower in search of Eagle.

"Alden reported a large sighting of hellhounds near the shipyard," Eagle reported when I approached.

He was our best sniper, steady under pressure, and reliable in a fight. He'd stepped up and been invaluable since Labyrinth's death. He would make a solid addition to Marinah's guard, though I kept that thought to myself. Marinah had to choose her own people. She'd make the right decision. I just hoped it was soon.

"Alden sent the message about twenty minutes ago," he continued.

We kept telegraphs in key locations throughout the island. Hellhounds were attracted to electronic devices, so the early telegraph machines were a less dangerous option due to the smaller amount of electricity they needed. They still caused trouble, but not as much as pre-hellhound electronics or devices that worked wirelessly.

"We ran into twelve at the airport," I told him. "Now there are a dozen less to worry about. Feel like taking a ride?"

Eagle glanced around, his expression shifting curiously. "Where's Beck?"

Usually, I couldn't get rid of Beck. He was always a step behind me, watching my six while I watched Marinah's.

"He's helping his mate with the children we retrieved," I said.

Eagle blinked, then let out a quiet chuckle, shaking his head. Even he had trouble picturing Beck in that role.

"It happens to the best of us," I told him with a knowing smile.

Eagle grimaced, but I didn't call him on it. One day, he'd understand.

We took the motorbikes.

Riding felt like freedom. Like an escape. But now that Marinah ran things, I didn't feel the same pull to the open road. I'd rather be at her side than chasing the wind. Unfortunately, duty kept us apart most days, though even when I wasn't with her, I felt her.

It was something in our mate bond, a steady hum beneath my skin, always letting me know where she was. If we were miles apart, the connection wasn't as strong, but at the citadel, it was constant. I could sense when she was happy or agitated.

Since she became pregnant, the bond had deepened. Maybe "tether" was a better word for it. We were tied together by something unexplainable.

I pushed the thoughts aside and let myself enjoy the ride. The steady thrum of the motorbike beneath me, the wind slicing past. It was a fleeting moment of sanity before reality crashed back.

We pulled into the shipyard.

Alden stood with a group of Shadow Warriors, all in their beast forms, their postures tense, their watchful eyes scanning the area. As soon as Alden spotted us, he strode toward me.

"I have something strange to report," he said.

I waited, but when he didn't immediately continue, I prompted, "Report."

His gaze flicked to the others before settling back on me. "There were thirty in this group of hounds."

I exhaled sharply. "That's larger than the pack that attacked us at the airport."

"That's not the strange part." He hesitated, something uneasy flickering across his expression. "One of them was big. Really big and he looked different. He seemed to have control over the others. They obeyed him."

I stilled. "Obeyed?"

Alden nodded grimly. "Yes. Not in a way we fully understood. More like grunts and gestures. But the group split off, and only half of them attacked us. It was coordinated. The big one got away."

My stomach tightened. That wasn't just bad news; it was hell of dangerous.

"How big?" I asked.

"As big as one of us in Shadow Warrior form."

Fuck me.

"What direction did they go?"

"We aren't sure. That's what we were discussing when you arrived. The hellhounds made a tactical attack. They knew what they were doing and allowed the others to escape. We've never seen them behave like this. No one around with whistles but us. When we tried the whistles, they did nothing."

The implications settled inside me. The Federation had somehow nullified the whistles, which was bad news. A creature leading the hellhounds could be catastrophic.

"Are the fifteen dead?" I asked.

"Yes."

I nodded. "We need one alive. Next time, keep that in mind."

Alden gave a sharp nod. "Understood."

"Injuries?"

"A few scratches and bites. We took the antivenom this morning. It's still working."

He hesitated.

"What else?" I pressed.

His expression darkened. "The strange one had blue eyes."

Fuck me twice. Shadow Warriors had blue eyes and hellhounds always had black eyes.

As large as a Shadow Warrior and with the same eye color. This smelled like rotten fish.

"Eagle, set up here until Alden returns." Eagle pulled his rifle off his bike. I turned my attention back to Alden. "Take five Warriors and track the hellhounds. Do not engage unless it's absolutely necessary."

"Got it."

I had to speak with Marinah about going on high alert and canceling leave for the Warriors. Most Warriors headed to the southern part of the island to see their families or relax with single friends. If they stayed at the citadel, they invariably got roped into work. This was another change Marinah had imposed. She wanted them to have time away. Unfortunately, she wouldn't place the same parameters on herself. Funny how I never minded the constant grind of leadership until it fell on her shoulders.

I returned to the bike and drove the curves at top speed. Marinah needed this information immediately. She also needed sleep. I had a feeling my news would ruin that.

I worried about Marinah and our child constantly. Control had been my foundation since I accepted that I was a Shadow Warrior. I had no control over her pregnancy. The baby could arrive at any time. There could be complications. Marinah could die in childbirth.

The thought seized my chest, and it felt like a heavy weight took my breath. If I let myself dwell on the what-ifs, I spiraled and had a harder time handling Beast. Marinah was essentially my heart. I needed her in order to breathe.

Mate, Beast grumbled softly.

When I reached our room, I found Marinah sleeping on top of the bedspread. Two covered trays rested on the small table on the other side of the room. Our dinner. It was unlike her to pass up food, even for sleep. It showed how tired she was.

I decided to eat and let her rest for another hour. She'd be pissed when I woke her, but she needed the down time.

I watched her while I ate. She'd called me creepy for doing it before, but I'd caught her doing the same thing. The truth was, we were happiest when we shared the same space. We didn't care if we were making love or fighting hellhounds. Being close was what mattered.

While I watched her, my thoughts circled back to Alden's report.

We had always wondered what would happen if a Shadow Warrior became a hellhound. We kept tight control of our numbers, and there was only one Warrior unaccounted for.

Knet.

CHAPTER THIRTEEN

Marinah

I OPENED MY EYES and found King lying beside me, his body warm against mine. Those piercing blue eyes were locked onto me.

I smiled sleepily. "What time is it?"

"Around 1 a.m.," he murmured. He brushed a few stray strands of hair from my face, then placed his hand on my stomach. "How are you feeling?"

I loved everything about this man. Whether he was soft and warm like now, or angry and frustrated. He could be in human or his beast form; it didn't matter. I wasn't sure how I got this lucky. I knew when he was near. King said it was the mate bond, but it went past that. Our energy was aligned, and I had no other way to explain it.

A thought suddenly struck me.

King always pushed me to rest. He wouldn't be lying here awake, watching me like this, unless something was wrong.

I tensed. "What is it?" I asked, propping myself on one elbow.

Instead of answering, he slid out of bed, walked around to my side, and took my hand. With a firm but gentle pull, he helped me sit upright, lifted me, giant belly and all, and carried me to a chair, resting me on his lap.

"I waited longer than I should," he admitted. "But you needed sleep. You can yell at me after we figure this out."

Unease ran through me. "You're scaring me," I said, my voice tight with growing wariness.

He explained what Alden said. I listened in silent horror. Our worst nightmare was turning into reality. King didn't need to tell me who it was.

"Knet," I spat, already picturing my Nova teeth sinking into his skull, one powerful bite crushing his brain to pulp.

Kill, Ms. Beast whispered inside me.

She was right. We didn't need Nova to kill Knet.

"It has to be," King said.

"Do you think they injected him with their serum and then killed him?" I asked, my mind racing through the possibilities.

His jaw clenched. "Alden said he appeared to be in control. If the Federation murdered him, would he be working with them? He may have volunteered. There's no telling what types of experiments they're doing. No matter what our small group of scientists discover, we're always a step or ten behind the Federation. Right now, we don't have the information we need."

I exhaled sharply, trying to piece it together. "We know it's because Barnes and possibly his wife helped create the first hellhound."

King nodded.

"What about the hounds they created at the settlement?" I asked. "The ones who slaughtered the children?" My hands fisted in the blanket. "I don't see how they would kill their own children if they had any form of control."

"Until we capture one, we have no way of knowing."

"You said our whistles didn't work. Was Knet controlling them verbally?" I pressed and continued. "They had to have made him with the hellhound serum. It's the only thing that makes sense. I agree with you, Knet hates us enough to volunteer."

"He does. I have Alden tracking them now while Eagle holds the shipyard. I told them not to engage unless necessary."

"Why?"

"We're stretched too thin."

I stared at him for several seconds, then shook my head in frustration. I knew what had to be done. "Have the entire island placed on high alert. All Shadow Warriors at their assigned stations. No time off until the island is safe from this current threat."

"I'll see it done."

"I am pissed off that you let me sleep, but we'll deal with that later." I folded my arms. "What really infuriates me is that Lesley Barnes has the information we need. I broke her damn leg, and she still wouldn't talk." My jaw tightened. "We need a torture expert. Or something."

King's expression darkened. "Or something. My answer is to simply kill her. She's not worth the headache she causes."

I smirked. "What if we use her as bait?"

King's lips pulled back in an evil grin. "Okay, maybe I like your plan more than mine." He tilted his head slightly, watching me. "Do you have a plan?"

"Not yet, but I will," I said as my head spun through possibilities.

"Are the new children settled?" he asked.

"They're in the lower hall. I had beds moved in, and we'll sort out additional details tomorrow. Two of the older teens will attend the meeting in the morning." I shrugged. "I guess this morning."

His gaze held mine. "And what's your plan for right now?" His voice dipped slightly, the heat behind his eyes unmistakable.

"Not that," I said, leaning in and giving him a quick kiss before moving away. "I need food delivered to the argument room, and my guards there as soon as possible."

King sighed dramatically but stood and placed me on my feet.

"Unfortunately, I need to pee first," I said.

He chuckled.

I narrowed my eyes. "After our prince is born, you and I are going to have a long discussion about appropriate times to laugh. We'll be in warrior forms with claws bared."

His grin widened. "I can't wait."

Then he pulled me in close, and just before our lips met, he whispered, "Our princess."

He stole my breath and gave me no chance to argue about our child. Within a minute, the sudden need for the bathroom cut our make-out session short. Frustrated but refocused, I told King to gather the guard.

"I had sent Nokita south to be with Maylin, so we were down one. No, two, with Alden out chasing hellhounds."

"Okay. We'll make do."

While King gathered the men, I went to the argument room, my gaze drawn to Labyrinth's chair. I had to replace him, but how could I? He had been a man of few words, and he hadn't always been on my side, but he stood with me when I made the final decision. A small smile tugged at my lips at the memory of him going head-to-head with Beck.

I began eating the food on the table allowing memories of Labyrinth to fill me until my grin was a full smile. It still hurt to think of him, but my chest lightened just a bit.

Nokita entered the room, and my smile disappeared.

"I thought you were going to Maylin," I said.

"She's coming here. I stopped at the shipyard and spoke to Eagle. He told me what happened. I sent Warriors to escort Maylin and Che here. She should arrive tomorrow." His expression darkened. "The large hellhound is a problem."

I exhaled sharply. "You must be thinking what we are."

"Knet," he growled, the name carrying a sharp edge of rage.

King strode in, dropping into the seat beside me. "He's mine," he declared.

I gave him a warning look, a low growl escaping before I spoke. "Beck said those same words before, but Nova has a special place in her black heart for him."

King held up his hands. "I don't mess with Nova."

"What if the first person to find him gets the honor of killing him?" Nokita suggested.

Axel, Cabel, and Beck entered just in time to catch that last part.

"Who are we talking about killing?" Beck asked.

"Knet," the three of us answered in unison.

Beck gave a nod of approval. "I would like nothing better than ending his miserable life, but I'm with Nokita. Whoever finds him first gets the kill."

Axel didn't join the discussion. He looked tired. It seemed to be a constant state with him lately. When this was over, he was getting a vacation.

I sighed. "We have bigger problems to discuss. Unfortunately, we might need Knet alive." I turned to King. "Would you like to sum things up?"

King laid out what happened at the shipyard.

The room charged with K-5. Expressions hardened, hands fisted, and eyes gleamed. Even Axel, the most level-headed of us, looked furious.

Knet had already signed his death warrant, but this new information elevated the need by ten notches.

"The Federation has been experimenting with their unnatural serum to create hellhounds," I said. "It's most likely been happening since the beginning, which is why they're always ahead of us. If we take

Knet alive, we can put our science to work, figure out exactly what he is, and how to eliminate these new hellhounds who follow him."

I gave them a moment before asking, "Do any of you want to add something?"

"He'll be coming after you," King said, his eyes locked on mine.

"He will," I admitted.

"I disagree," Beck cut in.

I groaned internally. Beck always disagreed.

"He wants you dead, but he'll go for the bigger picture too. He'll do his best to hurt the people on the island. It will appeal to him just as much. You're well-guarded. He knows that. He'll target the soft spots, the places where he can kill the most people because that will cause you mental anguish. The only good news is that if he's on the island, we will find him."

"Dammit," I muttered. "I hate when you're right."

"I try," Beck said with a smirk.

The door swung open, and Alden entered. The look on his face didn't give me much hope. He sat down, exhaling sharply.

"They went into the water a mile from the ship-yard. After that? No idea. We scouted the shore for miles in both directions. Nothing."

I turned to Beck. "Give him your thoughts."

Beck repeated himself.

"Makes sense," Alden said. "What are we going to do about it?" His eyes landed on me.

"For starters, we go on high alert," I said. "Get word to your men that there is no time off until we're secure. Knet is on the island, or close to it. We have no idea how many hounds are with him. We need to keep Knet from attacking humans." I turned to Nokita. "How's the sub coming along?"

We had an older submarine he'd been scavenging parts for. There was also the submersible. It was useful for scouting and minor runs, but not much else. Right now, our best advantage was having the sub in the water.

"It should be operational after I make a few minor adjustments," Nokita said. "I took it out for a test run two days ago. The oxygen gauge decided to act up, but I have a spare and can replace it within the hour. If I were Knet, I would attack the shipyard."

"They failed before," I replied.

"Yes, they did," Nokita said, "it's why it makes a good target. We won't suspect it."

I nodded my head. He had a good point. "The Federation is transporting this new group of hell-hounds to the island somehow. We need to stop them. It's either by ship or submarine. What are the capabilities of ours?"

Nokita leaned back slightly, arms crossed. "As you know, it's not a modern craft. No high-tech systems, no fancy tracking. But that's actually an advantage. I have seventy men ready to go but I could run it with a twenty-man crew if I had to. The men have been training hard. The islanders can fight, but they're not Warriors. In the sub, it doesn't matter. Everyone is even."

He glanced around the room, then zeroed in on Beck, who waved him to continue. "Rodrigo knows everything I do, and he's been training the men for submarine combat. We have four torpedoes in the front, two in the rear. A direct hit could take down or cripple a large ship, but the torpedoes are old, tracking could fail, or they could malfunction completely. Tactical positioning and surprise are our best weapons."

"And the mines?" I asked.

"We have them in the shipyard harbor and Warrior Bay," Nokita confirmed. The Bay was close to the citadel. "They're remotely detonated. If we use them right, we could catch their sub by drawing it closer. The mines give us an advantage."

I was impressed. More than that, I liked the idea of the islanders having a way to fight without risking hellhound bites or scratches. How to use Lesley Barnes as a decoy was also swirling in my head.

"Give me an update tomorrow once the oxygen gauge is replaced," I said.

A yawn crept up before I stopped it. I was so tired. I glanced at the clock. It was after three. No wonder my brain was barely functioning.

"Tell me what I'm missing," I said, rubbing my eyes. "I'm too tired to think straight."

King leaned forward. "You mentioned using the president's wife as bait."

That's right. Lesley. Decoy. "I'm open to ideas. There's got to be a way to use her even if Barnes doesn't want her back."

King took my hand. "What if we reconvene in the morning? We can iron this out when we're more rested, then call in the teens for the next meeting."

I wanted to argue, but exhaustion made my thoughts blur together. I don't think it had ever been this bad. Pregnancy was to blame, and there was nothing I could do about it.

"Sounds like a plan," I muttered around another yawn.

King stood and, before I could protest, he scooped me into his arms.

"Really?" I grumbled.

He ignored me, carrying me from the room like I weighed nothing.

I gave up and snuggled into him. Sleep took over before we were halfway to the room.

Chapter Fourteen

Marinah

FOOD WAITED FOR ME when I opened my eyes. I slept like the dead and only woke up because of the delicious aroma filling the room. King entered the bedroom wet and naked, fresh from a shower.

"Did I sleep for three days?" I asked.

He smiled. "Only eight hours. I moved back the meetings." He held up a hand. "You needed the sleep, and it's not up for debate."

"Who's the boss of this outfit?" I muttered.

"You are, but you're pregnant, took a hellhound bite last night, and overextended yourself. I'm your mate, and I have a say when it comes to your well-being the same way you have a say when it comes to mine."

"But you never listen to me when you overdo it," I challenged.

"You are pregnant," he said with finality in his voice.

"Argh." I tossed a pillow at him.

He caught it and tossed it back. "You're always cranky when you're hungry."

He walked over and helped me up. It was impossible not to lean into his naked body, but my bladder couldn't wait, so it was a very short snuggle. He had his pants on when I came back but his chest was still available for perusal. I liked his chest and secretly smiled because before we were together, I told myself he had too much muscle. It was a lie. He had the perfect amount and my mouth watered for more than food. Leading the Shadow Warriors and being in charge of the island was not kind to our sex life.

As always, I ate with single-minded purpose. King sampled his food at a slower pace.

"Do you feel better?" he asked.

I took inventory. "My back isn't as sore, which is a plus. The bites from last night aren't affecting me or the prince at all. He's performing in his first gymnastics meet right now. Hopefully, I eat so much, he's incapable of tumbling in such tight quarters." I held up my hand. "Do not say it."

King smiled. "Tell me about the teenagers."

I did.

"They *can* fight," he acknowledged.

"They can, but the danger is too high. We need an antidote for humans. I'm frustrated that we haven't moved forward in that regard."

"It might never happen," King said.

"That's what bothers me," I replied sadly. "When did you tell the guards to meet?"

"They're waiting for you in the conference room."

I gave King the evil eye and shoved a piece of sausage into my mouth before standing. "You can be entirely too frustrating, but I do feel better after sleep and food. I'm in such a good mood, I'll wait to start bitching at you."

He smiled, and we left the room.

Two people were missing when we entered the argument room. My eyebrows rose.

"Missy is in labor," Nokita said.

I turned and glared at King.

He shrugged. "Axel thought it would be a few hours."

"You didn't think to mention it while we ate breakfast?"

He shrugged again, but kept his mouth shut. He pulled out my chair, and I slapped his hand away. My last nerve was wondering if duct tape was an acceptable form of punishment. Not for his mouth. I had another body part in mind. I'd tape the appendage

I was thinking of to his thigh so he pulled out hair when he walked.

"Did anyone come up with an idea to use Lesley as leverage against the Federation?" I asked as calmly as possible. I was at a loss no matter how much I thought about it.

"We could shoot her and be done with it," Nokita said.

"You're as bloodthirsty as King, and not helping," I replied with a sharp look.

"Your mate didn't disappear and run to the other side of the island to escape that woman," he threw back.

I covered my eyes and leaned my elbows on the table. I may have growled.

"What if we implanted a locator device on her and gave her back?" Cabel suggested.

"Hmm." I turned to Axel. "Is it possible?"

"It would be a homing device for hellhounds," he replied. "There's also no way we could do it without an incision, which would leave a scar."

"What if one of us was captured with the barnacle and we carried the tracking device?" Cabel asked.

That gave me pause, but then I shook my head. "They might kill the Shadow Warrior immediately, or worse, turn the sacrificial Warrior into a hellhound like Knet. We can't chance it."

"Knet seems to have control over whatever the hell he's turned into," Nokita said. "He knows our secrets, and he is stalking us on our own damn island. We need to do something." There was pain and anger in his words. He was usually reasonable, but Knet's defection and Labyrinth's death had gotten to him.

"It's a death sentence for the Warrior," I said. "We can't risk it. We have families and people who love us."

"I don't," said Alden. "I'm willing to volunteer."

Everyone looked at him.

"I agree with Cabel. We've made little forward progress," he said. "We got lucky before the Federation attacked. We knew they were coming and still had casualties. We need to do something unexpected. I'm willing to go."

I stared at him for a moment. My mind snapped to a certain young woman who liked him. I turned to King, and he looked just as shook up as I was. It would be a suicide mission.

"I will think about it," I told him. "I'm not saying yes or no right now. This needs to be thought through before we try something so rash. You also need to know that you are part of my family and I love you like a brother."

Alden's face flushed.

"I think it's a good plan," volunteered Cabel saving Alden from further embarrassment.

Of course he did. Everyone was challenging Beck's spot for being a pain in my ass.

"I have a meeting about the children and need to get it started," I said. "Cabel and Alden can think about the problems associated with Alden's plan and if there is any way around those problems. After the meeting about the children, I would like to speak with Eagle and Rodrigo. Can you arrange it?" I asked Nokita.

He looked perplexed, and I knew it was because of Rodrigo. Eagle, not so much. He was the person we needed to take Labyrinth's place, even though it was hard. We couldn't be shorthanded right now, especially if we put Alden's harebrained plan into action.

"I'll see it done," Nokita agreed carefully.

"King, find the teenagers and send them here," I told him.

"I would like to speak to you for a moment," he said.

"If it's about Rodrigo, I'm angry with you for not mentioning Missy's labor, and won't answer your questions until I've settled something with him."

King grumbled.

"I would also like an update on Missy. I don't know how long the meeting with the kids will last."

"I'll take care of it," King said begrudgingly.

"I knew I could count on you," I replied sardonically.

In less than sixty seconds, I was left alone. I placed a hand on my belly. "Your father is a jackass sometimes," I whispered, "but you will love him as much as I do."

The baby didn't stir. He had finally exhausted himself after endless somersaults. I was okay with that.

CHAPTER FIFTEEN

Marinah

THE MEETING WITH DESMOND, Julia, and several of the women who wanted to help and more than likely adopt went longer than expected. The women stayed silent because Desmond made himself a problem again.

"We did fine on our own," he said angrily.

"From what Julia told us, you didn't," I replied, keeping my tone as even as possible.

He turned his eyes to me, and Ms. Beast grumbled. "People get sick. That's what went wrong. If we hadn't gotten sick, we would still be at our home."

"We were near starving," Julia said, giving her brother a hard stare. "That's why we stayed at the outpost after we recovered. You always seem to forget that part."

He went silent, and I took a minute to regroup.

"The people in this room want the same thing," I finally said. "We want everyone on the island safe, fed, and to have a roof over their heads. Families are willing to take in the children and provide love and care. Children are treasured here, and they want it to be a permanent solution." I stared at Desmond. "The kids trust you. Help them and give them a chance to be part of a family."

His sneer was his answer, and I turned to Julia. "We have doctors and food stores. We have well-built homes and an underground network of tunnels if the island is attacked. Work details are chosen, not assigned in most cases, and the harder the work, the more time off. Shadow Warriors guard this island, but humans are the most valuable part of this world. It's their island. You and the children could make it yours too."

Her eyes slid to Desmond, then back to me. "My brother believes everyone is out to get us. We've trusted people before." She looked down for a moment before meeting Desmond's eyes. "What choice do we have? They flew us here. Are we going to swim back?" She touched his arm. "I know you love the kids as much as I do, but they are too young to care for each other or for themselves. They need help. We need help."

"If we do this," Desmond said, "we take away our options."

Julia threw her hands up in the air. "What options?" She looked at me. "He doesn't want this to be his fault if it goes bad. He won't agree, but I will."

Desmond pushed his chair back and stormed from the room.

"I'm sorry," Julia said. "He's not a bad person; we've just been through so much." She turned her attention to Maria. "Cade needs someone to love him. He is the neediest child we have."

"I have love for him now," Maria replied in stilted English.

Julia smiled at her. "He needs you, and I feel that you will give him a good home." She wiped tears from her eyes. "May I visit him occasionally?"

Maria wiped her own tears. "Mi casa su casa, my home is yours. Gracias, señorita, gracias."

Julia focused on me again. "Would it be possible to interview those willing to take in the children? I would need an interpreter."

"Yes, we have many bilingual islanders and even some Shadow Warriors. Whatever will make this easier for you."

"Desmond needs something to do, or he'll be a bigger problem."

"What about working with one of our defense units?" I asked. "They are made up of islanders and Shadow Warriors. The southern part of the island has its own protection unit. He can choose where he goes."

"That would be perfect for him, but convincing him to do it could take a bit. Are women trained too, because I would be interested?"

"Yes, but I know something you might enjoy more. One of our near-teens has teamed up with a Shadow Warrior. They want to train children to protect themselves. They could use help and having more than one training group would be a plus. A few of the new children will stay here but most will go to the southern part of the island where it's safer. If Desmond chooses to go there, you could go with him and train kids who are interested."

Julia smiled. "Desmond lives to fight. I want to be able to protect myself and others if needed, but I don't have the killer instinct Desmond has."

"Even without the killer instinct, you were very good at killing a hellhound," I said. "Having you help train the younger generation would be a huge bonus."

"Thank you, Mark and Suzie, the other teens with us would want to help too."

"The four of you are old enough to live on your own. We have several homes available that would fit, but you could also choose families willing to take you in."

Her relief was obvious. "Our own home would sweeten the deal for Desmond."

"It's a plan then," I told her.

We set up a block of time for the parent interviews.

I walked Julia to the training gym so she could officially meet Togg. We found him talking to Desmond about killing hellhounds.

"We confuse them," Desmond said. "We work strategically to take them down so we can stay away from their teeth and claws."

"You do a damned good job of it too," I said.

He went silent, and his shoulders stiffened.

"Julia will tell you what we discussed. Julia, this is Togg. Ruth's mother is having a baby, and you'll meet her later."

With a silent sigh of relief, I left and headed to the med bay.

"You're in big trouble," Ruth said as soon as she saw me.

"What's new?" I quipped. "I'm always in trouble."

"Beck is unhappy with you for letting my mom ride on the airplane. He says she could have had the baby on the plane."

Missy hadn't asked my opinion, and she reminded me of that when I told her she couldn't go. She stopped me and said she had several more weeks until she gave birth. When I tried to argue, she held up her hand. "I'm tired of being useless. I've put up with that bitch in the holding cell for weeks now, and you're lucky I didn't blow my brains out. If I need to climb into the wheel well, I will be on that plane."

I looked at Ruth and tried to hold back some of my frustration. "Tell Beck I'll meet him on the training field whenever he wants to take it up with me."

She giggled just a bit before the corners of her mouth turned down. "Human parents don't want their children learning to fight. Or at least they don't want them learning from me. I'm trying to hold onto my patience and see it from their perspective, but I'm having trouble."

She said human like she wasn't one. I had a feeling she didn't think of herself that way.

"Julia, one of the teenagers who arrived last night may be able to help. She will be going to the southern part of the island, and I've offered her a chance to train with the adults and to set up classes for the youth. After your brother is born, you need to meet with her and share ideas."

Ruth's jaw set stubbornly, but I cut her off. "Julia is older than you, and within a couple of years, you will be training with the adults too. I plan to address the lack of parent support for your endeavor when I meet with the kitchen staff again. That should give you a few children to work with. More will follow if they see the good it does. Julia has good fighting techniques, and you can all learn from each other. Use Togg too."

She rolled her eyes at the mention of Togg. "He has a good heart, but he's bossy. He's disappointed in the parents too. He told me you were going to assign him someplace else on the island, and he would rather stay at the citadel."

I hadn't told him I was sending him south, but it was easy to figure out. I liked that he was bossy with Ruth. She needed someone looking over her shoulder. I didn't entirely trust this new Ruth, but only time would tell.

The door opened, and Axel, looking tired, walked from the medical room. He smiled when he saw me. "Mom and baby are healthy." He turned to Ruth. "They said for you to go in and meet your new brother."

"Yippee," Ruth shouted.

"Quietly," Axel admonished.

She didn't acknowledge his order, just rushed into the room.

Axel closed the door behind her and gave me a not-so-nice stare.

"I know," I said before he started his lecture. "Missy shouldn't have been on that plane. I take full responsibility."

His anger was on full steam. "Part of being our leader is making hard choices. You gave into Missy because you feel bad that she had to care for Mrs. Barnes. It's no excuse." His hard eyes drilled into me.

Ms. Beast took notice, and I held her back. Axel was right. I deserved this lecture. I had made a bad choice due to guilt. I looked away.

The warmth of his hand settled on my shoulder. "You will make many mistakes, but if this one had gone south, you would never forgive yourself. The baby is in excellent condition, and so is Missy. She told Beck to keep his mouth shut, or he could find another room to sleep in." Axel chuckled. "That guarantees even with a screaming newborn, Beck will sleep in Missy's bed until hell freezes over."

I looked into Axel's eyes again. "Thank you. I know I'll make mistakes, but you're right. Harm to the baby or Missy would have been shattering."

"I need to examine you and check in on the little princess." Laughter flashed in his eyes as he spoke.

"As my doctor, as well as King's, you are not allowed to take sides. Please call this baby an 'it,' if you must," I grumbled.

"That won't happen. I'll say prince to King and princess to you and keep it equal."

This time I growled, even if it was good-naturedly.

After Axel had me in a medical gown and sitting on one of his tables, he examined my wounds, which were almost healed.

"Pregnancy is increasing your healing ability. I don't remember reading anything about this in the men's texts. Have you run across it in the women's?"

The damned journal! My great-grandmother made it frustrating enough that I had to fight throwing the book across the room each time I settled down to decipher more.

"That bad, I take it?" Axel said, looking at my face.

"Worse. I wish my grandmother Veda had written it. She at least would make sense. It's like entire sections are left out. I thought Endura gave the journal to me to help. For each small bit of information I learn, it causes ten more questions that I don't have answers to. On top of that, deciphering takes more time than I have. When I think I've figured out a word or two, something changes, and it doesn't make sense. People think English is hard, but they have never attempted to read my great-grandmother's writings."

Axel just shook his head and changed the subject while he measured my belly and did all the other things he needed to do that made him feel better. He kept a written log, which I peeked at.

"An inch?" I questioned. His chart showed my stomach had expanded, and it had only been twenty-four hours since the last measurement.

"Yes, this little princess is growing fast."

"I may need to give birth in my Warrior form so he doesn't kill me coming out."

"Hmm," Axel said. "Have you seen anything like that in the texts?"

"No, I was joking. You think that's what I should do?" I asked.

"I have no medical opinion one way or the other. So far, you and the baby are healthy. Tomorrow, I'll take measurements again and do a vaginal exam."

"Hopefully the Federation will attack in the next few hours and ruin your plans."

He laughed.

I'd had to get over my aversion to a friend seeing parts of me that should stay hidden, but I was still uncomfortable.

Ruth stuck her head into the room. "Do you want to meet my baby brother?"

Chapter Sixteen

Marinah

"H E'S PRECIOUS," I SAID, ignoring Beck's glare. If I looked him in the eyes, Ms. Beast would take offense. I didn't want K-5 to spike because Beck had a right to be angry. "Have you decided on a name?" I asked Missy.

"He," she pointed to the scowling father, "doesn't want a junior. I think we've decided on Barrett."

Beck gave a solemn nod and said, "Barrett." It was the first word he spoke since I entered the room.

I knew he needed time to get past his anger, and that wouldn't happen with me here.

"I will take my leave," I said. "If there is anything you need, Missy, just send word."

She cast a furious glare at Beck. "Your frown had better turn upside down before she leaves this room," she said like she was scolding a child.

He threw his hands into the air. "You should not have been on that flight, and you know it," he said.

"Get over yourself. We're fine, and you are being a jerk."

"I'm leaving now," I said, walking to the door.

"Beck," Missy ground between her teeth.

He gave a heavy sigh. "Forgive me, my Queen. I'm grumpy because my mate took risks she shouldn't have."

"Understood," I replied. "I'll check in later this afternoon."

I left quickly.

Ruth wasn't in the hall, so I headed back to the training facility. Ruth, Julia, and Desmond were circling Togg with wooden knives, using the technique I'd seen at the airport and talking Ruth through it. Togg looked thrilled to play the hellhound, though thankfully he hadn't shifted forms. For the majority of Shadow Warriors, gaining control of Beast after a shift took time, and the last thing we needed was an accident.

They took a break, and Desmond, who had noticed me, explained how they came up with the technique.

"We were getting attacked by hellhounds when we went out scavenging for food and other items. If it was a larger pack, we retreated before they saw us, but if it was only one or two, we engaged and discovered what worked best. It confuses the hounds. While they're watching one of us, the others attack from different angles at different intervals. We haven't lost anyone since we discovered how well it works."

I walked forward. "Would you be willing to train us? I'm talking about Shadow Warriors and our human fighters?"

Desmond, who had donned his perpetual scowl, shrugged.

"If he won't, I will," said Julia.

"Could I speak with you and Desmond alone?" I asked.

"Sure." Julia followed me to the office, and a reluctant Desmond came behind her.

"Our doctor, who is a Shadow Warrior, and his mate, who is one of our best medical assistants, would like to adopt a child. Due to their work schedule, they prefer one of the older children."

"Why don't they have their own?" Desmond asked suspiciously.

"Axel is mated to Garrett. They are unable to have a child. I'm requesting you put them on the interview list. Garrett is at the southern part of the island right now, and Axel delivered a baby, or he would have been at our earlier meeting. They are both wonderful, and any child would be lucky to have them as fathers."

"Of course," said Julia, and looked at her brother with an arched brow.

He gave a frustrated sigh. "You know I don't care about *that*," he hesitated. "I just feel like we're being set up. This," he pointed around the room, "the entire place is too good to be true. What aren't you telling us?"

"The Federation could attack any moment," I said plainly. "They've attacked us before. We're gearing up to put an end to their threat, and we have every intention of winning. It's why we are all training so hard, and that includes the islanders. Most will stay behind and protect the island. We will leave Shadow Warriors too. Some of the humans want to join our fight and will be coming with us. But there's always the chance we lose. If that happens, no one on the island will be safe."

"Will the outposts fight with you?" Julia asked.

"Yes, at least the ones we help protect. Tully, Second Son, and Territory Three have just joined us. We've sent Warriors to them. That's why you came here. For the time being, this is the safest place, or at least the southern part of the island is."

I could see Desmond's mind racing, and waited for his comments.

"If I train with your men, will you take me to fight the Federation too?"

"How old are you?" I asked.

"I'll be sixteen next month."

"Yes, if you work hard and the Warrior team you're assigned to thinks you're an asset, you can fight with us. After what I've seen you do, I don't think there will be a problem."

For the first time, Desmond relaxed. "I want to kill Federation officers more than hellhounds."

"You'll have the opportunity for both."

"What about me?" Julia asked.

"How old are you?"

"I'm six months from fifteen."

"The island and the children here can use you more."

She shrugged. "Okay, I had to ask." She smiled. "There are six-year-old twins who might be perfect for your doctor and his mate. A boy and a girl."

I smiled back. "Meet Axel and Garrett first and ask your questions. I think the twins would be perfect. If they're willing, the final decision is yours and Desmond's."

Even Desmond seemed happy when they rejoined Togg and Ruth.

I went to the kitchens for food, and to enroll juveniles in Ruth's fighting group. It went better than I expected, and there would be children at the following morning's session.

I also discovered I was a huge fan of mamey sapote.

Overall, the day was positive, and I had no idea why a sense of dread settled in the pit of my stomach. It had to be that outside of Knet, things were running too smoothly.

CHAPTER SEVENTEEN

Marinah

DESMOND WAS A HELL of a fighter. He'd been working with Nokita's group for two days. King gave me updates, and today I wanted to see for myself. Nokita had a tight smile on his face. Maylin had not returned from the southern part of the island, and I could see the strain it was causing. We'd sent a message after she didn't arrive. There was some holdup with a patient. Maylin was one of Axel's many assistants, though she should have been taking time off since the birth of her third child. Hopefully, she would arrive at the citadel within the next hour or two.

Desmond had a sword and was fighting against a life-size hellhound dummy. The early morning sun cast long shadows across the training yard, making the dummy look almost alive. It stood hunched on its wooden frame, proportioned with tightly wrapped straw and coarse canvas, painted black with crudely painted red eyes because someone had a sense of humor and thought it a great touch. The teeth and claws were splintered wooden stakes carved to resemble those on an actual hellhound.

Desmond clutched a practice sword, like he was born with it, and circled the dummy. Sweat beaded on his temples, clinging to wisps of hair due to the humidity, which was on the extreme side today. He might not be facing a real hellhound, but he approached it like he was.

The initiated attack wasn't a charge. He feinted to the left, shifted his weight, and dropped his right shoulder as if to strike a high diagonal. The dummy, naturally, didn't react, but Desmond used the motion to practice his footwork, pivoting swiftly, bringing his left leg back for balance. His gaze never left the painted eyes of his target.

The first strike was a horizontal sweep, aiming for the hellhound's mid-section where its guts would be. The blunted edge of the sword thwacked against the tightly packed straw. The dummy shuddered on its frame and a few wisps of straw fluttered free.

He reset, and his next thrust connected with the neck. He spun away, practicing a defensive maneuver, a quick sidestep and a low block that would deflect a clawed swipe. He ended the movement with a short, sharp cut to the dummy's foreleg. Thwack.

He moved around the dummy, assessing angles, practicing different entries. He tried a high overhead chop, and the sword came down with a powerful thud, striking the dummy's canvas head. He followed it up with a rapid series of slashes across its torso. The straw flew, tiny pieces showering down.

With a sudden burst of power, he whirled, bringing the sword around in a wide, sweeping arc. It struck the dummy's wooden support with a resounding crack, splitting the timber. The straw hellhound teetered, then toppled over, landing with a soft thud.

Desmond's chest heaved, the sword held loosely in his hand.

"He's too damned good for his age," Nokita said.

I'd wondered how the children survived, and now I knew. They had their own personal ninja, and I had a feeling the other teens were just as deadly. The outposts would have been smarter to take lessons from them and keep them around.

"I know this is practice, but he needs to put hounds down as quickly as possible and not play with them," I observed. "It is, however, damned impressive to watch."

Nokita nodded.

I wandered away and checked on the junior squad next. In just two days, they were up to eight children, not including Ruth and Julia. Togg watched and gave pointers.

"How are they doing?" I asked him.

"They're little killers," he said with a grin. "I don't think we realize how uncertain and scary their world actually is. Their confidence went up ten degrees after yesterday's training, and it was noticeable when they arrived this morning. I've given each of them a knife, and they'll be carrying them wherever they go.

"Some look too young to carry knives."

"They understand that they're weapons and they won't use them as toys," he assured me. "I want them to learn to shoot as soon as possible."

The kids looked to be between the ages of eight and fourteen. After seeing what Desmond could do, I had no doubt these children could eventually protect themselves. I didn't like the idea of killers, though. We needed peace, but then again, even if we defeated the Federation, hellhounds weren't going anywhere. People, including children, needed to be prepared.

"I do not want them carrying guns," I said bluntly.

Togg smiled. "That wasn't the plan. They need to understand how guns work. I want shooting practice to be a weekly thing. They'll also have training in archery"

"I won't object. Kamen is one of the guards bringing Maylin back. When he returns, he'll go back to armory duty. Ask him how much ammo he can spare. The shooting will be limited, but you're right, they need to understand the basics."

My next stop was Axel at the med bay. I found Garrett inside the first room. He had returned to the citadel before the sun rose. He and Axel had their meeting with Desmond and Julia earlier, and I wanted to see how it went.

"Becky and Derrick are coming for dinner this evening," Garrett told me. "We want this to be their decision."

"How do you feel about it?" I asked.

Garrett was a large man who had been special forces in the military before the hellhounds attacked. He served several years afterward and was one of the lucky ones who survived. An injury cut his career short, but he recovered, left the Federation stronghold, and became the governor of the outpost that Landan now oversaw.

"If they don't choose to stay with us, they may see a grown man cry," he said with a small smile. "I'm trying not to get my hopes up, but that may be a losing cause."

"You will make great parents. This will work out," I assured him. We had moved to the hall outside the largest medical bay. I turned when I heard someone running toward us.

"Maylin was attacked on her way here," Caleb said when he saw us. "Kamen escaped with the children. He just arrived, and they are safe. He said they were outnumbered, and the other two Warriors and Maylin could be dead. Maylin ordered him to keep the children safe."

My heart dropped into my stomach. "Find King and tell him to inform the guard to be in front of the citadel within ten minutes."

"Yes, my Queen," Caleb said.

Garrett looked at me, and I read the protest on his face.

"Don't start," I said. "I'm pregnant, not an invalid."

I moved past him and headed to my room to change into my Warrior clothes that would shift with me. The leather straps needed adjusting after I changed form. The pants stretched and had the expanding front panel now that I had a bowling ball for a stomach but they worked.

Even though I said I wouldn't ride again, the bikes were faster, so that's what we took. We were through the gates in nine minutes. We'd all shifted to Warrior form. Beck had been informed that he was in charge while we were gone. Axel would assist in every way he could so Beck wasn't disturbed. Unfortunately, that might be impossible.

Fury and fear shot through Nokita's expression. Kamen came with us, bringing our small force to six. It would have taken too long to form a larger group. Maylin's and Nokita's children were turned over to the women at the citadel. There was no keeping Nokita from this fight. He was out for blood.

"They were hellhounds with that thing leading them," Kamen said before the roar of motorcycle engines drowned out his voice.

I needed to wrap my claws around that *thing's* neck.

It took thirty minutes to get to the spot where they were attacked. We didn't see the two Shadow Warriors. A small curled-up form was on the road in front of us. Nokita was off his bike and running before the rest of us stopped.

He picked up an unmoving Maylin. I drew closer, but the wild look on his face made me stop in my tracks.

He stood still and lowered his cheek to her mouth. After several long seconds, he said, "She's breathing."

"She needs to be checked for bites and scratches," I said.

He turned away, his massive Warrior frame shaking. He wasn't controlling his rage, and I didn't want to be the focus of it. If she were bitten, there would be nothing we could do, so I didn't press the issue.

"Do we follow?" King growled.

"If we do, it weakens us." I looked at Kamen. "You think there were fifteen of them?" I asked.

"At least fifteen. Possibly one or two more."

"Maylin must get to Axel," I told a very angry King. I looked at Nokita. "Get on my bike and hold her," I told him. I shifted back to human form before he said anything. "It's the only way we'll have room." I hoped with the size of my stomach it wasn't a lie.

He turned to me, not moving.

"We must get her to Axel. If you want to drive, I'll hold her."

He finally shook his head, my words sinking in. It was a tight squeeze, but he managed to get on the bike with Maylin in his arms.

I drove at breakneck speed, hoping Maylin held on.

CHAPTER EIGHTEEN

King

AXEL RAN OUT THE front doors when we arrived at the citadel.

"She's breathing," Nokita told him. His next words held so much anguish. "She hasn't moved. I don't know if she's been infected."

"Follow me," Axel said.

I waited until they were inside.

"Getting Maylin away from him could be difficult. Do you want to handle it?" I asked Marinah.

"No, I'll be there in a few minutes. You have a better chance of talking him down; you went through this when I was bitten," she said.

I had threatened Axel and refused to do what he ordered. I injected Marinah with serum, even though it wouldn't have worked if she were human. All I could think about was saving her. Then I cut the dying flesh from her wounds. Axel couldn't get me to stop, even when she screamed. I'd gone over the edge.

This wouldn't be easy.

Marinah took off, walking as fast as she could with her enlarged stomach and disappeared. All I could think about was ripping Knet from limb to limb, slowly.

I entered the medical bay. Nokita placed Maylin on the examination table without argument. He looked at me. I could see defeat in his eyes. He thought she would die. Unlike me, he didn't feel he could fight it. The only thing that had saved Marinah was her being a Shadow Warrior. Maylin didn't have a chance.

I shook my head. "We are not giving up," I said.

"Nokita, help me get her clothing off," Axel said. "I don't see bites or scratches on exposed skin and I don't smell blood."

Nokita turned and followed the doctor's orders. Once she was naked, Axel examined her closely along with Nokita.

"Nothing but a large bump on the head," Axel said after a few minutes. "She has a concussion, and that's what I'm going to treat her for."

"Will she live?" Nokita asked.

"If I have anything to say about it, she will," Axel responded.

Nokita's shoulders slumped, and he swayed on his feet. I reached out and grasped his arm. He didn't seem to notice. When he looked at me, his eyes held hope and confusion.

"Why did they leave her alive?" he asked.

It was a very good question. With the two Shadow Warriors gone, it made no sense. Marinah was right, though. Searching for them immediately would have left us vulnerable, and it was more important to get Maylin to medical.

Marinah walked into the room fifteen minutes later. Axel updated her on Maylin's condition. She turned to me when he finished.

"Eagle is taking twenty men out to look for the two Warriors. If we don't find them on the island, we know they're using a submarine. It's the only answer." She paused a moment. "Rodrigo is waiting for me in the conference room. Would you like to attend?"

The rage she felt over Maylin overshadowed her angst with me. We left, but Marinah didn't speak while we walked. She stopped outside the conference room and tightened her chest straps so her breasts were covered. Having the men see her human breasts had stopped bothering me. It helped that they didn't stare, and now her nakedness seemed natural. Without being troubled over modesty, she shifted between forms more easily. Her Beast and Nova forms weren't an issue because her breasts became part of the new form and weren't obvious. It helped that the mating rage hadn't shown itself these past few months too.

Rodrigo stood when we entered. Marinah took a seat two down from him and turned her chair slightly so she faced him. I sat across the table from them. Rodrigo appeared nervous, his fingers lightly thrumming the table.

"I'll get straight to the point," Marinah said. "You've proved yourself. You love the people on this island, and you care about the Shadow Warriors."

"Si, Señora," he answered.

"I am filling a place on my guard. Eagle will be assigned to Labyrinth's position, but I also want to place someone from the island on the guard. That someone is you. When this hell is over, we will return the island to its people. That process needs to start now."

Rodrigo turned away from Marinah and looked at me. I simply nodded. This should have happened when I was in charge. The humans needed to be part of decisions that affected them. I couldn't think of a better person than Rodrigo.

"If you accept this offer, you will lead a contingent of men, both Shadow Warriors and humans. The inability of humans to survive a hellhound bite or scratch will keep your unit off the front lines unless it becomes absolutely necessary. I can promise that won't stop your men and women from fighting and seeing action. Your responsibilities will exceed your current ones. You will also be the human liaison for the island, which at times may prove the hardest part of the position. Do you need time to think about what I've said before giving me an answer?"

Rodrigo's expression changed. His eyes hardened slightly, but it seemed to be more with pride than anger. "You will not regret this," he said. "I need no time. We are proud people. This change is good."

"You will attend all guard meetings," Marinah told him. "You will also move into the citadel. Even with you and Eagle, Labyrinth's shoes will be almost impossible to fill. You report directly to me." She paused a moment. "Our meetings can be volatile. You need to hold your ground when you think you're right. Do not let the Warriors run over you. They respect you already, but as soon as you go against one of them, they will throw that out the window. Put them in their place if you need to, and that includes me. I make all final decisions after I hear all sides." She paused again. "We need you," she said earnestly.

"Mi madre y mi hermana, my mother and sister," he translated, though I understood him. "I care for them at our home. Would they be welcome?"

"Absolutely. I will have someone make accommodations for all of you. They will have full access to our amenities. Do they have jobs?" Marinah asked.

"My sister, yes, in agriculture. My mother cooks and cleans and cares for us."

"Your sister can be assigned the same job here, or she can choose something she would prefer. Your mother's duty will lighten. If she wants additional work, let me know, and I will find something for her. Hard work with few benefits comes with your new role, but your family will be cared for."

Rodrigo smiled, showing his teeth. He left after saying it would take him a day to move his mother and sister to the citadel. He agreed to attend the meeting the following morning, and Marinah would make the announcement. She turned to me after he left.

"I informed Eagle that he would be stepping into a guard position before he left to find the Warriors. Elright will take over Eagle's duties with the snipers, though Eagle will ultimately be in charge of them."

"You did good," I said.

She released a long breath. "Thank you."

"You fill in the places I missed. It hadn't occurred to me to assign a human to the guard."

"It was past time. They need to feel part of what we do."

"Have you received complaints?" I asked curiously.

Marinah had straightened out the problems with the island women, and things were running smoother than they ever had.

"Not exactly, but something was missing, and that something was having Rodrigo part of my guard," she said. "And, so you know in advance, the next addition to my guard will be a woman."

It was a promise, and I wouldn't dare object. There was a knock at the door.

"Enter," Marinah said.

Che walked in. Marinah was out of her seat and had him in her arms a second later.

"They hurt my mom," he cried.

"I know," she told him. "She wasn't bitten or scratched, though." She turned to me. "King will go check on her. The two of us will sit with your brothers so they are not afraid."

"Okay."

I crossed to them and wrapped both in my arms for just a moment before I walked out.

After receiving an update from Axel, I sat down quietly outside Maylin's room. All we could do was wait.

CHAPTER NINETEEN

Marinah

THE FOLLOWING MORNING, I went to the indoor training facility to speak with Ruth, Julia, and Togg.

"I'm impressed with what you've done in only a couple of days," I told them.

Alden entered. "Maylin regained consciousness," he said.

I approached the med bay and heard Maylin crying. I had only seen her cry when her first Shadow Warrior husband, Boot, died. Her toddler, known as Baby Boot, was named after his father. The new baby was named Labyrinth, nicknamed Laby, which he would someday hate.

I stepped inside, and King's eyes met mine. His tightly clenched hands and the burn in his eyes showed the rage he struggled to contain. He nodded at the door. I backed out, and he followed me. He placed a hand on my back and steered me farther down the hall away from the door.

"She positively identified Knet. He told her who he was. Maylin said his speaking ability was poor." King took a breath before he continued. "He injected her with the hellhound serum and told her it was a present for you."

I recoiled and took a full step back.

King wasn't finished. "They took the Warriors as hostages. One will be exchanged for Mrs. Barnes. The other will become whatever the hell Knet is. There will be no negotiations. One Warrior for her. We are to deliver her to the shipyard tomorrow at noon. If we don't, both Warriors will be turned into monsters."

I needed a few minutes to breathe and absorb this horror. King pulled me into his arms and rested his head on mine. "I'll hold you while you think," he said.

King understood. Right this moment, I didn't have a plan. Fury didn't adequately describe my feelings. Maylin would become one of those monsters when she died. If she were around her children and it happened, she would kill them. I couldn't begin to imagine what she was going through. And Nokita.

Yes, I wanted to kill Knet, but I wanted President Barnes even more. In my mind, he was the evil that permeated everything. Lesley Barnes wasn't far behind because I could feel her hatred in every fiber of my being. She was as good as, if not better than, her husband at hiding her distaste for everything Shadow Warrior.

I also wanted my country back. It would never return to what it had once been, but that wasn't necessarily a bad thing. We needed a do-over, and we had to do better.

My people, the Shadow Warriors, also deserved a good life. The deep-seated anger I carried and the lives I had taken were not me. Killing had been forced on me by the Federation. I wanted my soul back. My child deserved to grow up in a better world.

Maylin. My heart ached.

I stepped back and looked into King's eyes. "We give them Lesley. Once we have our Warrior back, we kill them all. I am done playing nice." I took several deep breaths. "We need to be smart. I'll meet with the guard in fifteen minutes. If Rodrigo is still at the citadel, notify him too.

I entered the argument room and found everyone but Eagle waiting for me. Their expressions said they knew what had been done to Maylin. They met my eyes, then glanced away. We were all on edge and knew that pushing Ms. Beast was not in anyone's best interest.

"I'll make this part quick." I said, then stopped when Eagle entered. "Please sit," I told him. "Rodrigo and Eagle have been added to the guard. The general consensus has been that Eagle should fill the spot Labyrinth held. I agree fully, but the island people need representation, and Rodrigo has earned a spot too. I want to be clear that he holds as much power as each of you, and his words hold just as much weight." She met the men's eyes before they looked away. Her heavy gaze stopped at Beck, and she waited for him to look up.

"Don't look at me," he said. "I'm currently in a new daddy state of bliss and agree fully with your decision." He turned to Rodrigo, reached past Nokita, and shook his hand. "Welcome." He then turned to Eagle and said it again.

"We are exchanging Mrs. Barnes for one of our Warriors," Marinah said after the men welcomed the new members. "The other will be turned into whatever it is that Knet has become."

Beck's daddy-bliss didn't last long. His seat flew back.

"Sit and keep your feelings to yourself until I am finished," I said and waited for him to sit. "At the moment, we do not have leverage unless we are willing to sacrifice both Warriors. Is there anyone who thinks we should sacrifice both?"

Thick energy swelled in the room as the K-5 spiked.

"They are good men," Beck said, his fury in overdrive.

"I'm aware of that. If you think I want one of our own turned into one of those monsters, you shouldn't be on my guard." Beck nearly choked on the words forming in his throat, and I growled. He looked down, and I continued. "Somehow Knet and his hellhounds have evaded us. We have no idea how long they have been on the island. My guess is they're using a submarine to hide in. Rodrigo and Nokita have ours ready, and the men have been training for this. We need to find the Federation sub before it leaves the island waters. I'm open to suggestions about anything I've said."

"May I speak?" Rodrigo asked.

"Yes," Marinah replied.

"The men are ready to blow the other sub from the water. If I were one of the Warriors taken, I would rather die than help the Federation's cause. If you plan to make the exchange, I have an idea." Marinah nodded at him to continue. "We have nothing that rivals what they inject into the innocent to turn them into monsters, but they do not know that, and we should use the terror they wield against them. Inject the Señora with something and make her think she will become one of the monsters."

Silence filled the room when he finished speaking. Slowly, I smiled.

"Son of a bitch," Alden said. "That's the devious shit we need to be handing out."

"I can inject her with saline," Axel said.

Beck also smiled at Rodrigo. "You're going to fit in perfectly."

"We need the exchange to take place before they know that she's been injected," Marinah said.

Caleb spoke up. "The woman never shuts up. Anyone who knows her would understand if she were gagged."

"I like it. Now for the hard part. We are sacrificing one of our own. Both of these men are single, but they have friends. They are one of us. I carry the burden for this death."

"We carry the burden," Beck said. "We should have found Knet by now. That is on all of us."

"I agree," said Nokita.

The other men gave their agreement too.

I released the air from my lungs. "Thank you, but the weight of this still falls on me." I held up a hand. "You feel it too, but the most important thing here is to find Knet and stop both Warriors from becoming monsters."

"They have superior science," said Alden, "but I keep wondering how Knet is able to control himself. Wouldn't a Warrior side with us?"

King finally spoke. "That thought has crossed my mind too. Could there be more than one serum? Or maybe a Shadow Warrior reacts differently. Our Warrior could possibly become something like Knet and keep his loyalty to us intact. I doubt Knet ever gave a fuck about us."

Marinah looked at Nokita and then Rodrigo. "We need you to find that submarine and stop it from leaving. They may be taking our Warrior back to the mainland. They may also experiment to see how he reacts. If the only way to stop that sub is to blow it out of the water, then do it."

Both Nokita and Rodrigo nodded.

CHAPTER TWENTY

Marinah

UNABLE TO GET COMFORTABLE in bed that night, I tossed and turned as much as my stomach allowed. A Shadow Warrior would die the following day. My brain raced for some way out as fury filled my thoughts. I couldn't do anything to stop it. The only thing I was sure of was turning into a hellhound was worse than death. I had given the order to kill our own man. A friend. One of us.

King's eyes were closed, and I hoped he was sleeping. Due to my squirming, the little prince woke up and did somersaults. He was working towards an Olympic gold medal in gymnastics.

I turned slightly and checked on King again. He didn't move, and his breathing remained even. If I stayed in the room, I would wake him. I carefully slipped from the bed and walked to one of my favorite courtyards. With a deep inhale, I let the scent of the ocean fill my lungs.

Tomorrow, I would be stoic in the face of what had to be done. Right now, I needed to let go. The tears started. After my Shadow Warrior form emerged, I seldom cried. I was usually too busy for tears. Now that I was in charge, it happened even less, or at least it did until pregnancy hormones took over. Tears disturbed King, and I tried to hide them when I could no longer hold back. He always seemed to know. Maybe my red eyes gave me away. His protective mode would go into overdrive, and when he wouldn't let up, I became angry. Anger was better than sadness in his book, and I was fairly sure he pissed me off on purpose.

I allowed the tears to run down my face without wiping them away. One day, we would have peace. Not everyone would survive until then. Losing Boot and Labyrinth was hard. Losing others would also be hard.

A small sound alerted me to King's presence as he slipped into my private hiding spot. His arms went around me, and he pulled me as close as my large belly allowed. His shirt grew wet, and he didn't seem to mind. My shoulders hitched, and he pulled me a bit tighter.

"I was trying to let you sleep," I told him when I could finally talk.

"You shouldn't do that," he replied huskily.

I pulled back and wiped my eyes. "It's the damned hormones. Sometimes I can't control them."

He smiled softly, and I knew he didn't believe me.

I shrugged. "You needed sleep."

"You need it more," he said.

"His highness is restless." I told him, and rubbed my hand over my stomach.

"Her highness is a night owl," he responded.

I could hear the smile in his voice. I did need King awake. His presence grounded me. With a sigh, I took his hand and threaded my fingers through his, resting both our hands on my stomach.

"I think I can sleep now," I said.

We walked to our room together. I had to be alert for whatever happened the following day. King held me close, and eventually I fell asleep without dreams.

The only thing good about the morning was the interaction with Mrs. Barnes. She had not been released from her room to perform her work duty. Alden, who had picked the short straw, was pacing before her door when I arrived with King, Axel, and Rodrigo, who wore leather straps on his chest like the rest of us. He proudly said his mother and sister had made it for him. I should have acted sooner to place him on the guard. He had a cunning brain that quickly saw through problems in ways we didn't. He'd given us a small chance to get both our men back.

Axel carried a medical kit that held what he would inject into Lesley's vein. He'd spoken at length to Amy about her injection. She told him the contents of the vial used on her had been pale pink. There had been no side effects except extreme terror over what had been done to her. Axel had used a drop of beet juice to get the slight pink coloration.

I had the pleasure of opening the door and entering the room first.

"You have some nerve," Lesley spit out angrily. "You make me work and then take it away at a whim. Why are you here?" Her eyes widened when she noticed the men entering after me.

"We have a present," I said. "It will go easier if you cooperate."

Axel walked to a side table and rested the zippered pouch on it. He unzipped the top and pulled out the syringe, followed by a vial filled with tinted pale pink saline.

Lesley watched closely. Then she noticed the color and lost control.

"You bitch," she screamed and ran straight at me. "You can't do this."

We'd rehearsed how this would go down. We wanted to know if Lesley knew about the injections. She'd answered our question. K-5 boiled inside me, and I could smell it from Axel and King too.

I grabbed Lesley's arm, spun her, and grabbed the back of her neck with my other hand. King got hold of her hands, pulled them behind her, and pulled her backward until she sat slightly sideways on the bed.

She swung her legs up, but Rodrigo grabbed them and went to the floor to hold them down.

"I take it you're going to fight?" I asked with a smile I didn't feel.

She'd known about the hellhound drug and lied to us.

"Don't do this," she begged. Terror filled her eyes and tears rolled down her cheeks. These might be the first real tears.

"Don't do what?" I asked innocently.

Axel came closer with the filled syringe, and Lesley started fighting again. I leaned forward, released my hold, and placed my knee against her chest, pushing her back. King restrained her arms above her head.

"You can't do this," she screamed.

"It will be over in a few seconds if you'll simply relax. You know how this goes. One injection, and we're done. At least for the foreseeable future."

"Noooo." This scream was so intense I wanted to cover my ears. I shouldn't be getting enjoyment out of this, but she deserved the same nightmare she'd given others. Amy had been held down too. I had no sympathy for the president's wife.

She tried to twist, but she couldn't escape the piercing of her skin and the cool liquid that entered the vein at the bend of her arm. Her screams turned into sobs.

"What have you done?" she finally whispered.

"Your husband holds two of our men. One is being returned in exchange for you, and the other will receive the injection you were given. He will be killed shortly after and become one of the monsters you are so afraid of becoming yourself."

We released her, and she curled into a ball, putting her back to us.

"During the exchange, we will have a sniper focused on you," I continued. "If anything goes wrong, you will receive a bullet to the chest. It will tear you apart, but leave your head intact so you will become a monster. We also have something you don't."

She lifted her head slightly, and she looked at me.

"An antidote. It's taken us months, and we have only a very small amount. If both our Warriors are returned, we will give you enough to reverse the effects."

"I will see you and that demon inside you dead before this is over," Lesley hissed in a voice filled with pure hatred.

Gone was the poor misunderstood woman she had been over the past few months. This was the real Lesley Barnes, wife to the president, scientist, and a monster in her own right. I resisted the urge to wrap my fingers around her throat and squeeze until she no longer breathed.

King lay a hand on my arm, and I gained back the control I was losing. Leslie wouldn't help herself to save our Warrior.

"The handoff is in a few hours. Until then, you'll remain here," I said, somehow keeping the fury from my tone.

We left. Alden and Rodrigo stayed to guard her. We would take no chances.

The others waited in the argument room.

"She knew," King said as soon as we'd taken our seats.

I looked at him. "She's a scientist like her husband. The two of them are responsible for this. They will ultimately pay with their lives. That is a promise."

Chapter Twenty-One

Marinah

WE WERE DEALING WITH several scenarios. While King and I faced what was happening at the docks, attacks at different locations on the island were a huge threat. At any other time, I would have sent King to the southern island to lead the men there. My pregnancy would turn the order into a full-out argument because, without even asking, I knew he wouldn't leave me.

Trusting anything the Federation said was suicide, and we had to be prepared on all fronts. Even with the entire island on high alert, we were vulnerable due to Knet. It all came down to how long he'd been on the island and what he'd seen. Could his new form even decipher what happened around him? I had so many questions, and we were out of time.

Ace and Trevor were the two Warriors being held. My stomach clenched when I thought about them. Both were good men whom I trusted implicitly. My heart felt like it weighed a hundred pounds.

Thankfully, after a restless morning, the prince had decided to sleep. King didn't want me at the exchange, but I'd vetoed him. Lesley would tell the Federation about my pregnancy, and there was no use hiding it.

We'd had to quickly implement safety measures for the shipyard. Eagle set snipers up in key locations the evening before. He left Elright in charge because he was acting as my personal sniper and he would take out any threat to me. The group with Elright was far enough away and was hard to spot. One of the old steel ships closest to dry land would be our fallback point if needed. The ship's hull, even rusted, could take a lot of damage.

The moment I saw Lesley trussed and carried to the dock with duct tape circling her head, a bit of evil glee entered the dark chaos filling my mind. The duct tape would be a bitch to get out of her hair. Her eyes locked on me, and they promised retribution. Bring it, I thought to myself. My hands hitched to end her miserable life right now.

I didn't take my eyes off hers, and slowly something else entered her gaze. Smugness? Maybe she was thinking that if we had an antidote, the Federation could make one too. Hell, they might already have one, and our plans were for nothing. Her reaction to the shot had been pure terror, so I doubted they had anything to counteract the serum. Our lie was a long shot, and getting both our Warriors back nearly impossible, but I wasn't giving up.

We had changed our mind about using the submarine to blow theirs out of the water. We knew Ace and Trevor would rather be dead than turned into hellhounds, but it didn't make it easier. I finally decided that giving away the fact we had a sub could hurt us more in the long game. When Knet was with us, the old sub hadn't been a consideration, and we'd done what we could to keep the secret intact. I hated these decisions, and I questioned myself continuously.

Beck hadn't been himself since his son was born and he barely argued with me. I wasn't sure about this calmer Beck, but I would take it while it lasted.

Ruth had been unusually quiet before I left. She seemed to understand the gravity of what was happening, even if she didn't have the specifics. I left her with Desmond and Julia. It was good for her to be around people her age who understood how she felt. Hopefully, they would guide her and not cause additional trouble. For now, all civilians at the citadel were below ground. We were taking fifty Shadow Warriors with us. Warriors were stationed at the citadel, and another group at the southern part of the island. Caleb had gone there to take command.

The baby was a hard knot in my belly. Axel assured me he would be okay. Well, he assured me she would be okay, but I only had energy to give him a hard stare.

We shifted form an hour before the exchange. If the Federation wanted to deal with the Shadow Warriors, that was exactly who they would get. They knew our secrets because of Knet. We needed each Warrior fully in control of their faculties for what could go down.

I stood at the shore, King, Beck, and Nokita beside me. Alden led the forces at the citadel, and Rodrigo manned the mini sub. Rodrigo's men, which he'd chosen the day before, moved the underwater mines away from the dock so the Federation sub could get closer. His job in the mini sub was to stay out of sight unless he had a chance at picking up one or both our Warriors from the water. The water near the shipyard was thick with fuel and death. Rodrigo knew the area like the back of his hand, and it wouldn't be a problem for him. Axel stayed behind our troops with Rodrigo's human soldiers guarding him for protection. Under no circumstances could we lose Axel.

We had planes ready to run interference if we were attacked by air. Though we hadn't pictured the scenario we faced today, we'd planned for so many possibilities that everything came together smoothly. And still, I had that nagging feeling that we'd overlooked something.

We waited at the end of the dock for about ten minutes. My body stiffened when a barely perceptible ripple in the water caught my eye. A dark column rose up. Droplets of water caught the sunlight as the periscope climbed higher. No splash, no churn, just a quiet, almost surgical penetration of the natural waves.

With a deep, resonant groan that vibrated through the air, the ocean's surface began to boil. A dark mass surged upward, displacing tons of water in a thunderous roar of foam and spray.

I wanted to look at King, but I kept my eyes on the enemy. This display was meant to intimidate. I almost laughed. No one with me was afraid of the Federation.

The hatch opened. A man carrying a rifle climbed out and took a position on the far, left side of the sub's deck. More men emerged until they lined the deck, holding their weapons at ready.

"Do we do anything this stupid looking?" King asked.

"No," Beck replied.

"They must have drilled for hours to get it right," Nokita added.

"Stop it," I muttered under my breath. "I'm trying to look properly cowed, and you're going to make me smile."

"Give the order, and the snipers will take them out," Beck said.

"Not now," I replied.

What came next was something out of a horror film. There was nothing sexy about our Shadow Warrior form unless you were one. King found my Warrior body appealing, and I returned the favor, but we were not Hollywood werewolves. We were hairy, muscled, killing machines, and built just for that purpose. The creature that emerged was hideous. Its arms were too short, its head too something. I wanted to say small, but the teeth made up for it. The leg joints bent at awkward angles, making it hunch its body as if trying to decide whether to walk on two legs or four.

Knet.

Two soldiers on the sub's deck turned slightly and pointed their rifles at the traitor. I found this interesting. They didn't trust him, which made them smarter than they appeared.

A tall man I didn't recognize came up next. He looked official, his parade uniform complete with firm creases and shiny pins to mark his significance.

Another man came out. He wore a lesser uniform and carried a megaphone. He handed it to the officer.

The shrill squeak made me fight covering my ears.

"My name is Admiral Fegan," he said after the squeal subsided. "I need to see that First Lady Barnes is unhurt before we proceed."

"Bring her forward," I said.

She was carried by a Warrior and placed on the ground beside me. I pulled a large knife and cut the bindings on her hands. I grabbed beneath her arm and lifted her so she stood beside me.

The admiral showed no reaction to her condition. He said something to the soldier beside him, and within a minute, Ace appeared, followed by Trevor. Both men were chained. They looked straight at us, and my heart clenched. They were ready to die, and more than anything, I wanted them to live. They didn't show fear; they showed fury. Two men to either side of them had stepped back and pointed their rifles at them.

A yellow, square-shaped object was pulled from the hatch with a rope. A man tossed it over the side and pulled a cord so a raft inflated. The admiral said something to the soldier beside him again. The soldier took Ace's arm and led him toward the hatch.

Ace gave us one last look, nodded his head, and went below. My heart broke. Trevor's beast roiled, and I worried he wouldn't be able to control it.

"If he changes into one of those creatures, shoot him," the admiral bellowed into the megaphone so we would hear.

Trevor slowly gained control and kept his eyes trained on me. I could almost feel the red-hot rage pouring out of him. His head finally lowered, and he stared at the deck. We knew he would switch places with Ace if he could.

The admiral lifted the blowhorn again. "He will be placed in the raft alone. Do the same with the First Lady."

We had a small fishing boat waiting. While Trevor was placed in the raft, Mrs. Barnes was situated in the boat. She struggled with the tape but only managed to pull part of it from her mouth. Her face looked even more misshapen after her effort. With a last furious glare at me, she began rowing.

This was the most dangerous part for Trevor. Enemy guns were trained on him. His legs were still chained, and he had few options. I watched his face as he drew closer to Lesley. My vision and hearing were excellent as a Shadow Warrior.

"Trevor, no," I shouted when his body changed position and he made his intent to throw himself at Lesley. He would drown them both.

His head snapped up, and his shoulders relaxed.

I understood how he felt. His sacrifice wouldn't have the desired effect, though. We needed every Shadow Warrior we had for the coming battle that was long overdue.

Five minutes later, Trevor reached the dock. Mrs. Barnes reached the sub, and she was hustled down the hatch.

We stood staring at the admiral while he stared back. Then, he smiled. It sent shivers up my spine.

Someone yelled from behind us. "Hellhounds."

I looked toward the Federation sub. Knet and the admiral had gone below. Several of his men were trying to get down the hatch as fast as possible.

"Take them out," I commanded.

Six Federation soldiers went down from sniper fire.

We fell back to the ship and took cover behind it. An explosion rocked beneath us.

CHAPTER TWENTY-TWO

Marinah

"Torpedoes," Nokita shouted. "They're aiming for the docks."

"Radio the planes and see if they can blow that damn sub from the water," I told him. "Everyone else on me," I shouted.

Another explosion detonated, sending debris in all directions. My side stung for a moment.

Kill, whispered Ms. Beast.

Yes, time to kill.

My sword was strapped on my back, and I never considered using it. My rage overshadowed everything else. I needed blood on my teeth and claws.

A hound zeroed in on me and launched itself. King leapt and intercepted before it reached me. I let out a cry of frustration, then quickly found my next target. There had to be over a hundred hellhounds. We'd checked the surrounding area throughout the night.

Where the hell were they coming from?

Within a few minutes, the air thickened with the scent of death, machine oil, and something similar to burnt hair. My guttural growl vibrated. I locked eyes with another hellhound. Its curved claws clicked on the ground as it ran forward, its hungry eyes glued to me.

I leapt, a blur of dark fury, and launched forward aiming my claws at the hellhound's throat. It jumped aside at the last moment, and I only managed to rake a furrow across its side. The hellhound turned, and its snapping jaws missed me by an inch. I lashed out again and penetrated its flank. The hound shrieked, twisted, and flew at me again.

I lifted my clawed foot and drove it into the beast's gut, then withdrew. It snarled and began to circle, feinting left, then right, its eyes fixed on me. Another low rumble emanated from my chest. The hellhound darted in again, this time aiming for my legs, a tactical lunge designed to bring me down. Its claws raked my thigh, tearing deep. Pain and rage kept me going.

The hound tried to bite my lower leg, but I brought my powerful fists down, one after the other, on the hellhound's hunched back; each blow landed with the force of a jackhammer. The hellhound tried to get away. I roared again.

Battles took place around me. Eagle was as good as his word and other than the hound I fought, the ones nearest me had their lives cut short by sniper fire. I bit into the hellhound's shoulder and grabbed its front leg. It tried to twist away, but I got my other clawed hand around its throat. My jaws replaced my hand, and I bit into putrid flesh. The hellhound thrashed wildly, its powerful legs kicking, its teeth snapping futilely. I jerked my head to the side and tore its body apart.

"Marinah," King called.

I looked in his direction. There were only a few hellhounds left. One of Rodrigo's human men lay on the ground. He'd been bitten.

I moved toward King while looking for another attack. A sudden sharp pain took my breath away, and I stopped. My eyes looked downward where liquid slipped between my legs. Another jagged pain ran through me, and I dropped to my knees.

My side hurt, the hellhound bite on my thigh burned, but the pain in my stomach overshadowed everything.

"She took a bite," King shouted to someone.

"Where are you injured?" Axel asked urgently.

"Thigh. My water broke, and something is stinging my side," I gasped.

Axel lay me on my back.

"She's got a piece of shrapnel above her hip. I need her back at the citadel."

"The baby," I said as another pain assaulted me.

King lifted me and started running toward the vehicles. I hurt so much I couldn't breathe, and the jostling didn't help.

"Can you get the shrapnel out?" King asked Axel after placing me in the back seat.

"She's losing blood, and I'm afraid she'll lose more. I can't do anything until I know what we're dealing with."

"Fuck," King said.

Chapter Twenty-Three

King

MARINAH MOANED LOUDLY. BECK drove the vehicle while I sat in the back, holding her, with Axel squatting between the front seats, facing us. We were still in Warrior form, and the heavy weight of K-5 filled the vehicle.

"Should she shift?" I asked Axel, while trying to keep my voice calm for Marinah's sake.

"I'm unsure," he replied, while checking the pulse at her wrist. "I'll know for sure once I see how deep the shrapnel goes."

He turned and rummaged through the medical bag he'd dropped into the floorboard of the passenger seat. He pulled out tubing and a saline bag.

"I need to get an IV into her. I don't think the bleeding is dangerous, but I'll feel better once I have a line in. Hold her arm steady for me."

"Are you with me, Marinah?" I asked.

"Hurts," she said between tightly clenched teeth.

I rearranged her so I could hold her arm out to Axel. She groaned again, and her body curled tightly against the pain. Axel got the needle in. My heart felt like it was pounding through my chest.

"Hold on," I told her.

"Holding," she ground out.

"Give her something for pain," I demanded.

"No," both Axel and Marinah said at the same time.

I growled low in my throat, but didn't argue.

We pulled into the courtyard, and Axel jumped out. I tried to move toward the door, but Marinah grabbed my arm, her claws digging in.

"Don't move me right now," she gasped out.

"Get Kenneth and a stretcher," Axel shouted.

I held Marinah while she panted. I realized blood saturated the front of me. I tried to take the second hellhound from her, but another attacked.

"I'm going to shift," she gasped again.

"I've got you," I said.

"I would rather check the shrapnel wound first," Axel told her.

"I don't know if I can stop it," she moaned.

Kenneth arrived at the car. I placed her on the stretcher. Axel handed me the saline bag and began pushing Marinah toward the medical bay.

"She has shrapnel embedded in her side, and her water broke," he told Kenneth. "We'll need blood just in case. I may need to do a cesarean. When we get to the surgical room, set everything up for me."

"Got it," Kenneth replied.

He had been one of the Federation fighters who attacked the island as a red stripe. He had medical experience and had turned into an asset.

"Where's Garrett?" I asked after we arrived at the medical bays.

"Southern part of the island in case there was trouble. You need to check on them while I examine Marinah," Axel said.

"Beck's got it under control. Your job is my mate, and my job is to stand by her."

Axel lifted a hand with scissors and brought them to the straps covering Marinah's chest.

"No, not the straps," she said.

Axel ignored her, and she growled. The growl turned into a moan.

"I let you do your job without interference, and by damned, you're going to let me do mine," Axel lectured. He proceeded to cut her clothes from her body. "Help me roll her to her side," he said when he finished.

Two inches of shrapnel stuck out. The piece was about a quarter-inch thick. Dammit, how much was inside her?

"Check the baby's heart rate," Axel told Kenneth who was working busily around the room grabbing supplies.

A stethoscope was placed on Marinah's belly.

"Stable," Kenneth said after thirty seconds.

"Grab a blood bag before I remove this. Her name is on the bags I want," he ordered after he knew the baby was okay.

"Marinah," Axel told her. "I'm going to give you a local before I remove the shrapnel. I may need to cut into you, so I know what I'm dealing with."

"Do it," she ground out. "And hurry. I need to shift."

The pain was bad. Marinah never stayed silent, and she'd barely said ten words since she went to her knees at the shipyard. My concern for her overshadowed thoughts of our child. I couldn't lose her. This was my worst nightmare.

Axel put another line in her arm for the blood and administered the local. He looked up at me. K-5 burned in his eyes. "If you stop me from anything I need to do, I'll have you removed. Do we understand each other?"

I grunted, but he continued to stare. "Fine," I said like a petulant child.

The doctor cut her skin along the edge of the shrapnel. I held Marinah's hand.

"It's approximately three inches deep. It doesn't look like it hit anything vital. This will hurt." He didn't give her a chance to object. Using forceps, he slowly removed the metal.

Marinah's groan was louder.

Axel quickly squeezed a clear substance onto the wound.

"Superglue," he said. "You can shift now," he told Marinah.

Marinah's shifts were usually fast and explosive.

"No, no, no," she screamed, shaking her head while her body contorted.

I looked at Axel. He shook his head.

Her Nova exploded. She jumped from the table, knocking over the IV stand and a medical tray set up beside her. In two leaps, she was in the corner, her eyes burning with fury.

Everyone froze.

Her nova form was larger than my Warrior's form and far more deadly. Marinah's control of it had grown, but these were extenuating circumstances.

Barely above a whisper, I said her name.

She growled, her large teeth on full display. Her eyes didn't seem to focus on anything.

"Everyone needs to leave," I said. "Move slowly and stay as far away from her as you can."

Marinah's gaze followed Axel and Kenneth as they exited.

"Marinah, you're safe. The baby is coming. The baby is safe."

She stared at me for a moment before she threw her head back and made a sound I had never heard before. It was somewhere between pain, rage, and fear. Her entire body shook. Her large, clawed hand went to her stomach. Her eyes darkened further; the brown with golden flakes became pure obsidian.

This scenario hadn't occurred to me.

I took a step closer, and her jaws opened, showing a mouth full of huge teeth.

"Marinah, it's me. I won't let anything bad happen to you or our baby. I love you."

I kept my voice low as I took one step, then two. When I was close enough, I lifted my arms and lowered my head. She lowered herself slightly and rested her forehead against mine.

"You're okay," I assured her. "The baby is coming, and it would be easier if you were in human form. I'll shift with you." I moved my head an inch back and looked into her haunting eyes. I saw recognition.

"Shift with me," I said again, and let my form morph to human.

Marinah screamed, but at the same time, her body flowed into her human form. She'd pulled out the IV. I called for Axel, and he came in alone.

"Help her," I said.

"Lay her down."

Before I could do it, Marinah spoke. "No, stand me up. I feel too vulnerable lying on that damn medical bed."

"It's only me and Axel," I said. "Do what you need to do."

She looked at Axel. "Is the baby okay?"

"I need to check," he said. "Can I listen to the heartbeat?"

She leaned all her weight against me and gave a soft moan. Axel came closer, went to a knee, and listened.

"The baby's fine," he assured her. "Mothers gave birth out of bed long before some quack had them lay down. We've spoken about this. You need to feel safe. It's time to check you vaginally, though. Can you lean against King while I see where you're at?"

"Yes," she said. Her lips trembled, and tears streamed down her face. "I couldn't stop Nova," she said at last.

"You're scared," Axel told her. "I expected this. The fight at the shipyard didn't help. Unless I need assistance, everyone but the three of us will stay out of the room."

Her head turned, and she looked into my eyes. "Don't leave me," she whispered.

Axel kneeled in front of her while mine and Marinah's eyes stayed locked. "I'm not going anywhere. Our daughter will be here soon. I wouldn't miss it for the world."

After Nova's appearance, a steady calm filled me. The wound from the shrapnel was more than survivable. We could do this.

Chapter Twenty-Four

Marinah

IT SEEMED LIKE HOURS passed.

"You're doing great," Axel assured me.

"That's because it isn't you doing this," I grumbled between gasps while King assisted me as I walked from one side of the room to the other.

"You are correct. None of us would be here if childbirth was the man's job."

Everything hurt, and there was no possible way I could smile, much less laugh.

"No one told me it would hurt like this," I said.

"That's one of the miraculous things about childbirth. Once the baby is born, the pain becomes a distant memory."

Another contraction hit. Without King, I would have fallen to the floor.

"I'll never forget this pain," I said in a raspy voice.

Time passed until the contractions became one long pain without end. I gripped King's hand, squeezing hard as the wave continued. It squeezed my lower back in an all-consuming vise then wrapped around my abdomen.

"It's getting worse," I gasped, focusing on slow, steady breaths I'd practiced, trying to ride the peak that was now steady torture without end.

"You don't have long now," Axel said. "I'm going to check you again."

The seemingly endless contraction receded a small bit, leaving me momentarily breathless.

"Ten centimeters!" Axel announced, a bright, triumphant note in his voice. "And fully effaced. It's time to push."

A surge of adrenaline, mixed with a healthy dose of terror, flooded me. This felt monumental. King squeezed my hand, leaning in to whisper, "You've got this."

"Okay, Marinah," Axel's voice coaxed. "Next contraction, you push. Take a big breath at the start, hold it, and bear down."

The next contraction rolled in, a monstrous wave I couldn't escape. I took a ragged, deep breath, held it, and bore down with everything I had. Every muscle in my core screamed in protest, but a primal urge took over. I could feel the immense pressure and a raw burning sensation between my legs.

"Good, good push! Keep going, I can see the head!"

King remained a rock beside me, holding me steady in a squat position. He offered quiet encouragement, reminding me to breathe deeply between pushes.

After what felt like an eternity, but was probably only a few intense pushes, Axel suddenly exclaimed, "Okay, Marinah, one more big push! You're almost there! I need a good push for the shoulders!"

I bore down, a guttural cry tearing from my throat, fueled by sheer exhaustion and the fierce desire to meet my child. There was a final, stretching burn, a sensation of immense release, and then—

Axel lifted the baby and placed it into King's arm. King's other arm stayed around me.

A small but powerful cry filled the room.

My baby. My perfect, squalling baby, who looked so tiny with his father holding him. Tears blurred my vision as I took in the details of the wrinkled face, dark wet hair, eyes squeezed shut. I glanced at King. Tears streamed down his face as he stared in wonder at the child we created.

Axel gently nudged my belly. "Just a few more pushes for the placenta, Marinah. You're doing great." It felt like a minor aftershock compared to the earthquake that had just passed.

A few minutes later, King handed the baby back to Axel and assisted me to the hospital bed. I lay back, and Axel placed the baby on my chest. I listened to the tiny whimpers. The room was a bubble of warmth filled with a sense of peace. The pain was already a distant echo, replaced by an overwhelming, primal love.

"You have a daughter," Axel said.

A daughter. I hadn't even cared. I leaned down and kissed her blood-smeared head before looking up at King.

"I knew it was a girl," he said with cocky assuredness. "A beautiful, perfect baby girl." He leaned down and kissed my forehead. "I love you. I love you both."

I couldn't stop the tears. I'd been so worried, even before the shit that went down at the shipyard. I'd stayed busy so I didn't have time to think about the what-ifs. They encroached every time I had a quiet moment. And now she was here. Our miracle.

I glanced around the room. Axel had left us alone. That reassured me more than anything that our baby was okay.

"I don't want to let her go," I said, looking at her tiny body.

She began crying again and I brought her to my chest. Her little mouth turned to my warmth with the cutest of lip movements. I adjusted her to my breast. She struggled a bit, and I remembered what Missy had told me. With a little help, she began sucking. Nothing had ever felt so right in the world.

"You're beautiful," King whispered.

Five minutes later, Maylin stuck her head into the room. "Axel wanted me to assist getting the baby cleaned and you too, Marinah. I also wish to meet your daughter."

I smiled at her as she walked closer. She looked better, but I could tell she was putting on a show for us. She had insisted on working even though Axel argued that she should rest for a day or two. The island was full of stubborn women.

"The announcement hasn't been made. That is for the father. I will make sure both mother and baby are clean and comfortable."

King leaned down and kissed my lips. "They can wait," he said.

"It's okay," I told him. "Inform the guard and give us about thirty minutes. I love you."

He leaned lower and kissed the baby's head. He stood and looked at me. "Our princess is perfect."

"Yes, she is."

Chapter Twenty-Five

King

E AGLE, ALDEN, AND RODRIGO waited outside the med bay. They stood against the hallway walls. I couldn't stop my smile even if I wanted to.

"The princess of the Shadow Warriors has arrived," I said after taking two steps from the room.

A cheer went up. Eagle hugged me. Rodrigo shook my hand and said congratulations in Spanish. Alden slammed his palms into my back.

"The islanders are waiting for news," Rodrigo said. "May I tell them?"

"Yes."

He began walking away, then stopped and turned. "You know she will be spoiled?"

I couldn't help the laugh that escaped. "Mostly by her father."

"How is Marinah?" Alden asked.

"She's fine now. Her Nova made an appearance, giving us a few tense minutes, but the rest went smoothly. The shrapnel caused no harm to the baby."

Eagle's expression changed. "When are we putting an end to this?"

I knew exactly what he was asking. "As soon as Marinah is healed we will move forward. It's past time to fight for peace."

Our families had to be safe. With the Federation in control, it would never happen. I also suspected if they weren't already pushing around the rest of the surviving world, it would happen soon.

Marinah and the baby were moved into our room a few hours later. They were both sleeping now. We hadn't named the baby, but we would discuss it again after Marinah rested.

There was a soft knock on the door. I opened it and saw Beck. I quietly entered the hall and closed the door behind me.

"One casualty," Beck said. "It was one of Rodrigo's men. A hellhound bit him, and he died shortly after."

I was furious that the hellhounds evaded our search.

"We know what Knet's assignment was," Beck continued. "There was a hidden tunnel a mile from the shipyard. Who knows how long he's been collecting hellhounds. Some of the debris was cleared and the men could see holding cells. Small detonations were used to free them. They tend to head towards water and we think that's what drew them to the shipyard."

It didn't make sense.

Beck stared at me and gave his next news. "A human detonated the charges."

My eyes burned. "Is he alive?" I asked.

"Alive and terrified."

"Do not kill him. Place a guard outside the room. I'm not leaving Marinah tonight. Tomorrow will be soon enough."

"Do you want guards on your room?" Beck asked.

I smiled, showing my very human teeth. "If someone tries to hurt Marinah or our child, they will die violently, so no, we will be safe."

"We are still on high alert. No one will get to this room," Beck promised.

I nodded and went back to sit and watch my mate and child.

A little girl. Her eyes were blue like mine, but her face was all Marinah. She weighed sixteen pounds and still looked entirely too small. I was a father. This was something I thought would never happen. Too much fighting and killing for so long.

I passed out in the early morning hours. When the baby stirred, light was just coming through the window. Marinah woke instantly.

"She's wet," Marinah said at the exact moment the baby let out a loud cry that built even though Marinah picked her up.

"And hungry," I said. "I'll grab a diaper."

The women on the island had brought baskets of cloth diapers with lanolized wool wraps to go over them to keep the cloth from leaking. They explained the diapering process to Marinah, so I simply handed her the diaper. She looked at it for a second before taking the old one off. The baby screamed throughout the process. Her tiny legs stiffened while the old diaper was removed. Marinah seemed to have a difficult time, and I had no idea how to help.

The baby's cries grew louder and her lower lip trembled. She had a good, strong set of lungs. As soon as she was dry, Marinah brought her to her breast. The screaming stopped, though soft, heartfelt whimpers continued. I lay down beside them.

"We need a name," I said.

"I truly thought she would be a he," Marinah said with a sigh. "I had a dozen male names chosen. Did you think of girl names?"

"Not a one," I admitted. "I didn't want to test fate."

"We can wait. The perfect name will come to us when we know more about her personality."

"That works for me." I touched my daughter's cheek with the back of my finger. "She's so soft. It's hard to believe she wasn't here yesterday." I rubbed her cheek again. "How are you feeling?"

"Tired, but not too sore. I really want a shower."

"After feeding, I'll hold her, and you can take your time. Food should arrive soon."

Marinah laughed. "I don't think I've gone this long without thinking about food since I became pregnant."

"You can eat before the shower."

"No, shower first. A mountain of food afterward. The hellhounds attacked us from behind, and they shouldn't have been on the island. Have you discovered anything?"

I told her about the Federation soldier on lockdown and how the hellhounds escaped detection.

"When are you going to question the soldier?" she asked.

"He'll wait for as long as we need him to."

"The sooner the better. He might know about their future plans."

"They're always planning something," I said. Frustration laced through the words.

She took my hand and squeezed my fingers. We would face whatever they threw at us together.

Chapter Twenty-Six

King

THE FEDERATION SOLDIER WASN'T in good condition. A Shadow Warrior's claw had left a deep wound in his leg. The bandage around it was bloody. He glanced at me when I entered the cell, then tightly shut his eyes. Trevor stood against the far wall, staring daggers at the man. He'd asked Beck if he could stand guard, and Beck allowed it. I wasn't so sure. Trevor looked like a man out for blood. Fury radiated off him as he fought to control his beast. I nodded at him, then adjusted the leather straps on my chest. "Look at me," I told the prisoner. His eyes opened a sliver, and my Beast exploded. Gaining control so quickly after the change was a new phenomenon. I wasn't quite where Marinah was, but

I was damn close. I took three steps toward the man, lifted him by the collar of his shirt, and said, very distinctly, "You will tell me everything you know. I can make your death quick, or I can eat you from your feet up, and keep you alive through most of it."

"Kill me," he said. "I know little, and nothing I tell you will help. They have my family. My children. I had no choice." He closed his eyes again.

A loud growl came from across the room. Trevor had been unable to stop his shift, and he was now in Beast form. His control would be erratic for up to an hour, and I didn't want him killing the prisoner before it was time. I directed my stare at him and growled. He stayed where he was.

"Anything you say will help," I said through elongated jaws with huge teeth that could easily circle the prisoner's head.

"They are planning to attack soon. You have no chance. They will overwhelm your forces with hellhounds. They also made that thing from a Shadow Warrior. He bullies the hounds into going where he wants them to and they don't fight back against him." Something in his eyes died. There was no fight left, only resignation and his entire body went limp.

"When are they coming?" I demanded.

"I do not know the exact time, but soon."

"How many soldiers?"

He shrugged and I shook him.

"I don't know." He squeaked.

"Were you captured?"

"Yes."

"From where?"

"Tully."

"They took your family?"

"A large group of us were on our way to Outpost Three to trade with them. The soldiers captured us at the midway point. I did what they said, even though I knew they would not spare my family." He lifted his chin slightly. "Kill me. I do not want to live."

"What is your name?" I asked.

"Evan Pycos. It doesn't matter, though. I want to die."

"Why do you think your family is dead?"

He looked down, then back up. "They want as many hellhounds as possible for the fight against you. They are killing everyone they find and turning them into those monsters. They captured about twenty of us. Men, women, and children. Then they injected us with the hellhound evil. They told us what they wanted and asked for a volunteer. No one stepped forward, and they shot an entire family. That's when I raised my hand. They moved my family to the side and killed everyone else. My children witnessed the slaughter." He looked down again. "They moved the dead into a huge cage, and an hour later, hellhounds rose. My daughter wouldn't stop screaming, and a soldier backhanded her. One of her baby teeth flew out and she didn't move after that. I should have let them kill me and my family immediately."

"Did you see them kill the other members of your family?"

"No, they were taken away, and I was told exactly what they expected from me. It was a suicide mission, and I knew it. That's why I know my family is dead. The Federation didn't expect me to survive."

"How did you survive?"

"I dug a shallow hole and buried myself with sand until I heard the high-pitched sound from the submarine."

"And?" I asked when he didn't continue.

"I hit the detonation switch and released the hounds."

"Even knowing your family was most likely dead?" I growled.

"Yes." His eyes lifted to mine again. "I am a coward. You need to kill me."

He wanted to suffer for what he'd done. He wanted to die because his family was dead, and he hadn't been strong enough to watch them die or to die with them. He *was* a coward. He needed someone else to end his miserable life. I was very tempted.

"I have a better idea," I told him. "You deserve the death you seek."

He gulped.

"You will die on our front lines at the hands of the Federation when they attack." I released him.

He collapsed to his knees. "Please end this. I can't take it." He began crying.

I wanted to strangle him. I turned to Trevor. "Guard him closely so he doesn't kill himself." I didn't think he was capable of doing it, but I wanted to be sure. "Do not harm him in any way. Do you have enough control for this assignment?"

Trevor looked at the prisoner before momentarily meeting my eyes.

"Yes, King."

If Trevor did kill him, his punishment wouldn't be severe, but I didn't say so.

I left the cell and returned to my wife and child. Marinah sat in the chair by the table, feeding our daughter again. For such a tiny thing, she enjoyed her food as much as her mother. Marinah slowly munched on food from a plate on the table.

"You should be in bed," I said after kissing her on the cheek.

"My, what big teeth you have, oh great one." She grinned, then shifted her attention to the baby. Her eyes grew soft, and a smile curved her lips. I would carry this picture in my head for the rest of my life. They were so incredibly beautiful.

I shifted to human form and knelt at Marinah's knees. I ran one finger across the baby's cheek. She was our future, and it was worth risking everything to know she would survive.

Marinah leaned forward and kissed the top of my head. I straightened and looked up at her. "Your thoughts are in turmoil," she said. "We planned to take time after the birth and relax, even if for only a few days. That was unrealistic of us. We need to be fighting for a peaceful world she can grow up in."

"My thoughts show so loudly?"

"You are my mate. We have the same thoughts." She reached her hand out and ran her fingers over the stubble on my jaw. I took her hand and kissed the backs of her fingers. I placed her hand over my heart. "I love you."

"I love you."

We gazed at each other for what seemed an eternity. I felt her deep inside me. Mates. I don't know if our connection had ever been this powerful.

"What did the prisoner say?" Marinah finally asked.

I stood, adjusted my chest straps and took the chair beside her. I recounted the man's story.

"Do you think they killed his family?" Marinah asked.

"Most likely. Putting him in battle is risky because he might kill one of us. Killing him instantly was too good for him."

"We'll think about our options," she said.

"Do we wait for the attack, or do we preempt it?" I asked.

Someone knocked on the door. I opened it with a growl, upset that our time together was being interrupted. Beck stood there.

"There's a ship in the citadel harbor."

"Just one ship?"

"Yes, it's filled with women. They want to see Nikayla."

"Who?"

"Your child, though they said Marinah's child. They claim to be Shadow."

CHAPTER TWENTY-SEVEN

Marinah

THE BABY HAD FALLEN asleep a few minutes before. I lifted her to my shoulder while staring at Beck in shock. It took a moment to form a sentence.

"The Shadow women are here?"

His expression showed something. Not quite disdain, but something close. "If they are who they say they are, then yes, they are here. We shouldn't trust them."

I stood up and gave Beck my hard stare. "Shut up. No one asked you."

King made a noise low in his throat. It sounded like a laugh. I ignored him and directed my command at Beck. "Escort their representatives into the citadel and take them to the sitting room. Have food and drink delivered while they wait for me."

"Sitting room?" Beck questioned like I'd grown two heads.

"Yes, the room on the bottom floor with comfortable couches and chairs." I had trouble not adding "duh" to the command. It was rarely used but it was a place for guests and any idiot knew that. Okay, it was obvious one did not. "Make them feel welcome, and if I hear you haven't done as I've asked, I'll send you to the southern part of the island until I calm down." I glared. "It could take a year or more. Have I made myself clear?"

Beck stared for a split second too long before lowering his gaze. "Yes, Alpha."

"Why are you standing still? Hurry," I said and made a shooing motion with my hand.

A second after he left, King began laughing. It didn't help the turmoil rolling through my stomach.

"You deal with him so much better than I ever did," he said when he could speak.

"Take her." The baby had fallen asleep, and I thrust her gently into King's arms. I needed a very quick shower before facing the women. My brain began going in a hundred different directions.

"What do I do if she cries?" King asked, looking at me like I was out of my mind for handing him the baby. He must have forgotten caring for her when

I took the long shower. I was slightly upset that he hadn't assisted earlier when I changed her diaper. I'd struggled, and he'd only watched. That would end right now.

I looked at his chest that was covered in straps. "You have large pecs; she might enjoy one."

He looked down, then up. The expression on his face said I had to be joking. I left him standing there with his child in his arms. If a Shadow Warrior couldn't handle his own child, he needed to kick himself in his own ass.

Men.

I scrubbed myself thoroughly, got out of the shower, and found one of the thick pads the women made for me. They had thought of everything. If it would have been left to me, I would be wearing a T-shirt between my thighs. My old clothes from before I was pregnant were tight, but they would work.

I gave a long sigh. King and I had set aside time after the baby's birth to simply be a family. With all that happened these past few days, family time had to wait. I had no aches or pains left from labor and delivery. Shadow Warrior healing was miraculous. The only thing bothering me was an overall sense of tiredness. I needed the downtime I wouldn't get. I smiled and shook my head. Forward, oh great leader of the Shadow Warriors.

Ms. Beast whispered inside me. *Baby.*

She had been unusually quiet. I couldn't sense Nova at all but didn't have time to worry about it.

I left the bathroom and found King sitting in the chair I'd vacated. The baby slept. He gave me a relieved look. It would become abundantly clear very quickly that raising our child was a team effort. He led the Warriors before me, and if he could do that, he could handle one small infant.

"I'm going to speak with the women alone," I said. "I'll send someone for the baby if I decide it's safe."

He nodded his head like he'd expected this and he was resigned. Her last diaper had been black tar. King needed a good, solid dose of newborn poop, but I most likely wouldn't get that lucky.

How many Shadow Warriors does it take to change a dirty diaper? I thought to myself as I quickly left the room.

I turned several corners and almost ran into Cosway.

"You had the baby?" she asked with a wide smile.

"She's with King. He's learning to be a dad. Could you come with me now? The Shadow women are here, and I think they want to see the baby, but I need to know what their intent is first."

"Yes, I will protect you," Cosway said.

I didn't correct her. Cosway thought about life very differently from the rest of us. Her simple ways didn't show how smart she was, but I knew the truth and had no problem listening to her wisdom.

I entered the sitting room. Beck stood inside the door along with Caleb. My eyes zeroed in on Endura, who walked toward me. Her calming essence was in full force along with a smile that enveloped me with serenity.

She wore jeans and a T-shirt, which made her appearance disconcerting for some odd reason. I always pictured her in the same loose cotton dress that had flowed around her the first time we met. She looked different now. More modern.

I turned to the men. "You may leave," I told them.

Caleb moved immediately, but Beck hesitated. I narrowed my eyes, and he followed Caleb.

"It's good to see you," I said when I turned back to Endura.

"I did not think we would meet again," she said, and before I asked why, she continued, "You have had the child."

"How did you know I was pregnant?" I asked instead of answering.

She turned to another woman, about ten years older. "This is Amissa. She sees that which has not happened."

Amissa was dressed very similarly to Endura, but her T-shirt held the slogan, "I predict I need more coffee." Did this mean she had a sense of humor? It was something lacking in our current world. Fighting hellhounds will do that to a person.

Amissa bowed her head.

"You see the future?" I asked somewhat skeptically.

Amissa looked into my eyes. "The gift was passed down from my mother. I knew you were having a daughter. A few weeks ago, I understood that we, the Shadows, have a part in what is to come. We are here to protect Nikayla."

Beck had said the name, but it had no effect on me. Now, it hit like a lightning strike, and I stepped back slightly. I looked at Cosway, and she appeared shell-shocked. Then her eyes took on a dreamy look, and her lips curved upward. She swayed slightly.

I looked back at the women. "Can she feel your essence?"

Endura smiled. "Most humans cannot, but she does feel it. She has a pure heart."

Strange. I knew there was nothing pure about mine, but the essence was stronger since they said that name. Nikayla. It buzzed strangely through my body.

"Who is Nikayla?" I asked.

The women smiled.

"She is your daughter," Amissa said. "Nikayla is her given name."

"You seem very sure," I replied a little stiffly.

"When you hold her and say the name, you will know."

I already knew, but that didn't mean I liked this mystic shit.

"Why Nikayla?"

Amissa smiled again. "The name has two powerful meanings. The first, 'No One is Like God.' Your enemies think they are God. Nikayla strikes that down. The second meaning is 'Victory of the People.'"

Hmm. The name continued to buzz as I repeated it inside my head. "Is this why you are willing to fight now?" I tried to keep ire from the words but failed.

"We are not here to fight. Our presence will help in some way. The prophecies are never clear, but I know we must be here while you wage war on the continent. If you survive the coming battle, Nikayla will assure lasting peace."

What could I say to that? A lot, but I decided it best to think about it before I caused an incident.

"How many women did you bring with you?"

Endura gave a small laugh and spoke, "One hundred and forty women and children took the voyage with us. No one stayed behind."

This shocked me. They had all come. "What about your husbands?"

"We have no husbands. The men who lived with us left to fight. We told them not to return. Most died early in the hellhound battles. We do not make binding ties with the men who father our children. It is a lesson we learned several generations ago."

I wasn't going to touch that.

"May we see Nikayla?" Endura asked.

There it was again. Maybe "buzz" was the wrong word. "Zing" fit better.

"I am Cosway. I will fetch Nikayla," she said and smiled at the two women before she left the room.

Cosway had accepted what the women said. I couldn't believe someone else was naming mine and King's child, but arguing against it seemed futile.

"What condition are those who traveled with you in?" I asked.

"They are tired of being cooped up on the ship. We bring no illness with us, just grumpy children who wish to run and play without boundaries," Endura replied.

"We can provide rooms, food, and a place for the children to run. My worry is that if the Warriors leave the island, your unwillingness to fight will endanger those who stay behind." I shook my head before Endura could speak. "I'm not saying you will bring danger, but if they need to protect their families and you, more of the island people will die."

It was Amissa who spoke. "We are tasked with keeping your child safe and will give our lives to do so. We will not endanger the people here."

Endura nodded in agreement.

I wasn't sure how I felt about any of this, but I needed more time to think on it.

"Then welcome to my home," I said.

Chapter Twenty-Eight

King

THE BABY SLEPT WHILE I studied her. I'd held other babies for a short time, but this was different. Marinah and I created her. She seemed so delicate. Too delicate. I knew she would grow strong but her vulnerability while she lay in my arms was jarring.

Protect baby.

Beast said it almost like a reverent whisper which was damned strange.

With our life, I assured him with more command than usual.

I swear he purred.

The baby's smell seeped into my senses and my body tingled with a strange awareness. Love rolled through me. The overwhelming urge to fight that usually surrounded me was missing. I would protect my child at all costs, but the sense of calm I felt was strange. The bloodlust I'd carried with me since the Federation betrayed my uncle was missing.

I stood carefully when a knock sounded at the door. The unique scent of flowers and herbs told me who was in the hall. I opened the door. Cosway looked at me before her gaze turned to the bundle on my shoulder.

"May I?" she asked and placed her hands out.

I'd almost killed this woman because I thought she was a man with half his screws loose. The killing would have been a mercy. I wasn't happy when I discovered she was indeed a woman. But I was wrong. She'd helped Marinah find balance in the chaos that surrounded her after she went nova. Cosway used meditation. I had laughed and shook my head at first. Now the Shadow Warriors embraced it. In a way, meditation was similar to how the baby affected me and my beast.

I placed my child in her arms. She smiled down at her then turned and took a step down the hall. I grabbed her shoulder.

"I did not say you could take her away," I said somewhat sternly.

Her eyes remained calm. "The Shadow wish to see Nikayla. It is my job to take her to them. They are safe and would not harm the child of the queen."

Interesting. I looked at the sleeping baby's face. The name Nikayla chimed through my brain. Very interesting.

"I will accompany you." The baby was going nowhere without me or Marinah."

"Of course," Cosway said, almost like she had a say.

Beast didn't grumble. His restraint was odd. Hell, the feelings I had were more than odd. I needed to question Marinah about these changes. I didn't think Beck or Nokita would be much help. They had never said anything had affected them strangely after their children were born.

I followed Cosway to Marinah. I recognized one of the women immediately. The other was a stranger.

"King, I would like to introduce you to Endura and Amissa," Marinah said.

The women bowed their heads slightly before looking me in the eyes. Beast didn't grumble. Cosway handed the baby to Marinah and the woman named Amissa stepped forward. She placed one finger on the baby's temple.

"Nikayla, not a God but the victory of the people," she said softly and smiled.

That damned tingle happened again and Marinah actually jumped slightly. She turned to me, her eyes larger than normal.

"Amissa sees into the future and the future has named our daughter Nikayla."

What could I say? I wasn't sure I believed in someone's ability to read the future but there was no denying our baby's name.

"I made a promise to Labyrinth our child would be named after him," Marinah said. "She can have more than one middle name if you would like to offer one."

The Shadow Warriors had adopted one name when we joined the war against hellhounds. We had left our human identities behind.

"I wish the name to be Greystone."

"Nikayla Labyrinth Greystone. It's the perfect name," Marinah said.

As soon as the words left her mouth, the tingle returned with more force. If the name appeared mysteriously on our child's skin, I wouldn't have been surprised. Slowly, the world returned to normal or as normal as it had been since Marinah entered my life.

"May I," Endura asked.

Marinah handed Nikayla to her. Endura gently kissed her forehead then handed her to Amissa who did the same. The baby was then placed back in Marinah's arms. I saw something in my mate's eyes that surprised me.

Peace.

CHAPTER TWENTY-NINE

Marinah

DUE TO NIKAYLA, COSWAY insisted we take a car to Warrior Bay. I had no idea Cosway could drive. She often surprised me in small ways like this. She disappeared for days at a time, and even when I questioned her, she never revealed where she went. Ms. Beast felt no danger from her, so I let it pass. Cosway was what you would call a free spirit. She danced to the tune of her own drum, and it was what I loved most about her.

Endura and Amissa seemed drawn to her, just as I was.

Caleb was our escort, and he rode in the front passenger seat. I sat in the middle of the backseat, holding Nikayla, with Endura and Amissa on either side of me. The baby slept peacefully and didn't stir during the short ride.

When we stepped from the car, the ocean breeze was welcoming. Women began walking down the gangway. Endura and Amissa stood solemnly and watched. Women and children came one after the other. The children were female, which was a bit disconcerting. Shadow Warriors produced male off-spring.

Their clothing ranged from jeans and T-shirts to dresses. There were a few babies held in women's arms. I was curious about their lives. These were the women descended from those who left the Shadow Warriors and went out on their own several generations before. The history texts King gave me told nothing about their lives after they disappeared.

Blue-eyed gazes stared at me. Or maybe it was Nikayla who held their attention. They stopped ten feet from where we stood. I couldn't deny the serenity they emitted. Caleb, who had walked beside me, backed up a few feet. I turned and looked at him, but he was watching the women with a strange look on his face. It wasn't fear.

Endura had told me they did not share their essence with Shadow Warriors. She never said they couldn't.

Endura followed my gaze. "We no longer teach the children to shield their essence. He is feeling it."

I turned away from Caleb and returned the stares of the women. Some of them peered quickly at Caleb before turning back to me. They didn't exactly have anger in their expressions, but it was definitely not joy.

Endura spread her arms wide. "We are welcome here. Marinah has given birth, and Nikayla is among us."

It was the baby who drew their attention. I looked down at Nikayla. Her large blue eyes were open. I smiled at her because there was no other choice. I turned her and lifted her in my arms because it felt like the right thing to do. Endura's smile encouraged me.

"They will not harm her. They wish to add their blessing to mine and Amissa's."

Ms. Beast purred. This felt right. It was as if something had been missing. I hadn't known it was missing, but pieces simply clicked into place.

Tears slowly ran down my cheeks and energy swelled around us. It was the opposite of K-5, which carried rage, but at the same time, more powerful. The Shadow Warriors lost so much when the women left them.

I lowered Nikayla and walked forward. When I reached the women, gentle hands reached out and touched my arms. They also touched Nikayla's head. My newborn child stared. Her wide eyes held knowledge, which was impossible.

"She's beautiful," one woman said.

"May I see her, mommy?" a little girl asked.

I took a knee and showed the little girl my child. More of the children stepped forward. Their hands going to Nikayla's head, their eyes showing wonder.

"She has blue eyes like us," another child said.

The essence these children carried was stronger than the adult women. Or maybe it was simply less controlled. I had so much to learn. Somehow I had to convince the women to stay and balance the Warrior aggression. Being around them was like meditation on steroids.

When I discovered I was a Shadow Warrior, pieces of my life made sense, and I finally felt that I had come home. The key element I hadn't known I was missing were other women. Shadow Women.

I looked behind me and saw a similar expression on Caleb's face. He looked shell-shocked, just as Cosway had.

A little girl, maybe three or four years old, touched my leg. I peered down at her and smiled. She wore a knee-length blue dress with small, colorful flowers. Her slightly chubby cheeks had dimples.

"I brought this for Nikayla. I don't think she's able to hold her yet. Will you give her the doll?"

The doll's dress was made of the same cotton that the little girl wore, and the styles were identical.

"What is your name?" I asked.

"Sweeting," she said and lifted the doll to me.

I took it. "She is beautiful, and Nikayla will love her."

Sweeting wrapped her arms around my legs and hugged me. She then turned and ran to a woman who I assumed was her mother. She smiled at me.

Amissa placed her arms out, and I handed the baby to her. She walked forward and was surrounded by the women and children. She lifted Nikayla in her arms.

"Nikayla is ours to protect." She turned to me. "No harm will come to your child."

I was no longer worried about them when it came to Nikayla. It felt like it was meant to be. Crazy, maybe, but our world was already insane. My thoughts went to the Shadow Warrior he-men who were not ready for this punch to the gut. Caleb continued to look shaken. I would leave my child in capable hands when I went to fight the Federation.

And I was ready for the fight. Ready to end the war and return to peace.

CHAPTER THIRTY

Marinah

WHEN I FINALLY RETURNED to my room, I was exhausted. Mikayla began to fuss. She decided fussing wasn't getting her anywhere and screams might work faster while I changed her diaper.

I'd arranged transportation to the citadel for the women and children. We were now at full capacity. There were buildings surrounding us that held human families. Some unmarried Shadow Warriors turned several buildings into dorm-like living quarters. If the outposts sent more children, we would have trouble fitting them here.

"There, there," I told Nikayla when I lifted her to my breast and she gave up her tears so she could latch onto my nipple. A few whimpers interspersed with the sucking noises made my heart swell.

Nikayla's tiny fingers wrapped around one of mine when she finally relaxed. Her large blue eyes opened. They said most babies were born with blue eyes and they could change. Mine were brown which was strange for a Shadow Warrior. Hers matched her father's perfectly and I had a feeling; they would stay blue.

"What wonders do you hold?" I asked softly.

Neither King nor the Shadows knew what to expect from her. Amissa said she would assure lasting peace. Getting to that peace was my job.

Nikayla eventually stopped nursing and fell asleep. I placed her in the center of our bed. A soft knock sounded at the door. Axel and Garret stood waiting.

"You just couldn't stay away could you?" I asked Garret.

He smiled and tried looking over my shoulder and into the room.

"I am sorry I wasn't here for the birth. This man," he nodded to Axel, "insisted I care for other patients while he had all the fun. Where is the princess?"

I gave an internal groan. If people continued calling her princess, spoiled rotten would be an understatement. I didn't want to ruin Garret's mood so I let it go. For now.

"She's sleeping but you can come in. I haven't noticed that talking disturbs her. Please take one of the chairs."

"I came to see how *you* are doing," Axel said, after we were seated.

"Of course you did." I smiled. "A little tired, but overall, I feel good."

"A little tired in Marinah speak means you are exhausted and overdoing it. You need protein and sleep. The second part, I can do nothing about unless I drug you. The first part I can handle. I'll speak with the kitchen staff and make sure you are given an overabundance of meat."

Just the thought sent queasiness through my stomach. My internal protein regulator knew exactly what I needed. "Check to see if they have tofu," I said. "Lots and lots of tofu."

Axel's face scrunched.

"I lived off tofu and vegetable proteins until the hellhounds attacked the first time. For some reason, I'm craving tofu."

"What about beans and rice?" he asked.

My stomach gave a small rumble. "Those sound wonderful too."

"Interesting," the doctor said.

"Is that good interesting, or bad interesting?"

"I'm unsure. Ask me in a week or two so I have time to study this strange phenomenon. As far as

I know the word tofu has never been spoken by a Shadow Warrior in my lifetime."

I shook my head slightly and grinned. I wanted what I wanted.

Garret kept looking toward the bed or I should say the middle of the bed.

"Go ahead and pick her up," I told him.

He did exactly that. I won't say he ran to the bed, but he had the baby in his arms within seconds.

"Meet Nikayla Labyrinth Greystone," I told them.

"Quite the name," Axel said.

She'll need to grow into it," I said with a smile. "Did you hear about the Shadows arrival?"

"Yes. I want to introduce myself and see if anyone needs medical attention," Axel replied.

"From what I saw, they were healthy but you should introduce yourself." I remembered the looks they'd cast at Caleb. "Don't expect instant com-radery," I said. "They gave Caleb the cold shoulder."

"I'll keep that in mind," Axel replied.

"You can go alone," Garret said. "I'm going to hold Nikayla for as long as she and her mother allow."

The baby squirmed a bit and he raised her to his shoulder and gently pat her back. Within a minute a small burp released and she settled down.

"I forgot about burping," I said slightly panicked.

Garret laughed. "I had younger sisters and brothers who I cared for while my mom and dad worked. I can give you all the pointers you need."

I didn't ask about his family because he'd always seemed content. For the most part, families surviving the apocalypse were rare. Cuba, the island where we stayed had a better family ratio than most places but the hellhounds and the fallout after the electro-magnetic pulses had still taken a toll. Shadow Warriors lost nearly everyone. We seldom discussed our previous families.

With everything that had happened since my labor pains started, I just remembered his dinner with the two young kids.

"What happened with the twins. How did your evening go?"

Garret's eyes went even brighter. "The dinner was perfect. Becky and Derrick want to live with us. Suzie, one of the older teens is moving in with us too." He hesitated.

"Go on," I told him.

"She doesn't want to fight with Ruth's group. She's willing to care for the twins when we're at work. She told us she would find another job if we didn't need her."

"But she can fight," I said carefully.

"She can, but she would rather help in other ways. She's worried that she will be forced into being a soldier. Her parents were taken years ago by the Federation. They hid her beneath the floorboards so she would survive. She never saw them again and believes they are dead. She learned to fight because she had no choice."

"She will make a wonderful addition to your quickly growing family," I assured him.

His shoulders relaxed and he put all his attention into cuddling Nikayla.

"How do you feel about your instant family?" I asked Axel.

His eyes shifted to Garret who was looking at the baby. I saw so much love in his expression. "Like I have the family I thought would never be mine. The twins are a delightful handful. Thank you for putting a good word in for us."

"I'm glad it worked out. Now go and check on the women." I looked at Garret and then turned back to Axel. "The baby hog has this covered and while he holds her, I'm going to lay down and rest."

Axel nodded, rose from his chair, and left me alone with Nikayla and Garret.

"I won't take the princess from the room," Garret said after Axel closed the door behind him. "Sleep if you can. I'm sure food will arrive within the hour now that Axel wants you fed."

I yawned. "Thank you. I don't know when King will return."

"I have it covered."

I smiled but didn't hear Garret say anything more because I fell asleep.

A very fussy baby woke me. My mind felt cloudy from the nap and it took a moment to realize it was King jostling Nikayla as he carried her around the room.

"Bring her here," I said, lifting my arms. "How long did I sleep?"

"Three hours. I sent your food back to the kitchen to let you rest."

My stomach growled. "I'll feed her and then I need to eat. Did you change her?"

"Was I supposed to?" King asked with true curiosity.

I laughed as I put her to my breast. "We have a lot to learn. I forgot to burp her earlier. And yes, she needs to be changed regularly."

"What if I become the hunter and kill our food, while you change diapers?" He looked completely serious.

"What if I hunt and you change diapers?" I countered.

"Is this a negotiation?" he asked.

"No because you're not getting out of diaper duty. And you don't have time to hunt."

"It was worth a try."

"Grab a diaper and cover. I'll show you how to do a poor job of it as soon as she finishes eating."

Noises came from Nikayla's stomach followed by loud gas and the smell of poop.

"We need a nanny," King said. "If not, I'll make time to hunt." He placed his hand on his heart as a promise.

"Watch it or I'll will one of the guards to interrupt and tell me there's been a catastrophe that needs my attention. You'll be left alone with *your daughter* and then what will you do?"

"Call the other guards to save me," he said.

Nikayla finished nursing and I went through the finer points of diaper changing.

"What is that gunk?" King asked when he saw what was in her diaper.

"Axel told me it's part of the process after a baby is born and not to worry about it. I'll let you do the cleaning."

"With what, a bulldozer?" King asked.

"Haha, grab one of the cloths stacked in the cabinet in the bathroom and get it wet. This will be good for you."

"You'll need to make this a command or it won't work."

"Sure thing. I command you to clean every dirty diaper Nikayla has from now until she's potty trained. Does that work for you?"

"I take it back. I'm happy cleaning this one." He winked at me before entering the bathroom.

"You know this is disgusting, right?" he asked when the job was about half finished.

"She's staring at you and listening to your words," I reminded him.

King looked up from his task. And changed his tone. Not baby words but softer. "Okay, not disgusting, but definitely, not sweet either."

She sneezed.

"What did you do?" I asked.

"I didn't do anything. Is it normal for babies to sneeze?"

"I have no idea. When you're done, could you find Axel and send him here? Afterward stop at the kitchen and bring my food up. I'm starving."

King went fast after that. Her diaper looked a little less secure than the ones I'd done, but I knew mine needed work too. I was more worried about the sneeze.

I studied Nikayla after King left. She didn't look sick, but she'd been passed around to the women on the ship. I shouldn't have allowed it. I examined her chest and back then her arms and legs looking for any sign of illness.

King entered the room carrying a large tray of food.

"Where's Axel?" I asked.

"He's doing doctor things. He said sneezing is normal."

"He didn't want to examine her?"

"He wasn't the slightest bit moved to check her. We may need a new pediatrician."

"He's the only certified doctor on the island," I replied.

"There is that. I threatened him and he laughed at me. Even Garret laughed. This entire baby thing is hard work."

I gave him a bland look. "For whom?"

He set the tray down on the table and reached for Nikayla. "For both of us. Try not to think about the diaper I just changed or you won't be able to eat."

I loved him so much. I looked at our daughter and realized that love could expand in your heart to infinite proportions.

We had to fight for our family, the island, and the people holding out in the U.S. to rebuild the country that we wanted to return to.

We would win this war.

CHAPTER THIRTY-ONE

Marinah

THERE WAS NO TIME to relax after Nikayla's birth. I stayed in full work mode with the added responsibility of a newborn. I didn't resent my child; I resented everything that took me away from her. I wanted cuddle time and to learn her likes and dislikes. A wet or dirty diaper or a hungry belly were easy to decipher, but there was so much more. She liked bright colors. I learned this when one of the island women came in to change the bedding. She was dressed in a brightly colored dress, and Nikayla's eyes followed her.

Later that day, the woman, Carla, brought a mobile she made from an old dress similar to the one she wore. She had cut and stuffed the fabric in different shapes, hung them with string, and attached them to a dowel. We'd failed to use the crib, but after the new toy was set up with Carla's help, Nikayla lay in it and eventually fell asleep.

Endura and Amissa became my personal shadows. I was accustomed to having security when I left the citadel, but not while inside.

"There must be something else you could be doing other than following me around," I finally snapped.

Endura gave a soft smile. "We're here to assist with the baby. You should allow us to take her back to our rooms and care for her while you handle the things that are pressing on you."

"What's pressing on me is the fact you say I will leave Nikayla shortly. I want to spend as much time with her as possible, even if it means toting her around with me."

"I understand," Endura said.

I wanted to gripe at her some more, but that damn mellow essence kicked my butt, and my irked mood disappeared. I couldn't even complain because when Nikayla was content, she gave off the same vibes. I calmed when she did. Ms. Beast felt the same. Nova hadn't shown herself since the baby was born three days before.

On day four, Amissa approached me with Endura behind her. She had a piece of fabric in her hands.

"This is for you?"

I had no idea what it was.

"Allow Endura to hold the baby, and I will show you how it works." I turned Nikayla over, and Amissa wrapped the cloth around me. I finally understood.

It was a garment to hold the baby, and it allowed me to keep my hands free. With a few adjustments, Nikayla hung contentedly against my chest while she slept.

"Thank you," I said. "Did you make it?"

"It belonged to one of our babies who outgrew it. We want to help, not hinder you. If that's more time with the baby, we will see you get it."

"Again, thank you," I said.

"Is there anything else we could help with?"

"If you could figure out how to acquire tofu, I most likely wouldn't snap at everyone so much." I smiled good-humoredly. I was embarrassed over how I'd treated these women the day before.

Amissa gave me a huge grin. "We have a large supply of soybeans with us. It's one of our main farming crops, and one that's helped us survive. I will give some to the kitchen staff and help prepare it so they know how."

I stared in open-mouth shock. "You brought soybeans?" I couldn't have heard her right.

"Yes, we are vegetarian and eat quite a bit of it. Your island has a wide variety of beans, which is also good for us, but we brought our own food so we would not be a burden."

"You aren't," I assured both women. "We will gladly share what we have, especially in exchange for the soy."

"Anything we can do to help," Endura said.

"I'm having trouble with the timeline you gave me," I said hesitantly. "I've reached out to the homesteads looking for information about the Federation's movements. They haven't seen anything. I feel like the situation is up in the air, and it makes me apprehensive. I took that out on you yesterday. Forgive me, please."

"We are facing our own troubles," Endura replied. "The Shadow Warriors make us feel unstable. We didn't expect it to be this hard."

"Are they bothering you?" I asked. Maybe I needed to knock a few heads.

"They stare when they think we are not watching, but one or more of the women is always watching. We had hoped to help the island people, but you have everything organized, and we find ourselves at loose ends."

"Do you do any type of self-defense training?"

"We do. Hapkido and Aikido are our main focus, but we also practice Tai Chi for relaxation. We're unsure where to practice."

"We have a training field that would do nicely. Would you consider working with the Shadow Warriors?" I held a hand up at the expression that crossed her face. "They are beyond curious. If I allowed them to work with you, they would get over their infatuation quickly. You would be training them. I've already incorporated meditation into their daily routine. Your brand of self-defense training would be good for them."

Amissa placed her hand on Endura's arm. "It would be a good thing," she said. "We need to heal the past. Would one-hour a day work?"

"That would be perfect."

"I will hold a meeting with my personal guard. These are the men who lead the Warriors in battle. If you're okay with starting tomorrow morning, I will see it done."

"Tomorrow will work. We will head to our rooms, pick up soybeans, and take them to the kitchen."

Nikayla started fussing. It's time for her to eat and take a nap. I need one too. If you run into a problem, send someone for me."

"Thank you," they said before leaving me.

My Warrior body healed at a miraculous rate, but I was tired from the all-night feedings. I saw it with King too. We worked as a team, which meant we were both cranky.

I lay with Nikayla and thought about the Shadow Warriors. They were fascinated by the women. I had given the order that they would not approach or speak to them unless the women opened the communication. I hadn't mentioned staring at them, but from the way it sounded, the women stared too.

I finally fell asleep and woke about two hours later. I changed and fed Nikayla and decided to visit the quarters I'd given to the women.

They had an entire wing. I looked around at what they had done. It was set up with their personal belongings, which included colorful silks and wall hangings that fit in with the Cuban accents.

They passed the baby around and admired her while I looked on nervously. They were strangers, and it was hard for me. But Ms. Beast didn't grumble. I was glad I went to see them.

I ran into Caleb after I left the women. "Have the guard meet me in the argument room in one hour."

He nodded, did an about-face, and returned in the direction he came from. I took a breath, turned around, and went back to the women's quarters. They agreed to watch Nikayla during the meeting.

"I will play with her," Sweeting said. "She will be happy."

That more than anything soothed my heart.

An hour later, the men stared at me expectantly.

"You will begin training with the Shadow Women tomorrow morning. They will teach you Hapkido, Aikido, and Tai Chi for one hour each day. You will use it as your warm-up." I stopped Beck's next words with a flash of my eyes. "This is an order. The men are staring at the women, and the women at the men. You do not fear them, but they fear you. You will follow their dictates until the training is finished. It replaces the morning meditation."

I looked around the room. "Is this understood?"

They weren't happy, but they didn't argue.

King gave a nod.

CHAPTER THIRTY-TWO

Marinah

ON THE DAY NIKAYLA turned two weeks old, I was dead to the world and had no idea what time it was when Beck pounded on our door. King answered.

"Landan is on the radio. He needs to speak with Marinah immediately," Beck all but yelled into the room so I would hear.

I quickly pulled on clothes. Beck had disturbed Nikayla, and she began to fuss.

"I'll change Nikayla and bring her to you; go," King said.

I charged after Beck.

"What did Landan say?" I asked.

"They found the Federation's stronghold."

I tore into our communications room and hit the talk button on the radio. "It's Marinah."

"This is Landan. My scouts located the main Federation camp on the Louisiana coast. They estimate two thousand troops. Most are seasoned soldiers with only a few red stripes. There are five ships in the gulf, and those ships are preparing to leave. The troop numbers do not include men aboard the vessels. There is another main camp of soldiers about a hundred miles from us, deep in the city. The majority are red stripes, but they also have hellhounds in semi-trucks. They've been moving in soldiers slowly. I didn't get the information until yesterday evening. I was radioing you this morning to tell you about those soldiers, but my other scouts just returned with the new information."

"What time is it now?" I asked.

"3 a.m."

I was awake, but my lack of sleep made me feel sluggish. "Where is the main camp staging?"

"The area was difficult to get to, and my men found it purely by accident. It's surrounded by swamps about fifty miles from New Orleans."

New Orleans was demolished by bomb strikes after the first electromagnetic pulses hit. Survivors either joined the Federation or headed west to outpost territories.

"Why do they think it's a main camp?" I asked.

"President Barnes was identified. One of my scouts escaped as a red stripe years ago, and he is very familiar with Barnes."

My heart began beating double time. "Did he see Mrs. Barnes?"

"Was Mrs. Barnes identified?" Landan asked someone in the room with him. His voice was slightly muffled, so he must have turned away from the microphone.

"I didn't see her," came a reply.

"Would you know her if you did see her?"

"Yes."

"Marinah, did you catch that?"

"Yes," I said. "Any sign of a submarine?"

"No, and I asked specifically about it."

"What about hellhounds?"

"There are semi-trucks in both camps. If they have hellhounds in them, and if they're filled to capacity, you're looking at a thousand hounds at the main camp. The camp in our territory holds another two thousand troops. The trucks are also being used defensively and surround the camps. At the Louisiana camp, the scouts watched them load large amounts of supplies on two ships, with three others waiting in the harbor. They think those were already loaded. One ship can carry a thousand men."

I took a moment to absorb what he was saying.

"Do you want to send your children to the island along with non-combatants?"

"My best guess is they're planning to attack on two fronts: your island by sea and possibly air, and us by land and air. They have over twenty airplanes. It's too late to send our children to you. It took the Louisiana scouts thirty-six hours to get here, and the attacks could come at any time."

"I'll meet with my guard and get back to you within the hour," I said.

"That works. We've been preparing for this, and all outposts within two hundred miles are with us for the battle. Out," said Landan.

The radio went silent.

"Gather the guard," I told Beck.

We turned toward the door due to a screaming child in the hall.

"My signal to haul ass," Beck said. "I have my own screaming child to deal with."

King entered as Beck ran out. King looked at the two radio operators and nodded at the door. They made a quick exit, and he handed Nikayla to me. I pulled my shirt up and gave her what she needed while I explained the conversation with Landan.

"Two fronts for the attack makes sense," King said after the baby settled.

I was staring down at her and felt tears welling in my eyes. How the fuck could I leave her behind, especially with a pending attack? King understood.

"We can stay here and fight them in our territory," he said.

I shook my head. "We must take out Barnes. If the ships and planes make it here, President Barnes won't be with them. He's a coward. We need to wipe out his land troops."

"Why do you think they're staging so many troops on land away from Landan's territory?" King asked.

I didn't even need to think about it. "They're preparing to take over the island after we're defeated. The president and his wife will come her for the celebration after the danger has passed."

"They won't win the island."

I smiled, and anyone else would have run. "No, they won't, but they don't know that."

"What are you thinking?"

I looked into the eyes of the man I loved. "We will divide the Shadow Warriors into three units. It means we are outnumbered on all fronts by two to one. The Shadow Warriors are the only hope and we knew it would come to this."

"Agreed. Do you think Nikayla's had enough to settle down so we can meet with the guard?"

"It's possible."

"I need your help getting this thing situated on me." He lifted the baby carrier that I'd noticed when he walked in.

"On you?"

"You wave your hands when you're agitated, and I think it will be safer for her if she's attached to me." He smiled in a way that let me know he was joking even though he had a point. Two minutes later, she fell asleep again. I stepped to the door and looked outside. The radio operators stood at attention. "Here," I said, and placed Nikayla in the closest man's arms so I could help King.

It took about five minutes to get him situated, and then we added Nikayla. She didn't stir. King's huge muscles made the straps appear small. I couldn't help but grin at how adorable they looked. I received a stern expression from King but didn't have time to tease him. We had to get to the argument room.

CHAPTER THIRTY-THREE

King

MARINAH'S GUARD WAITED. SOMEONE had been smart enough to place a carafe of coffee in the center of the table. I made a cup for my mate and handed it to her. The baby had fussed throughout the night, and now that we were awake, Mikayla was sound asleep.

Beck stared at me, then covered his eyes for a moment. "If Missy sees you in that thing, my life will be over."

I lifted a brow. "It's called bonding. You should try it."

Beck rolled his eyes.

"If the two of you are finished sizing up your manhood, we need to start the meeting," Marinah said.

"My manhood is not in question," Beck grumbled.

"I didn't say it was. You'll be carrying Barrett around as soon as Missy gets her hands on one of these contraptions. You and King will set a new fashion trend."

Beck shut up.

"We know where Barnes is," Marinah said. She then explained everything Landan relayed to her.

"Are you basing your decision on the Shadow Women's witch doctor?" Beck asked.

Marinah glared, and he lowered his eyes. "Everything they've said is happening. I was skeptical, but that's rapidly changing. Regardless if Amissa is right or wrong, it doesn't change the intel from Landan, so shut the hell up or help."

Beck's good mood and unwillingness to argue hadn't lasted long. He was back to his old self where he had to argue over everything simply because he could.

Marinah looked around the room. "We're here to decide on a course of action. We'll make more concrete battle plans in our next meeting an hour from now. Landan needs to know I'm sending one-third of our troops in his direction."

Beck started to say something, and Marinah's hand came up.

"One-third to him, one-third stays on the island, and the rest are with me and King." She explained her reasoning, and I saw subtle agreement around the room.

"Beck, would you like to share your thoughts?" she asked with enough syrup in her voice to make him hesitate.

"Should you or King stay here on the island?" he finally asked, which surprised me.

"The Shadow Women are here to protect our children," Marinah said. "King won't go without me, nor I without him." She didn't look at me. "We'll discuss our strategy once I've spoken to Landan. I'm heading back to the control room to radio him. Discuss your views with King while I'm gone."

"You said, 'our children'?" Beck questioned.

"Yes. Their job is to assure our children survive. Our children: human, Shadow, and Shadow Warrior, are the future. We need to plan our strategy and know while we fight, the children are in capable hands."

"How are their hands capable if they don't fight?" He wouldn't let it go.

"You have been working with the women. Their tactics are defensive. Do you feel they lack the ability to defend the children?" Marinah demanded.

"I haven't had enough time to make that decision."

"Good," said Marinah so sweetly, I knew Beck was in trouble. "I've made the decision for you."

She stood, walked around, and kissed Nikayla's head, before walking out.

"Is there anyone else you need to piss off?" Nokita asked Beck.

K-5 spiked.

"That's enough," I told them. "We've been given orders, and we have a lot to do." I cupped the back of Nikayla's head. "Having children gives us more to fight for, and it puts us more on edge. That includes Marinah. It's time to end the Federation's reign of terror. Who is with me?"

Caleb's fist hit the table. "I'm for ending the Federation."

More fists landed on the table until it was only Beck left.

"I'm angry enough that if I hit the damn thing, it will break," he said and followed it up with a grin. "We have a war to win."

CHAPTER THIRTY-FOUR

Marinah

"How will you survive if you send that number of troops?" Landan asked, his voice dropping.

The governor didn't know how many Shadow Warriors we had, and any guess he made was likely far lower than actuality. We were sending a thousand Shadow Warriors his way. I didn't tell him a third. I trusted Landan, but this kind of information had to be kept hidden. It was one of the reasons the Federation sent me to the island to begin with. I was a glorified spy, along with being a sacrificial lamb. They wanted to know the number of Shadow Warriors on the island, their weapons, and anything else that would help destroy them. Those days were long over, and I was their enemy now, exactly like I wanted it.

"We are fighting for our lives, and we will win this," I told him. "The Warriors will begin flying out this afternoon and arrive at your end tonight. We are sending tents and supplies with them."

"Okay, we'll be ready."

"Weapons and ammunition too. We have a large stockpile."

Ten seconds of silence met this declaration.

"Thank you, Marinah. Good luck on your end," he finally said.

I sat for several minutes after radio silence filled the small room. The island and Landan's outposts would be the safest. The Warriors with me would be in the most danger. Deciding who would go to Louisiana would be hard. There was no way we would get through this without casualties.

My thoughts turned to Nikayla. I couldn't imagine not seeing her grow up, but with or without me, I wanted her to live under the banner of peace. I felt as if my entire life had been heading to this one point in time.

We had to win. There was too much at stake. If President Barnes escaped, we were going after him this time. We would track him until he was eliminated. I stood and headed back to the argument room. Only Axel sat inside.

"King sent everyone for food, and they will be back in thirty minutes. He has breakfast waiting in your room," he said.

"Why aren't you eating?" I asked.

"I will, but I needed to say something before the next meeting." He stood up and faced me, shoulders squared. "I'm going with you. Garret and Kenneth will remain on the island." He shook his head before I argued. "You need me. And you owe this to me. I will not stay behind when you are taking the biggest risk. If anyone can keep you alive other than King and your Nova, it's me."

I walked over and hugged him. He'd been on my side since the day I arrived on the island. At times, he was my only friend. Boot finally came around, but in the beginning, it was Axel. After a tight squeeze, I pulled away.

"You're right. We need you. Thank you."

"I'll bitch and grumble about every scrape and bruise. Thank me after we kick the Federation's ass."

"That's a deal."

I found King in our room with a fussy baby.

"She's hungry, and I seriously doubt one of my pecs will make her happy."

"It was worth a try." I gave him a comical look of defeat. "The food smells delicious."

King's nose wrinkled. "There is something called tofu on your plate," he grumbled.

"That's why it smells so good. I've been requesting tofu, and it turns out the Shadow Women brought it with them."

"You're actually craving that sh, I mean, um, food?"

I huffed out a laugh. "Amissa believes the baby craves it, and I'm tuned into her wants and needs. I can't argue because the thought of meat turns my stomach."

"I hope you don't mind, but I'll stick to bacon." He lifted a piece and placed it in his mouth.

It did absolutely nothing for me. Gone were the days I could eat a pound of the stuff in one sitting.

"How did Landan take the news?" King asked after we finished the first round of food.

"Surprised we're sending so many Shadow Warriors. Thrilled about the guns and ammo."

King contemplated my answer. "He needs us. I hope they don't stab us in the back afterward."

I placed my hand over his. "They will not do what the Federation did to you. It's different now. They know who the enemy is."

His gaze remained on mine. "What would you do if they did turn on us?"

"End them. Nikayla will grow up in peace. I will eliminate each and every threat, no matter where it comes from."

He smiled, a wicked, satisfied grin. "I will always have your back."

"I know."

He leaned over and kissed me softly on the lips.

"It's time to go to the meeting," I said with a catch in my voice.

"Finish your breakfast. They will wait."

"I'll drop Nikayla off with Amissa and Endura."

"I don't mind carrying her," King said. There was a softness in his eyes when he said it. Soft and King had never gone hand in hand. Our child tempted me with tofu and him with gentleness.

"I'm worried you will need to behead Beck. I'll take Nikayla to the women."

We finished our meal.

"We will leave at daybreak," I told the Shadow Women. "You will be escorted to the southern part of the island and wait there in the tunnels. It's possible fighting will reach you."

Amissa grabbed Endura's fingers and squeezed them. "We are ready. Fighting is not something we are looking forward to, but we will protect the children."

"I know," I told her. "Nikayla is in good hands."

I left them with my child and went to the argument room where the others waited.

"We will start this meeting with meditation. We need clear minds to make decisions."

No one argued, and it was hard not to grin when I remembered how this went down in the beginning.

Five minutes of silence later, I opened my eyes. Beck was staring at me; the rest, including King, had their eyes closed. I winked at Beck, and he gave an almost imperceptible grumble.

The presence of K-5 was low. It would change as soon as Beck decided he didn't like something, but for a few minutes, we were calm.

"I want the submarine here guarding the island," I told Nokita.

"Good call," he said. If he had doubts, he didn't show it.

"I won't be on it," he said. "My fighting skills are useless if I command the craft. Alfred will be in charge of sixty men. He knows the submarine like I do."

I wasn't sure why that relieved my mind, but it did. Nokita was too valuable as a fighter to have him on the sub.

"Do the men understand the danger of their job?"

"Yes."

I inhaled slowly. The men onboard were human. It shouldn't matter to me, but I saw Shadow Warriors as the protectors. I was wrong though. All of us were fighting for our lives and for peace. People would die, and I couldn't dwell on it.

"After this meeting, we will meet with Alfred and anyone else you think needs to be informed of our plans," I told him. "It's vital that the sub takes out a ship or two before those ships reach the island."

I looked around the table and stopped at Rodrigo. "Have you made your decision?"

He nodded solemnly. "I will stay here and defend my people. My men were given the choice, and we are staying behind."

I looked at my guard again. I cared about them. They cared about me.

"We have family and friends on this island. It's our home, and the only way we can defend it is to wipe out the Federation. The Warriors going to Landan's territory will leave late this afternoon. The rest of us have tonight to say our goodbyes. We leave at dawn. Our destination is a small landing field, fifty miles from the Louisiana coast. Landan has people waiting for us. Axel and King are coming with my team." I looked at Beck. "Is Missy planning to fight?"

His neutral expression turned to exasperation. "She's exhausted from the birth but I can't stop her. Half her archers will stay under Rodrigo's command here at the citadel, and the rest will go with her once we decide where she can me most strategic. They've been training for close-quarter combat."

"And you?" I asked. From the look on his face, I knew he didn't like what he had to say next.

"Missy wants me with Landan to protect her friends." He shook his head in resignation. "Can you spare me?"

Beck guarded King's back and it had been that way since Caleb stepped down as King's second. When I took command, it didn't change. King had my back, and Beck had his. This couldn't be easy for the grumpy Shadow Warrior.

"Landan needs you, and I feel better knowing you're with him. Inform your men that they leave this evening. Nokita?"

"I want to go with you and King." His eyes flashed with anger. "I want revenge for Maylin."

"How does Maylin feel?"

"That she needs to be kept under guard and no one can risk that she will die and turn into a monster. The Shadow Women have agreed to watch our children." He grit his teeth and then forced himself to relax. "They also agreed to do what needs to be done if the worst happens. I don't think I could. I am more useful to you."

"Then you're with us." Nokita and his family didn't deserve this. He would get his revenge.

I turned my attention back to Rodrigo. "You will command five hundred Shadow Warriors here at the citadel. You are their leader. Trevor will be your second, if you approve."

"He is out for blood. I need him."

I looked at Caleb, Eagle, and then Alden. "What is your decision?"

"With you," said Alden.

"The island with Rodrigo," Caleb tossed out.

"Eagle?" I asked when he didn't immediately answer.

"With you. Elright will keep half the snipers and the rest will come with us."

These men knew their job. "It's settled. Meet with your commanders and give them their orders."

Chapter Thirty-Five

King

THOUGH IT SEEMED LIKE a long day, it also flew by. Marinah and I ate a quiet dinner while Nikayla slept in her crib.

"A penny for your thoughts," I said.

She smiled. "My thoughts are worth at least a nickel."

"My father said it to me when I was quiet," I told her. "It's funny that I almost gave him back the same joke once."

"You don't often speak of your father," I said.

"Greystone took his place after I discovered what I was. Before that, the sun rose and set on him. My worship turned to almost hatred after I knew what

Shadow Warrior meant. I blamed him for my mother leaving too."

"Did you forgive him before his death?"

"Yes, and I told him so the night before he left to fight hellhounds." I let out a short chuckle. "I was a true pain in the ass as a teenager. Not even Ruth holds a candle to the shit I pulled."

"He would be proud of you," I said.

"Maybe. He was a man of peace. He blamed the first Shadow Warriors for the loss of the women. He felt that peace was the only way they would return."

"Did he love your mother?"

"Yes. It was hard on him when she left us. He doubled down on his feeling that peace was the answer."

"How do you feel about it now?"

I looked into her eyes, seeing her sincerity and curiosity. "I agree with my father and with Greystone. A war was coming, and we had to understand our history. But my father was right too. Living in peace is the only answer."

Marinah stood and walked over to me. I put my arms out and pulled her onto my lap. She was the part of me that craved the end of a violent reign. I didn't want her or Nikayla in danger. When it came to fighting, her Nova form was stronger than my Beast form, and still I worried.

She cupped my face. "We will destroy the Federation and kill Barnes and Knet."

"Do you think Knet will be on the ships coming to the island?"

She inhaled. "I hope not, but if he is, someone else will end his miserable existence."

"I love you," I said.

She pressed her lips to mine. "I love you," she whispered after pulling away slightly. "I'm still bleeding, and Axel says no sex until it stops. More than anything, I want to make love with you."

I gave her a leering smile. "We can make out and fool around without that getting in the way, if you're up to it."

"The biggest question here is, are you up to it?" She wiggled her eyebrows.

"Yes to making out and fooling around. I can wait for the rest."

I saw her expression change, and I wouldn't let her say it. "We will defeat the Federation. You and I will raise our daughter and find a place to call home."

We hadn't been to our home on the southern part of the island in months. We managed one escape for three days to our small private island two months ago. I was willing to leave both behind to find somewhere permanent that we never had to leave. To do that, President Barnes had to die, and the Federation had to end its reign of terror.

I stood with Marinah in my arms and carried her to bed. I lowered her, then lifted her shirt above her head. Nikayla began to fuss, and we both groaned.

"I'll grab a diaper and bring her to you."

"I love you," she said again.

"Hold that thought."

Our make out session was short but it was all Marinah could handle. She needed sleep.

Marinah left a little before midnight to see the first round of planes off. I stayed with Nikayla. Watching her sleep had become special. We had created a miracle. I'm sure all parents thought this, but Nikayla was the first female Shadow Warrior born to Shadow parents, and every tiny inch of her truly was a miracle.

I was as worried as Marinah about leaving her. I didn't have the same faith in the Shadow Women that Marinah did. I trusted her judgment, though. I lifted Nikayla to my shoulder and carried her to the chair. She didn't stir. I gently rocked my upper body and held her against me.

A tingling started where her head rested and traveled downward. A wave of peace came over me, utterly disarming.

Baby, Beast whispered inside me.

Marinah had tried to explain the sense of calm she felt around the Shadow Women. Now I understood. My daughter was giving it to me. I had no doubt she would grow up to be as kickass as her mother, but she would also grow up with the Shadow Women influence that had been missing for generations. She wouldn't always be searching for something she thought she would never find. Marinah and I would give her the world.

Marinah walked in an hour after she left. I could see her exhaustion.

"Lie down before you fall," I said.

I was on the bed with Nikayla on my chest. She slept peacefully, still emanating calm. Marinah settled beside us and curled into me, her hand on the baby's back.

"They're on their way. Missy didn't cry until Beck left." Marinah looked into my eyes. "How do we leave our child?"

I had no idea, but Marinah didn't need to know that. "We leave her so she has a better world to grow up in. We'll be gone for a week at most. Hopefully only a few days. I'm sick of fucking around."

"I agree," she said. "President Barnes is as good as dead."

I smiled at her because this was the Marinah who would lead us into battle.

"Close your eyes and rest," I whispered. "Nikayla will wake up in another hour or two for a feeding."

Marinah's eyes drifted closed. Her hand remained on the baby's back. I brought my hand up and rested it on hers. I fell asleep holding them.

CHAPTER THIRTY-SIX

Marinah

LANDAN CONTACTED US BEFORE the sun came up. He'd sent a scout back with a radio for his men watching the Federation in Louisiana and one for those at the airport waiting on us. Radio frequencies attracted hellhounds, and they were a bigger problem when out in the open. We used them only for urgent communications, and this was urgent. Landan received word that the ships had left the harbor. The Federation's fleet was on its way to the island.

An hour later, Endura and Amissa stood at the entrance to the citadel, waiting patiently for me to hand Nikayla over. My arms were locked, and I would swear they actually ached. King had his hand on my back, his teeth clenched.

"She will survive," said Amissa. "This I promise you."

She didn't say that King and I would survive. This could be the last time I held my child. Nikayla's fingers closed around mine. She'd been up for several hours, which was unusual. Seeing her bright eyes with no fear and only trust almost undid me.

Maylin and Missy had already left for the southern part of the island. Ruth, Togg, and their small group of young fighters and families were with them, along with a large Shadow Warrior escort. The citadel's staff were given the choice to go. Most stayed and went down into the closest tunnels.

I hadn't seen Maylin since we discovered that she was injected with the damned serum that would change her into a hellhound when she died. I spoke to her briefly before they left.

"Ruth has sworn to take my head or have one of the Warriors do it if I die," she said.

Ruth was a child. This was something Maylin should not have asked, and she'd counted on Ruth's hatred of hellhounds to be greater than her feelings for Maylin. Che worshipped Ruth. The entire scenario was simply wrong.

"I had to." Her eyes held more emotion than I'd ever seen from her. "If I'm with Che and the babies, they must be safe from me. Ruth understands. She will see it done when some might hesitate."

I didn't agree, but what could I say?

I had to leave my child. I *would* kill Maylin if she were a threat. This was such a fucked-up world.

I couldn't seem to walk away. No one pressured me. They were holding the planes for us. I inhaled deeply, dipped my head and kissed Nikayla on the forehead, and turned her toward King. He gave her a kiss on the same spot mine landed. I closed my eyes and placed my arms out to Amissa.

When my arms were empty, King gathered me close. I opened my eyes and took the first step towards the future. I didn't look back until right before the car turned the corner. Amissa held Nikayla so her tiny head was upright and pointed in our direction. Shadow Warriors stood with the Shadow Women, waiting to escort them to the southern tunnels. Our child would be safe.

Fuck, this was nearly impossible.

King took my hand. I didn't cry. This wasn't the time.

When we arrived at the airport, I stepped into the muggy heat.

Desmond walked up to me. I had no idea how he'd gotten to the airport. "I want to go with you," he said.

Fury burned in his eyes. He was fifteen, and I didn't want to be responsible for him.

"Why?" I asked.

"I'm good at what I do. I kept the children alive, and I can help you. The enemy won't see me, and if they do, they won't suspect me."

He was a talented fighter, and there were other humans coming with us.

"You're on our plane. Does your sister know?"

"Yes, she didn't even beg me to stay." He didn't seem happy about that, and I almost smiled.

We boarded the plane, and the eyes of the men in the rows of seats held the same expression that was most likely on my face. They had left their loved ones behind, too. Some of us would not return. I was their leader, and I had to stay strong.

The plane's engines roared to life. We were on one of five passenger planes. They had been modified to carry and release a limited number of bombs. We had one official bomber. Nokita piloted it. The thing was rickety, but he'd worked on it for over a year now and trusted that it would do the job. We had to take out Federation ships. The submarine had left the evening before and was on course to intercept the ships, too.

The flight was smooth for the first two hours. Then a tense silence took over as we waited for the first sight of the enemy.

"Ahead," crackled over the speaker.

I stood with King, and we walked to the flight deck to see out the front windows.

The vast, open ocean stretched before us. The heavy, lumbering bomber, its belly loaded with missiles, flew to our right.

There was nothing King or I could do at this point. The Warriors' lives depended on our pilots' abilities to steer the planes clear of bullets from the Federation's ships, and we knew the large lumbering jets couldn't avoid them all.

"Target acquired!" came the crackle over the comms from the passenger plane on our left. "Three o'clock, five ships in formation!"

Nokita's voice came over the radio next. "Alpha 1, 2, and 3 disengage. We have this."

Our pilot steered the nose of the plane upward into the clouds. Alpha 4 and 5 would support Nokita in the attack.

We could not afford to lose the majority of our men, and splitting our forces was paramount. King and I returned to our seats. The men stared out the windows or looked straight ahead. No one spoke.

Behind us, the first explosion went off, rattling our plane. King lifted my hand and kissed the backs of my fingers. I clenched his hand tightly.

Another explosion, this one fainter.

The plane leveled out, and we resumed the flight to the Louisiana airstrip. King kept hold of my hand.

An hour later, we reached land and made a wide circle around the Federation camp so they wouldn't see us. At least if we were lucky.

Nokita

The bomber gave a slow, steady gurgle that was the best I could get out of the old engine. The enemy was below, and I banked sharply, lining up for the first run. Alarms would be blaring aboard the Federation ships, and men would be scrambling to their posts. I watched the lead ship's turrets swiveled in our direction. Bullets pummeled the sky.

"Now," I yelled.

A missile dropped and plummeted toward the lead vessel. It was a miss. Our six-man crew had no practice. This was a learn-on-the-fly scenario.

I made a sharp turn and went back in.

"Ready!" yelled one of my men. Below us, the bomber's internal systems hummed, and the bomb bay doors cycled shut. We were ready for another pass. I wouldn't keep the Federation waiting. My eyes locked onto the lead ship again.

I pushed the throttle forward, feeling the surge of power as the old engines strained. We were coming in low. Tracer rounds erupted from the ship's weapons system. They peppered our wings. I focused on the target.

"Damage?" I yelled out.

"We're good, Captain! Just cosmetic!" one of the men yelled back; his voice was a little too cheerful.

"Bombs away!" I shouted.

He hit the release. Another missile detached, tumbling toward the ship below.

A few seconds later, a blinding flash, followed by a loud boom, ripped through the air. A geyser of water and shrapnel flew skyward. The lead ship shuddered as several smaller explosions in the same vicinity rocked it.

"Fuck yes," I yelled, realizing we hit stored fuel.

A cheer went up from my men.

"Can anyone see a sign of our sub?" I yelled over the roar of the engine.

"Negative."

That wasn't a bad thing. It would stay deep. If the sub hadn't made it yet, their assault would happen without us. It was the old sub's maiden voyage, too. So damned many things could go wrong.

Alpha 5, acting as a diversion, swooped low, drawing heavy fire. It was the newest plane we had, which didn't say much. Not one of our air fleet was less than fifty years old.

Two seconds later, we took a volley from the second ship, and a sickening thud reverberated through the cockpit. The #3 engine sputtered, and a plume of black smoke erupted behind us. The plane bucked violently and I struggled to compensate. I fought the control column, wrestling the old bird back into line, my knuckles white on the yoke. I received a critical engine warning. This was no longer cosmetic.

If we pulled away now, we could possibly make it to the landing strip where Marinah waited. I peered at the crew. They were facing me and ready to die for our cause. I turned forward.

"Pull back," I yelled at the two other planes through the radio. "We're heading for land."

An explosion below us had everyone gazing downward. The second ship shuddered and smoked.

"Who made that hit?" I yelled.

Alpha 4 and then Alpha 5 replied, "Negative."

"It's got to be the sub," one of my men exclaimed.

Two ships down. The sub wouldn't communicate with us and give away their position, but they might be able to hear me. "We're heading back to land," I said. This let them know we were disengaging and heading to the landing strip.

A strange sensation traveled down my spine.

"Alpha 4, Alpha 5, take the lead."

I turned the bomber and circled back. I searched the water, having no idea what I was looking for. Another volley of bullets headed toward us. I banked to the right. I could see the third ship's crew clearly, and they weren't looking up. They were turned to the east.

An explosion from deep in the ocean rocked water and debris skyward.

The submarine. Our sub.

My heart dropped into my stomach.

All those brave men were gone.

And the Federation still had a submarine.

I banked the plane and turned toward the clear skies ahead. I was down an engine, and the men with me deserved to live. We had to make it to the landing strip.

CHAPTER THIRTY-SEVEN

Marinah

THE WARM AND HUMID air was very different from the island. It seemed heavier, and the sun a bit duller.

Landan's man, Stevens, met us after the semi-chilling landing on an airfield too short for the aircraft. "Almost" being the key word. Large airports in the U.S. were destroyed in the very beginning of the war. Some had been partially cleared, but they were heavily monitored by the Federation. Our pilots had practiced landing on smaller strips, but it didn't mean it was safe. I was glad to be on solid land.

Stevens was a burly, hairy mountain of a man who would be at home in one of the old prewar logging camps. His medium-toned skin was covered in a light coat of mud.

"Nice landings," he said after the third aircraft touched down.

We were standing under a makeshift lean-to that blocked a bit of sun. Shadow Warriors disembarked from the third plane and lined up in their units.

"My men and I want to get back to the outpost," Stevens said. "We will show you the camp and then leave, if you're good with that."

He was looking at me. I lifted my fist with my thumb pointing in Marinah's direction.

"She makes the decisions."

Marinah gave me a slight smile. I could have told him what she would say, but he hadn't looked at her once. It could be a "don't stare at a Shadow Warrior mate" thing that Landan taught him, or a "no way could a woman be in charge" thing.

"You're Marinah," Stevens said and placed his hand out. "I was expecting someone ten feet tall with hands the size of sledgehammers." He smiled at my mate, and Beast didn't so much as stir.

"Nice to meet you," she said. "You've given us a chance, and I can't thank you enough. I'll send five men with you and your team to check out the camp, if that works."

"Absolutely," he replied in his deep, rusty voice. "This is for you. It's a map of the area, along with other information that might be helpful." He handed over a brown leather satchel.

"I'll go with them to see the camp," I said.

"Choose the other four men," Marinah replied. "We'll wait for Nokita. Hopefully he's not too far behind."

What she didn't say was hopefully he made it, but we both knew the danger his mission posed.

Fifteen minutes later, I was tracking through swampland. The mosquitos that buzzed around us must have weighed a pound each. A slight exaggeration, but justifiable. We moved quietly, but couldn't stop the slaps on skin.

"We were being eaten alive like you are now," Stevens said. "One of our men covered himself in mud, and it worked."

I halted the team. "Mud up," I said and began to slather the brown gunk on my arms, neck, and face.

We set out again, and this time managed to move silently. I'd brought Desmond with me to see if he was as good as he said he was. I shouldn't have been surprised that the kid moved like a Shadow Warrior. Marinah called him a ninja and I had to agree.

It took two hours to reach the camp and find Stevens' man who waited for us. Lying on our bellies, in the same brown muck we smeared over ourselves, we got our first look.

The camp sprawled across a large area with the bay on one side and the swamp on another. Where we lay, the dense forest of cypress and tupelo trees rose from the murky water creating an eerie curtain that hid us.

There were a few small watercrafts in the bay but no ships. A sea of olive fatigues, most without the red shoulder stripes, walked on gravel that had been hastily laid over the damp ground. The air, thick with perpetual humidity, was choked with the acrid scent of diesel exhaust, soldier sweat, and something similar to dead fish.

Around the land perimeter were semi-trucks, parked bumper-to-bumper, their massive, dark forms creating a makeshift barricade. They also housed hellhounds, which didn't need air to breathe and could withstand the hotter-than-hell temps inside the trailers. The sheer scale of the camp was surprising.

We had half their number of Warriors if Nokita made it back with the other two planes.

Two-man armed patrols moved along the truck perimeter. The camp was a fortress carved out of the bay, but the swamp gave us an advantage.

"Desmond," I whispered. "See if you can locate the command center. Don't be seen."

He nodded and moved away. Sixty seconds later, he melted into the swamp. Twenty minutes he appeared again.

"Dead center," he whispered. "They have red stripe troops in tents surrounding two buildings with guards stationed at the doors." He grinned. "It was like a giant 'X' marking the spot."

I couldn't help grinning back.

We should attack at night and use the swamp to our advantage. The Federation had cleared the land and brought their fighting tactics with them. We had to strike quick, cause havoc, then move out and strike again at another entry point. I would discuss it with Marinah.

We watched for another thirty minutes, then headed back. We needed Nokita and the other two planes waiting at the landing strip.

CHAPTER THIRTY-EIGHT

Marinah

KING HAD BEEN GONE for an hour when the low rumble of engines sounded in the distance. I raised my arm and saw the bomber, followed by our other two planes. I was able to breathe again.

The old bomber limped toward the short runway. Bullet holes peppered its wings, some just pinpricks, others ragged tears in the metal skin. Along the edge of one wing, a larger, jagged rent marked where a direct hit had torn through.

One engine hung like a broken limb. A faint, acrid smell of burnt oil filled the air. The remaining engine on the other wing screamed in protest, its vibrations rattling the entire airframe. I couldn't believe it was still flying.

The plane swept in. The one engine roared, then whined as Nokita cut the power. The landing gear didn't deploy.

Thump! The undercarriage hit the dirt, hard. The plane bounced violently, threatening to veer off course. The dead engine on the port side dragged and tried to pull them off the runway. Sparks flew in all directions.

The groan of stressed metal filled my ears. The bomber shuddered, followed by the dip of its nose. With a final, protesting shudder, the plane came to a halt, its nose just inches from the edge of the swamp, its good wing drooping slightly. Shadow Warriors ran to the plane and began pushing it off the runway so the other two could land.

Nokita jumped from the back hatch.

He'd scared the shit out of me.

"Two ships are out of commission. I took down one, and the sub took down the other."

Something in his eyes gave me a clue. I waited.

He turned and looked at the next plane landing. When he looked back at me, I saw anger and devastation.

"Our submarine didn't make it. An enemy ship took it out."

Alfred. A kind man who worked with Rodrigo and Nokita. All those men gone.

I hugged Nokita to me. He patted my back uncomfortably. He'd worked on that sub for so long, and I knew its loss went deep, though not as deep as the loss of human life.

The rest of his crew walked up behind him. Nokita turned and shook their hands, thanking them.

"King is checking out the Federation camp. He should be back in another hour or two. We have tents set up for tonight, and we'll make our final plans after King returns."

Nokita began giving orders to his men. He placed all five pilots on standby. They would bomb the Federation camp when it was time.

Axel walked up to me. "I'm setting up one of the planes as a makeshift hospital for our wounded, if that's okay?"

"It works," I said. "We'll only use it as backup if we need the firepower."

He stared at me for a moment. "You need to bind your breasts," he finally said. "Cut back on your fluid intake, and only drink enough to stay hydrated. If we're back within a week, your milk will return."

As soon as the words left his mouth, I felt the ache in my breasts. Fuck. My heart ached with the need to hold and feed Nikayla.

I saw the look on Axel's face. "Do not hug me, or I will break down, which is very un-command-like. I've got this. Thank you for the advice."

I walked away because being near his sympathetic eyes was about to send me over the edge. I should have gone with King. Pitching tents hadn't kept me busy enough. I wiped sweat from my brow and waved away another swarm of mosquitos. The suckers were draining my blood dry, or at least that's what it felt like.

An hour later, King and his men returned, covered in mud. His white teeth showed when he grinned at me. "Mud's the answer," he said before he gave me a quick kiss. "It keeps the mosquitos away."

I turned and walked toward the swamp, which I'd been avoiding.

"Where are you going?" he asked.

"To take a mud bath, I hear they're in style."

"I'll help."

Between the two of us, we managed to smear the mud over me.

"Do I look as ridiculous as you?" I asked.

"Doubtful."

"You say the sweetest things." I inhaled deeply and gave him the news about our sub.

King looked off into the distance and didn't say anything. This hurt us. Yes, from a strategy standpoint, but more from the loss of life. I gave him a moment.

"Tell me about the camp," I finally said.

"We're taking off," Stevens called from about twenty feet away.

"Good luck and tell Landan to send news as soon as he can."

"Got it."

I turned back to King. "The camp?"

He hugged me first, and I accepted his embrace. We both needed the contact.

He explained what we were facing and laid out his plan.

"I like it," I said. "How many men do you think need to be on the strike teams?"

"Three teams, ten per team."

"Agreed," I said. "How was Desmond?"

"He got closer than I could have and located the heart of the camp. I was impressed. If we're lucky, Barnes was in one of the structures."

"I say we strike at 11 tonight and keep striking until morning. They'll send troops out as soon as the sun comes up, and that's when we send in the planes."

"Have you heard anything about the enemy sub?" King asked.

"No. I'm worried about it. It could be traveling with the Federation ships."

King understood. We'd left our baby on the island.

"What's the plan for right now?" King asked after a solemn moment.

"Besides the guards on the perimeter, the men need to rest and sleep if possible."

"Same goes for us." King looked at the sky. "I'll talk to the team leaders."

The team leaders were Nokita, Alden, and Eagle.

"They can point you to our tent. I'll see you there."

I lay on a cot inside our tent. It kept me out of the water, but was uncomfortable as hell. Melancholy set in. I stood up and slipped off my shirt. I tore a clean shirt into strips and used it to bind my aching breasts. Once I shifted to my Warrior form, my breasts wouldn't be a problem, but right now the heavy feeling added to my overall gloom.

I lay back on the cot and stared at the canvas ceiling about six feet above my head at the highest point. King walked in before I decided to attack the Federation right now in order to stay busy. Hunched over because his head hit the ceiling, he moved his cot next to mine and lay down. I was tall, and he was taller. His feet stuck out over a foot off the bottom while mine only hung about six inches over.

"You're not sleeping," he said.

"I was waiting for you."

"I miss her too." He took my hand and rubbed the backs of my fingers with his other one. "Close your eyes and think of mosquito swatters."

I chuckled softly. "You always know what to say to a girl."

"Good. I'll save the line and use it again."

I closed my eyes with no expectation that I would fall asleep. I was wrong.

The smell of food woke me. King wasn't in the tent. I would be pissed if he hadn't slept. I sat up and pressed on my bound breasts due to the ache. Missy and several other women on the island who had just had babies would keep Nikayla fed. I wanted to cry because it wasn't me holding and feeding her, but knew if I started, I might not stop.

I was stronger than this and would battle through. The first step was food. I left the tent and followed the smell.

Nokita approached. "No sign of Federation scouts or hellhounds in our area."

King walked up behind me. I felt him before he placed an arm around me. "Stevens said they haven't seen hellhounds in the area since arriving. If we're lucky, it will stay that way at least until the Federation releases theirs."

I nodded.

"How are you feeling?" he asked.

"Starving."

"I'll get you a plate. Find a seat."

The humans who came with us were assigned cooking and camp cleanup detail. They knew this before they made their decision to join our team. I was incredibly grateful and I hoped they didn't see battle. The loss of Alfred's men hung over me like a dark cloud.

The Warriors were mostly sitting on tree branches with their food in their laps while they ate. I had no problem doing the same, and neither did Nokita. King joined us a few minutes later.

"You're not eating?" I asked after he handed me a large serving on a paper plate.

"Had food an hour ago."

"Did you sleep?"

"For about two hours. I feel rested."

"Are you leading the strike teams?"

"Are you?"

I gave him my "don't fuck with me" expression.

"I want to, but I also realize it will weaken me for the bigger fight," he said.

"Same here."

"Then we wait together."

"Waiting sucks," I replied. Nokita started to say something, and I stopped him. "You're waiting too. Grab Eagle and bring him here. I haven't seen him since we landed."

"He's been doing sniper shit," Nokita said.

That made me smile. "I hope my plans for him won't ruin his sniper shit."

"My ears are burning," Eagle said and squatted beside us.

"You're leading a guerrilla style attack on the Federation camp. It will take two hours to get there, and the first strike will be at eleven tonight."

King outlined what he'd seen at the camp. "Take Desmond with you," he told Eagle.

"You don't need to twist my arm," Eagle replied. "I've seen him fight. He's also a fast runner, and I can use him for communication if something goes wrong." He thought about the task in front of him for a moment. "It's eight. I want to leave as soon as possible and scout the area first."

We went over the plan again, and then Eagle left to choose the strike teams. They left thirty minutes later. We would leave after midnight and find a halfway point to settle down in and wait. Between now and then, we would rest. Axel found us before we reached our tent.

"I have the med bay set up on Alpha 1."

"You'll be two hours from the action," I told him.

"No, I'll be with you. I have several men trained in emergency triage, and they will stay behind."

"Are you asking my permission, or making a statement?" I asked.

"Which one makes you feel better?" he replied.

"King, put him in his place, please."

King growled and stared. Axel smiled, then walked away.

"That was it, a growl?"

"He left us some alone time. That means it worked."

He was trying to keep my mind off Nikayla. "Let's lay on those damned uncomfortable military cots and pretend we're not going to be ripping out throats in a few hours."

"I thought you enjoyed ripping out throats," he teased.

"If I get a little more rest, I will." It was a lie. I wanted this battle over. I wanted King and I to survive.

I opened my eyes several hours later. King lay beside me, his eyes closed. "It's time to leave," I whispered. My internal clock knew we needed to hurry.

King's eyes popped open, and he sat up. I scrambled to my feet and tore off my shirt.

"What's this?" King asked and fingered the cloth wrapped tightly around my breasts.

"It keeps them from aching as much." I quickly removed them. "Help me with these straps." I picked up the leather chest contraption I usually wore.

King helped put it on, then loosened the individual straps. He placed his on quickly while I shifted into my Warrior form.

"Set?" I asked after he shifted.

"Let's do this," he said with his elongated jaws.

I grabbed the portable radio, adjusting for my claws, and carefully slid it into one of the pouches. So far, the Federation hadn't intercepted our communications. The radios we used had a high frequency range that allowed us to talk over long distances. The military radios the Federation used were on a lower frequency. Unless they had figured out our setup, especially if we kept communication to a minimum, we should be safe. Neither King nor I had seen a single hellhound since we landed. Chances were good the Federation had been collecting them for a while.

The strike team would head in our direction as soon as the Federation camp gained a semblance of order and went out to fight them. Eagle would run past us, and we, rested and ready for battle, would meet the enemy head on. The planes would drop their bombs over the Federation camp at the first hint of light and take out their supplies and hopefully some hellhounds. Eagle and his men would back us up if we ran into trouble. They would also transport the wounded to medical.

And all our plans could go to shit in an instant.

I focused on President Barnes. I wanted to see the instant he knew he would die.

Chapter Thirty-Nine

Rodrigo

WATER MINES WERE LOCATED in the citadel's bay. It kept the Federation ships from coming close to land. Chances were good they would send hellhounds into the water to attack as the first wave.

We could no longer count on the whistles. I wasn't sure why, but it didn't concern me. Keeping the people safe did.

Cabel stood at my side as I went over the tunnel charts. I glanced up at him and expected to see resentment that I was in charge. He had been second in command under King in the beginning. He married an island woman, and Beck took his place. I thought he would take it back eventually, but he didn't.

In the beginning, the Shadow Warriors gave me pause. I wasn't afraid because each day we'd battled hellhounds before they arrived meant someone died. I accepted my death as inevitable. My opinion of the Warriors changed when I saw them risk their lives for us and not just themselves. Humans simply stopped dying. The Shadow Warriors had the ability to change into big monsters, but more than that, they were also human with human wants and needs. There were grumbles from the island men when the Warriors began courting our women. I looked at it differently. The women had tucked away food storages and safe spaces, preparing for a major catastrophe for years. And they had done it with very few resources and no control. All they had were other women to keep their secrets and help them plan a safe haven. They saved so many of us when the hellhounds first attacked. Without them, many more men, women, and children would have died. If a woman wanted to marry a Shadow Warrior, they had the right.

The complaints stopped after the first year. Shadow Warriors became part of the island. We learned from them, and they learned from us. My hope was that when Marinah decided to leave, some Shadow Warriors would stay behind.

I realized Caleb was staring at me. I shrugged while searching for the English idiom equivalent of what just happened. "Lost in thought," I finally said, and hoped I'd gotten it right.

Caleb laughed and nodded in understanding.

It was now or never. "Would you rather be in charge?" I asked him.

Surprise showed on his face. "Marinah left you in charge for a reason," he said.

"What was that reason?"

I could see him searching for an answer, or maybe the right words, like me. "This island belongs to the people. The Shadow Warriors will leave and return to the U.S. after we win the war. You earned a guard position. Even my Mary thinks so. You make a good leader, and you know your people."

"When they leave, will you go with them?"

He shook his head. "My mate wishes to stay here, and I will stay with her. Our children will be raised here. My original country has a lot of changes to go through. The island is more settled, and I'm ready to sit in the sun and watch my children play on the beach. My family's home is here."

"You think you'll have time to sit on the beach?"

"I plan to make the time. I'd like to work on the island's security team, and hopefully that will work out. I also like agriculture, so my options are wide open." He winked at me.

I liked him. He would be good at both jobs, and I wanted him and Mary to stay.

"We need you," I said.

"Thank you. I'm glad you feel that way." He looked away for a moment before turning back. "I am here to assist you. The Warriors will follow you without hesitation, but use us wisely. We are mostly immune to hellhound bites and scratches. We are your best defense."

"I thank you. They will send the hounds in first."

"I agree. We should be on your front line."

I nodded and looked back down at the map and gestured away from the citadel tunnels. "They'll send in hounds at the shipyard, too. Those will head to the southern tunnels."

"I would wait until the main force of hellhounds is in position and blow the entire shipyard out of the water. Then I would place a large group of archers with incendiary arrows here," he pointed to the map at an area about a half-mile from the shipyard.

"Why not closer?" I asked.

Caleb smiled. "The hounds could be led by Knet. They will survive the main blast." He pointed again. "There are miles of road. They'll expect an assault closer to the first village. You want to keep them on their toes."

"I like the plan," I told him. "What if we add a few surprises?" I explained what I was thinking.

"That devious brain of yours will keep you out of trouble."

I laughed; thankful I had Cabel by my side.

We continued to discuss the preparations for another hour and then went our separate ways to put the plan into action. Word came that Nokita and his planes took out an enemy ship, and our sub took out another. I also learned that our sub was destroyed, and the Federation sub was unaccounted for. Many of my friends and family had died during the first hellhound war. But this loss felt different. I had trained those men, and part of me felt I should have died with them. The ships were on their way, and we had at most forty-eight hours to finish our preparations. There was no time to grieve. That would come later.

I stood behind a line of Warriors at the bay two days later. The gentle lapping of waves seemed to hold its breath as hellhounds emerged from the ocean. An explosion rent the air when one of the water mines detonated. It was followed by another. The hellhounds would clear the way for the soldiers, but we were ready.

Two enemy ships had appeared at Warrior Bay when the sun came up. That meant one was at the shipyard. From their hulls, small landing craft held Federation soldiers who waited for the hounds to do their damage. I lifted the binoculars, looking for the submarine, but didn't see it. I also searched for Knet.

I despised the man. He was truly the monster who betrayed the island.

The first hellhounds out of the water started their slow lope toward us.

"We've got this," Caleb said and smiled at me, his large teeth glinting in the early light.

"I will message Beck's mate and let her know the attack has started," I said. "My men are ready behind the wall."

The Warriors had shifted an hour before, and the first group met the hounds on the sand. I trusted them to stop as many as possible. We were prepared at the citadel and the surrounding buildings for those who made it through. Once the Warriors were behind our walled barriers, we would kill hounds and soldiers with our artillery. If any survived, we would kill them with our bare hands, if needed.

Thirty minutes later, the first Warriors ran inside the walls. The others followed in quick intervals. The giant gates closed behind them, and I gave the command, "Fire."

A volley of bullets released from both sides of a long, narrow alley that led to the gate we'd built after the last assault. Federation soldiers were caught in the crossfire and fell. When they went down, hellhounds that had survived pounced on them. Those men used whistles and I wondered if the frequency was somehow modified. If not, we'd been fooled.

The Warriors took up positions on the wall. A few minutes later, a large explosion rang out, and the gates were blown off their hinges. Warriors jumped into the fight, and the battle devolved into a brutal dance. The Warriors' speed and strength gave them an edge, but with the close-quarter combat, it was hard to tell who was winning.

"Engage," I yelled at my human army.

With swords and guns, men and women followed the Warriors into battle.

I struck down the first soldier who came within range. Around me, there was a whirlwind of fur, muscle, and razor-sharp teeth and claws. Most were Warriors. Loud roars echoed in my ears, along with gunshots and metal striking metal and flesh. Men went down around me. Some were ours. A hellhound charged me, and I jumped back to evade its claws. A Warrior landed on it and ripped the head from its body. It was Caleb, and he was grinning; blood dripping off his jaws.

As the sun broke over the horizon, the dead lay at our feet while Shadow Warriors and islanders looked around for more to kill.

Soldiers ran back toward the boats.

Caleb looked at me.

"They came here to kill, and they will not leave."

He grinned and took off, followed by Warriors and islanders.

With a final push, the Shadow Warriors and humans overwhelmed the last pockets of enemy soldiers. The beach was littered with fallen humans and hellhounds.

The ships opened fire, and our men fell back. We had one last surprise. Two airplanes came into view and dropped bombs from the sky. These were our reserve planes.

One ship took a direct hit to its bridge and exploded in a fiery inferno. The other took a less severe hit, but there was enough damage to cripple it. Flames tore out of both ships, and men jumped overboard.

That's when I saw the Federation submarine. Soldiers were diving into the water. Smoke poured from the hatch. Hellhounds burst out and tore into any man they could reach. If I had to guess, something went wrong and the Federation soldiers were paying the price.

I radioed the lead plane. "Target submarine."

The plane turned around and swooped in low and released a bomb. It was a direct hit.

"Para nuestros hombres valientes," I whispered.

The roar of battle slowly faded, replaced by the sounds of exhausted breathing and the gentle lapping of waves against the shore. Without compassion, not one enemy soldier made it out of the water. This was a battle to the death and we were finishing this war.

Chapter Forty

Missy

THE MASSIVE EXPLOSION AT the shipyard lit up the sky. A thrill went through my entire body. I was tired of war and living in fear. I wanted my family safe, and that included my bone-headed mate.

"Marriage is a human condition," he told me after I fell in love with him. It sounded stupid then, and now it was even more so. Yes, we were mates in his Shadow Warrior world, but my world counted, too. He would put a damn ring on my finger and marry me in front of our friends after this was over. If not, he would be looking for a new mate. Barrett deserved a real father, and so did Ruth, although she would say she was too old to care. Beck would do it for me and our children.

"Be ready," I called to the line of archers.

Shadow Warriors stood behind us. After we took out the first round of hellhounds, they would take over. Each archer had a ground quiver of incendiary arrows ready to fire. We kept our arms down to save our strength until it was time.

The road leading to our position had the ocean on one side and rock ledges on the other. The hounds could only come at us in tight groups. The arrows killed hellhounds if we struck the neck, and the explosion took their heads. We used actual hellhounds when we trained.

I'd tried to talk Ruth into archery. Even though she was a human child, and hellhound venom would kill her, she preferred close-up and personal attacks with a sword.

Ruth and her newly formed team of fighting youth were the last line of defense for the youngest children. If the hellhounds and soldiers got through us, the Shadow Warriors, and the Shadow Women, Ruth and her team would give their lives to protect the children. My daughter had sworn an unasked-for oath stating just that. I had no doubt she meant it. If we survived this attack and she lived to be an adult, she would be the youngest general in history, and no one would convince me otherwise. She'd told me that she and her fighters planned to hunt the hellhounds into oblivion when they were old enough.

Even though she caused continual havoc, I was damned proud of her. Barrett would be a handful, too. Children were the future.

We heard the horde before we saw them. Their lumbering gait defied the speed they were capable of. The morning was still cool but the breeze coming off the ocean carried the unmistakable odor of hellhounds.

"At ready," I said.

Fourteen arms lifted. We had formed two rows, with the first row taking a knee. My hands were steady, and my heart rate slowed. I took measured breaths and waited.

No matter how many times I face down hellhounds, I would never get over their horrifying appearance. Their eyes locked on us as they came closer. They never showed fear because they didn't feel it. Their brains were a one-cell organism living for death.

"Fire," I yelled.

One hound made it through the first volley. The standing archers fired as we reloaded. The single hound fell along with others behind him. They would be too close soon, but each row could get off two more rounds before we retreated.

Through the center of the horde, something emerged. The hounds were horrifying, but this creature was worse. It was more than double their size. I froze when its red-tinged eyes zeroed in on me. His jaw widened, and disturbingly huge teeth emerged in a semblance of a smile. He swept aside the hellhounds nearest him and charged.

"Retreat," I cried.

We turned and ran. Shadow Warriors interrupted the charge. Someone cried out. Then a Warrior's head flew a few feet away from me. If they couldn't hold the line, my archers didn't stand a chance. We had to protect the children and get to the larger force of Warriors.

"Run," I yelled.

I didn't turn and look at the sounds of death behind us.

The thing with the hellhounds was Knet. He would not kill my children.

More Warriors ran toward us. I saw Trevor and held up my hand to stop him from running past us.

"Knet is with them, and at least one Warrior is dead," I said as I gulped for air. "I need to get my archers in the windows, and your Warriors need to protect the tunnel entrances."

He stared at me for a moment. His gaze finally focused on the road behind us.

"Cal, take three Warriors and guard the entrance to the tunnel with the children. The rest of you with me. We stand our ground here. Knet is with the hellhounds."

The Warriors split into two groups.

"Hurry," I told the archers. We lifted our bags and ran again.

"There, there, and there. Find a window and hold your ground until you're out of arrows, then run for the nearest tunnel entrance," I directed. "The rest of you are with me."

We took the stairs two at a time until we were on the top floor. I had a baby less than a month ago, and my lower body ached from the long run. Adrenaline pumped through me, but I knew when it wore off, I would most likely collapse from exhaustion. I would kill my share of hellhounds before that happened.

The first group of monsters rushed in without Knet leading them. Where was he? We fired from eight different windows, working in tandem with another archer. I had two arrows left.

"When you're out, run," I told the man behind me.

"Si Señora," he replied, fired, and then stepped back for me to have my turn.

I had one arrow left when he turned and ran. The others around me retreated and I was the last one there. Over fifty hounds fought against the Shadow

Warriors below us. I looked for a hound that wasn't engaged when my bow was ripped away.

I barely had time to turn when a clawed hand encircled my throat.

Knet.

Thoughts snapped through my head. I wouldn't see my children grow old. I would never feel Beck's arms wrapped around me again. I was about to die.

Knet lifted his other hand while mine went to the knife at my waist. He saw the movement and gave me his demon smile. My hand closed around the pommel, and his hand waited to strike, the grin never leaving his monstrous face.

Claws grabbed Knet's shoulders and ripped him away from me. I flew to the side. I didn't know if Knet's claws had punctured skin or not. My fingers closed around the knife as I watched Trevor fight Knet.

Within seconds, I knew Trevor wouldn't win. Knet was larger and more powerful. The giant jaws opened, then closed on Trevor's throat. I saw my last arrow laying a few feet away. I dropped the knife, scooped up the arrow, and charged.

I went for the back of Knet's neck and shoved with all the force I had. I turned my head, knowing I would most likely die when the incendiary device detonated.

The small explosion took me off my feet. I landed on my ass with blood in my eyes and pain in my hands. Did I have hands?

I lifted the blackened appendages and saw stubs where fingers should be. I lay back and draped my arms on my chest. I stared up at the ceiling.

"Missy?" a raspy voice said from a great distance.

I turned my head slightly and saw a very bloody Trevor. His head was still connected to his neck and I guessed that's why he was able to talk. I giggled then gasped as pain radiated up my arms.

"Tell Beck it was me who killed Knet," I whispered as the light around me faded.

"No, dammit, you will tell him."

"Did we win?" I whispered.

Trevor was putting something tight around my hands. I didn't think it would matter. I forced the words from my lips again.

"Did we win?"

"Yes, now rest. I'll get you to Kenneth."

The world went dark.

Chapter Forty-One

Marinah

WE WAITED QUIETLY, HIDING in trees or taking cover in the dense foliage.

"Eagle is coming," one of the Warriors higher than my position called out.

I jumped down and intercepted him.

"They're ten minutes behind us. Soldiers, not hell-hounds. I think they're holding the hounds back in case they're attacked again."

"Rest a mile from here, and we'll meet you after we take care of the soldiers."

"Got it," he said. He waved his teams to follow him.

King's arm went across my shoulders. "Ready?" he asked.

"More than ready."

We faded into the swamp.

The camouflaged uniforms didn't hide the noise the soldiers made when they trampled through the mud and undergrowth. King and I had discussed the red stripes before we left the island. If they laid down their arms and took a knee, some might survive. We had to end this war. If they opposed us, they would die.

Red stripes showed predominantly on the arms of the soldiers in the lead. The Federation's fodder. Then came their well-trained military troops. We had hundreds of Shadow Warriors, but even though the soldiers outnumbered us, they didn't stand a chance.

The chorus of cicadas, usually deafening, fell silent.

We attacked.

Gunfire erupted.

The thick, humid air filled with the acrid scent of gunpowder quickly. I ripped a man nearly in half with one clawed hand. Next, a woman's head went flying with a strike from my other arm. We plowed through their soldiers, knocking guns from their hands and methodically killing them.

"Hold the line!" a human voice barked.

Bullets flew at us. Shadow Warriors went down. I kept moving forward.

I killed two men at one time by slicing their throats with my claws, picked up a woman and threw her at four soldiers. I was on them before they realized what happened. Even if I were trying, I couldn't keep track of how many soldiers I killed. They fell around me; their dying screams filling the swamp.

I eventually noticed soldiers running away.

"Throw down your arms and go to your knees, if you want to live," King shouted at the retreating red stripes.

There was a group of about twenty-five thirty yards from us. Several turned and dropped their weapons. The others quickly followed and went to their knees. All had red stripes on their sleeves.

Warriors chased the soldiers who kept retreating.

The men and women who surrendered watched their fellow soldiers die.

I growled low in my throat, and they turned. Their expressions showed that they expected death. I kicked a rifle out of a woman's reach.

"Do not move," I said.

The woman closed her eyes as I gathered more weapons. Warriors stepped in to help. Once the area was secure, I looked at the men and women on their knees.

"Rise," I said.

They looked at each other while I waited. First one, and then another rose.

"Cuff them," I said.

Shadow Warriors held flex cuffs on their straps. The soldiers were cuffed to each other.

"Head that way," I pointed in the direction we came from. "Another group of Warriors will point out the direction to take in about a mile. If you run, you will die in the swamp. If you lift a hand against one of mine, you will die. I am giving you one chance to survive. Start walking."

A woman stopped; the man cuffed to her jerked to a halt a moment later. "Thank you," the woman said.

I nodded.

A group of our men assisted Axel with the wounded Warriors.

The dead Federation soldiers at my feet left a hard knot in my gut, but it was too late for them. I lifted my sword and sliced through the first intact neck I came to. Other Warriors began the grisly task of beheading the fallen. From the corner of my eye, I noticed Desmond helping. He was too young for this but war was war and it always affected the young. I found two men alive and dispatched them quickly. They would not have survived their wounds.

King returned twenty minutes later. "Dead?" he asked and looked at the carnage around me.

"Dead for good," I replied.

"You're wounded," Axel said.

I ignored his statement. "What about our men? How many did we lose?"

Axel grumbled but answered. "Thirteen dead. Another twenty-two critical but they have a chance. Sixteen wounded but they are upright and healing. Now it's your turn."

"There's no time," I told him.

"Then why am I here?" he demanded.

"Because you're a pain in my ass. I don't have any serious wounds." I held up a clawed hand. "This is enemy blood."

King walked over and glared. I ignored him too. I need to check on Eagle.

He grumbled but pointed to my right. Eagle's men were lifting the injured and transporting them to Alpha 1. Eagle directed them but stayed behind after they left.

"We wait here and rest," I said.

Thankfully it was a large patch of dry land.

Axel examined me and complained even when he discovered the blood did in fact belong to the enemy. I was too tired to give him a hard time. He checked King and Eagle who were fine. Alden had a bullet in his upper thigh. Axel got to work and had it removed quickly. He then went man to man, in search of more injuries. He should have returned to the plane with Eagle's team, but the stubborn man wouldn't leave my side.

Just as sunlight came over the horizon, explosions lit up the sky about two miles from us. Our planes were taking out the Federation camp. It was time to run again.

"Return to the landing strip," I told Alden.

"My leg is good and is mostly healed. I can run."

I stared at him for a moment then nodded.

The ground beneath our feet rumbled as more explosions detonated. I heard an engine overhead and looked up. One of our planes roared above us.

When we arrived, the Federation camp was in disarray. Fires burned throughout.

The red stripes battled the hellhounds that managed to escape from the semi-trucks. We joined their battle and as long as they didn't turn their weapons in our direction, we didn't stop them.

After the hellhounds were defeated, I stood in even more carnage. The red stripes dropped their weapons and silently looked at us. Rifles were hurriedly collected.

I wanted the soldiers in charge. All that was here were red stripes. Where the hell were the commanders?

"Marinah," an unknown voice said behind me.

I turned and gazed at a man in his twenties with a red stripe on his uniform. He looked vaguely familiar, but I couldn't place him.

"I'm Terry Aims. I lived in Landan's camp. I was caught while patrolling."

I *had* seen him at Landan's outpost. He'd lost about twenty pounds, and his red hair was filthy, making it appear brown.

"We won't fight you." He waved his hands at the other red stripes. "We will fight with you, if you will have us?"

"Can you trust these soldiers enough for them to carry weapons?" I asked.

"Yes," he said. "They know the truth. They want the Federation destroyed as much as I do."

"Come with me," I said, walking away from the others. "I'm looking for those in charge."

"They're cowards and they left an hour ago," he said.

"Land, air, or vessel?" I asked.

He smiled. "By land in armored vehicles." His dull eyes brightened. "We've been placing salt in the gas tanks for months. It corrodes metal parts throughout the fuel system. It takes weeks to cause problems, and if we're lucky, they won't get far."

I smiled back at him, and he grimaced slightly. Shadow Warriors were not attractive in Beast form, and my display of teeth would make any non-Shadow Warrior cringe.

"Is President Barnes with them?"

"Yes."

"What about his wife?"

"She's more than his wife. She made the serum they injected into us. She's known as the brains behind the president. She's with him."

Fuck me. They would both die, and if I were lucky, my claws would have the honor.

"I was told there were more veteran soldiers here than red stripes." We'd killed a large number but it wasn't the number I was led to believe it was.

"They made some soldiers put on uniforms without the patches. It's always been one of their tactics." He looked around the camp before his eyes swung back to me. "I don't think you need to worry about veteran soldiers any longer."

I wasn't sure how to feel about this revelation and wasn't sure I could trust it.

"Move out," I told the Shadow Warriors. I turned to Terry. "If you and your group can keep up, follow us. We're going after the president. If one of you turns against us, you all die."

"We will keep up," Terry said.

The vehicle trail was easy to find. Once more, we ran.

According to one of the maps that Stevens gave me, there was an old highway three miles from our current location. We had to reach the vehicles before they hit the highway. Hopefully the salt in the tanks would make our job easier.

"Can you increase your speed?" I asked King.

He leaned over and rubbed his giant maw against mine. "We train for this."

I smiled. "Let's get Barnes."

We left Terry and his group in our dust, though dust wasn't the correct word. Muck, maybe?

One of the Warriors ran ahead and climbed a tree. He pointed to the east. "They stopped," he called out. "Several have their hoods up."

"Take three," I said, and it was passed down the line.

They crouched where they stopped. We were breathing deeply and needed a minute or three to align the part of ourselves that made us Warriors. King crouched beside me. I closed my eyes and took slow, deep breaths, using the limited time to meditate. I pushed K-5 through every part of my body, starting at my toes. It strengthened Ms. Beast, and she let out a hum of satisfaction. No sign of Nova, but she appeared when she pleased, and I wouldn't let thoughts of her hijack my meditation session.

Gone was any sense of peace Nikayla or the Shadow Women gave me. My mind was filled with bloodlust and revenge. The meditation focused my mind. The Barnes' would die.

CHAPTER FORTY-TWO

Beck

OUR SENTRIES REPORTED THAT the enemy camp was on the move. Our children and non-combatants were relocated to the Tully Outpost. Carmen stood on my right and Landan on my left.

Carmen and her group of mayors were approached by the Federation and asked to act as spies. It enabled us to feed the Federation the wrong information. Carmen knew where the future lay and it wasn't with the enemy.

"Is everyone ready?" I asked.

"My people are in position," Carmen said.

"Mine too," Landan added.

"It will take twenty minutes for the Shadow Warriors to get here after the attack begins. Can you hold out that long?"

"We don't have a choice," Landan said, "but we do have a few surprises."

"Do I need to know what those are?" I asked.

"No time," he replied then smiled. "But it's a good plan."

I rolled my eyes. I regarded Landan as a friend but sometimes I wanted to strangle him. I throttled the desire.

Twenty Warriors were hidden around the road the Federation would be using. Their job was to create chaos. That was more my style and I was joining them. Enough planning. I was ready to rip some heads off.

I found my men spread out on a steep incline looking down at the advancing soldiers who were roughly five hundred yards away. We stayed in human form. If something went wrong, we didn't want the Federation alerted that we had a large contingency of Shadow Warriors in the area. We needed them to attack the main outpost.

"There are six semi-trucks," the lead Warrior, Jackson, told me when I landed next to him.

"What's the troop count?"

"A thousand, maybe a few more."

I picked up the field glasses next to Jackson and gazed at the column of soldiers. Their commanders rode in open top military jeeps dressed in pristine uniforms with cocky hats that made them look like fools. The hats didn't shade their eyes or offer more than minimal sun protection. They were simply ornamental covers. The only way they would stay on was with glue. My lips turned up at the corners. I would need to pull one off to find out. Hopefully it would be painful.

"They're acting like this is some sort of military parade," Jackson said.

"They think they made a deal with some of the outposts and they're cocky."

"Would the mayors turn on us?"

"No. All the children are at Carmen's outpost and the Federation is attacking Landan."

"Heard the Federation's new Shadow Warrior recruitment slogan?" Jackson asked.

He was known for his bad jokes but I took the bait anyway.

"No, what is it?"

"Join us, we offer free dental and manicures."

"Can I push you down this cliff just to hear you scream?"

"You know you wanted to laugh."

I showed him my very human teeth and clacked them twice. "If you're done with the bullshit, you need to join your men. It's time for me to stir up trouble."

Jackson was leading our main group of Shadow Warriors who were purposefully lagging far enough behind the Federation troops that they wouldn't be seen. They would attack from behind during the battle. Jackson took off with a tip of his non-existent hat.

The line of soldiers and vehicles slowly rolled past our location. The perfect opportunity finally came. I tracked the rhythmic sway of the last semi-truck in the convoy. My hand went up signaling to the small group of Warriors around me to hold their position. Timing my jump with the subtle bounce of the trailer, I coiled my legs and launched from my position. There was a soft, almost imperceptible thud when I landed. The heavily armed soldiers marching on either side of the truck didn't notice.

I pressed myself flat against the warm, corrugated roof. Sixty seconds passed before I moved. My fingers found purchase on the back edge, clenching the metal until my feet found purchase on the narrow lip of the trailer's rear. The smell of diesel and dust was obnoxious to my sensitive nose. With one hand, I slowly reached for one of the heavy, rusted lockrods. I felt the satisfying click as the first rod disengaged, then the second. The large, double doors of the trailer were now unlatched.

I pushed the right door inward a few inches, just enough to confirm the cargo. Low growls rumbled from within. With a swift, powerful kick of my right foot, I sent the door slamming back against the trailer's side, opening it completely.

A torrent of snarling hellhounds tumbled out. They hit the ground with grunts and became disoriented for a split second before their predatory instincts kicked in. I scrambled back to the roof, my body going flat against the metal again.

The first screams were music to my ears. A grim smile touched my lips. The soldiers, caught completely off guard, stumbled and cried out as the monstrous hounds tore into their ranks. I peered over the side. Blood splattered the asphalt. Simultaneously, my Warriors, still in their human forms, opened fire from the roadside, spitting precise bursts into the pandemonium, aiming for the soldiers who hadn't yet been overwhelmed. One of my men launched a grenade with a practiced flick of his wrist. It landed with a dull clang amidst the struggling mass of men and monsters.

The ensuing explosion was a concussive roar followed by a shower of dirt, debris, and torn flesh. I launched myself from the truck, landing lightly on the ground amidst the swirling dust.

I scrambled up the rocks and melted back into the shadows of the cliffs and joined the Warriors.

Strike one complete.

CHAPTER FORTY-TWO

Marinah

"How MANY UNITS ARE down?" demanded a general. His voice was deep and carried in the open area.

He was easy to identify since he was nice enough to wear three stars on the lapel of his uniform.

"Too many. Our only way out is on foot," one of the red stripes answered.

"The fucking president does not go on foot," the commander yelled.

"I have two vehicles that are operational," the unfortunate man replied. "You would need to leave the hounds behind."

We hid twenty feet away. King was on the opposite side of the road. This was too easy, and something told me I wasn't seeing the entire picture. A man walked up to the two military personnel, and they both saluted.

"President Barnes," the higher official said.

"Why aren't we moving?"

Thoughts filled my head. We had a major problem. That man might look like the president, but it wasn't Barnes. Had Terry betrayed us? I signaled the Warriors to fall back. We made our way deeper into the swamp until King approached me.

"That wasn't Barnes," he said before I could.

"No, it wasn't."

"Terry?" King asked.

I shook my head. "I don't think so. It looks similar to Barnes, and if it were Terry, their vehicles wouldn't be damaged."

King growled.

"He could be anywhere by now," I said feeling frustration build inside me. "This was a decoy. They blew up their camp after we attacked it by air. They wanted us inside the camp and we evaded them."

King thought about it for a moment. "I want that fucking bastard. He can't escape."

"We need to head back to the harbor and find someone who knows where the hell Barnes is."

"We need rest," King said.

"I can keep going," I told him.

"All of us need rest and calories, or we'll be no good."

He knew how to get to me. I nodded. "Not here. I want us further from the fake president."

I turned and saw Terry. His face and those of his men were flushed. One vomited.

Terry had not betrayed us. It took only a few seconds to put the pieces together in my head. I waved him over and relayed what we'd seen.

Worry flashed in his eyes. "I know it was the president in the camp. If there's a decoy now, Barnes is still in the area," he said, looking defeated. "Are the soldiers on the road still alive?" he asked.

"Yes, we left them trying to figure out what to do."

"The other two vehicles won't make it far. With permission. Allow us to go after them."

"You're more exhausted than we are," I told him.

His jaw hardened. "You were right," he said, barely keeping the emotion from his voice. "We couldn't keep up with you, and if you are going after Barnes, we'll get there after the fight. The commanders in that convoy," he pointed in the direction of the road, "gave the order to inject us with their shit. They also gave the orders to kill some of these men's families to supply the semi-trucks with hellhounds. We want blood and we want our loved ones released from their hell. I'm asking you to give us a chance to pay them back."

"Those two vehicles could make it further than you think."

"I don't care."

"My Warriors need rest, and we need a place further away from here to do it safely. We won't be able to come to your aid."

"If we die, we die helping the cause. I'll ask the men, but I know what their answer is."

"Ask them," I said.

Terry and his group left fifteen minutes later. We gave them two days' worth of supplies. We found a location on higher ground an hour later. It kept us out of the swamp. King brought me a plate of food along with his own.

"I might be too tired to eat," I told him.

He took my clawed hand and turned it over, examining my palm. "It looks like you, but I don't think it is."

"Ha ha. I don't eat all the time."

"It would be impolite for me to disagree."

"Fine, I'll eat," I grumbled.

We began the ritual with our usual silence, though I didn't feel hungry. "I miss her," I finally said. "There's a hole in my heart, and it's killing me."

King placed his plate on the ground and pulled me into his arms before I could set mine down. He then situated me between his thighs.

"Eat."

The hole was still there, but the contact with my mate helped. He felt Nikayla's loss, too.

We finished our food, and King leaned back against a trunk with his arms still around me. Shadow Warriors liked it warm, and even in the humid heat, the feel of his arms let my mind rest until I fell asleep.

I woke instantly when he squeezed me.

"Three hours," he said to let me know how long I'd slept.

I yawned, turned my head, and gave him a pointed stare. "What about you?" I ground out.

His jaw did its rendition of a smile. "Yes, I woke up a few minutes before I woke you."

I was still tired. I looked around and saw the Warriors were no better off. Yawns and stretches took a few minutes as we gathered ourselves for the next run. The sun would go down within two hours. If we didn't hit major obstacles, we would be at the shore an hour before nightfall.

The radio crackled.

"This is Mike Two. We've got a Sierra in the harbor."

The radio went silent.

"Mike Two rendezvous in sixty."

Mike Two was one of several Warriors we left hiding outside the Federation camp to keep an eye out if anything changed. We were en route within five minutes.

We didn't encounter problems and had an hour of sunlight by the time we located the bay. Besides the water splashing against the shore, it seemed eerily quiet.

"Something isn't right," I told King.

"It's too quiet," he said.

I looked at a single ship and pulled out binoculars. I scanned the vessel slowly. Uniformed soldiers stood on the deck in key locations. Moving the binoculars back again, I noticed something strange. No movement.

I did it again.

"They're decoys dressed in Federation uniforms," I told King and handed him the glasses.

"Fuck. They're running us sideways."

"Yep. The crew must have slipped into the water and made it to shore. I need the other paperwork Landan provided from the area. We've got to find Barnes."

King left, then returned with the satchel that Stevens had given me. I pulled out the papers and rifled through them until I came to the one I'd glanced at before. New Orleans had a tunnel system along with catacombs. I myself wouldn't use the catacombs due to the probability of hellhounds, but the Federation was collecting the hounds, and the catacombs were a maybe. Each tunnel had a name that connected to another document that provided a map of that tunnel or tunnels.

Harvey, Belle Chasse, and the Houma Tunnels were possibilities. There were also service and utility tunnels, others abandoned and unused, and last were the catacombs. I flipped through the papers and handed King the info on three of them.

"Check through these. We're looking for the most likely tunnel system near here."

"New Orleans has a tunnel system?" he asked.

"More than one. President Barnes likes underground spaces. I guarantee he's set up in one of them."

I examined the maps closely. Houma Tunnel had an asterisk next to it. It was outside New Orleans and too far.

"This group of utility tunnels has promise," King said a few minutes later.

I was studying the Harvey Tunnel and only half listening.

"Look at this," King said and placed the map in front of me.

It did have promise, but Barnes wasn't there. I passed the Harvey Tunnel map to King. A minute later, he grinned. He saw exactly what I saw. It was large enough and perfectly located.

Nokita joined us.

"The figures on the ship are dummies," he said.

"We came to the same conclusion. President Barnes likes tunnels, and we think we know where he's at."

King handed him the Harvey map.

"Son of a bitch," Nokita said. He looked up, and his eyes wandered to the bay again. "Are we supposed to board that ship?"

This is what I got for having Barnes on the brain. I hadn't thought about the ship being a trap.

"That makes sense," I said. "I think we'll pass but we'll give them a reason to think they're plan worked. Radio alpha 2. They have a couple of spare bombs waiting to help."

My thoughts turned back to Barnes, and I included Lesley in those thoughts. They had become one and the same in my head. I lived underground for years. Lived in fear and uncertainty. The island had been a sanctuary of sunshine and hope. I was no longer the fearful Marinah, and she would never come back, but still the dark, endless, sun-free thought of tunnels sent a shiver down my spine. Destiny said this would end where it began.

Thirty minutes later, the ship in the harbor exploded.

"Let's find Harvey Tunnel," I said after the debris settled.

Chapter Forty-Three

Beck

WE MANAGED TWO MORE strikes and killed over one hundred soldiers and eliminated approximately the same number of hellhounds. They still had a large contingency of soldiers, but they were wary, which muddled their unit. Fear was a powerful weapon.

Through the field glasses, I saw one of the commanders walk up and down the line of troops, yelling something at them. I could hear the bellow but couldn't make out the words. His uniform was no longer pristine, which made my smile grow.

We took time to rest while we waited for Jackson. My brain wouldn't shut down. I missed my family and worried about them. Missy had changed my life.

Love was not an emotion I'd felt until I met her. Or more precisely, she shot me out of the sky. I was raised by my father, and he was not a kind man. He owned a farm and believed in hard work and no play. He literally worked me until I could barely walk. I stayed exhausted even as a young child. My teachers sent notes home saying I fell asleep in class. I became very good at forging his signature because I hated having my ass beat. I was unlucky enough to be born to the one Shadow Warrior who didn't appreciate children.

Now I had a son and a daughter and understood that my father was simply a cruel man. He taught me what not to be.

Ruth was a hellion, and I loved her just the way she was. And then there was Barrett. His small, innocent eyes followed me across a room. I never thought I would have a family or know love like I did now, but the minute I laid eyes on Missy, that view changed. Wanting her wasn't just sexual; I craved her in every fiber of my being. She was an amazing woman and a challenge. The fact she didn't put up with my shit only made the deal sweeter.

They would be okay. The island was the safest place for them. And still I worried.

Jackson finally arrived. We set off at a fast jog to make up time. A plume of smoke rose above the town, and we ran even faster. When we topped the ridge, all hell had broken loose below. The air in the outpost was thick with the acrid stench of burning wood, mingling with the metallic tang of fresh blood. The hellhounds tore into human flesh, indiscriminately killing both those who wore uniforms and those in civilian clothes.

We were now in Warrior form. I led the charge. The outlying homes were demolished husks, engulfed in flames that licked at the sky. I felt a grim satisfaction that this particular destruction hadn't been the Federation's doing. Landan and Carmen had most likely detonated the homes when the soldiers entered the town.

My attention snapped to the nearest hellhound, a hulking mass of muscle. I moved, a low growl rumbling in my chest. It spun, sensing my approach, and leapt, its fangs bared. I sidestepped the attack and raked my claws across its throat. A wet, tearing sound filled my ears. Before it could fall, still thrashing, I grabbed a Federation soldier with my other hand, his surprised grunt cut short as I slammed his body into the wounded hellhound. The beast, in its frenzy, bit the man's arm, nearly severing it with a sickening crunch. I delivered another brutal slice of my claws, taking its head off. The hellhound's body collapsed, and the soldier rolled to the ground, his eyes staring blankly at the smoke-filled sky. My gaze swept the chaotic scene and found something else to kill.

Minutes felt like hours. I dismembered, I tore, I crushed. The air thrummed with the impact of my blows, the cries of the hounds, and the desperate screams of soldiers.

Suddenly, two hellhounds, larger than the first, landed on me at the same time, their combined weight threatening to pin me. Their claws raked at my fur-covered limbs. I tore them off, one with each hand, and clapped their heads together. I wedged one beneath my armpit to secure it, and with a savage twist, I severed the head of the other. I released it and let its body flop to the ground. The other hound wrenched from my hold. I faced it, and it came in low, aiming for my legs. I anticipated the move and grabbed its head. With a surge of power, I swung the snarling beast around like a grotesque club, knocking down two soldiers who were attempting to flank me. I brought the hellhound's thrashing body up, its legs flailing, and with a final, brutal thrust, I impaled it on a jagged, broken piece of farm equipment. It was a rusted plow blade that protruded from the wreckage of a blown-up barn. I quickly killed the soldiers.

Slowly, the sounds of battle grew weaker, replaced by the groans of the wounded and the crackle of burning structures. The sporadic gunfire became less frequent, then ceased.

My beast wanted to continue killing, but I throttled him as I noticed the outpost's humans stood upright in the middle of the dead. A few cheers went up. Slowly, others joined in.

It was a good day to die, but a better day to live.

CHAPTER FORTY-FOUR

Marinah

THE FEDERATION SET UP the entrance to the Harvey Tunnel much like they had for their last set of tunnels. Tents and trailers surrounded the entrance. When I had lived below ground, they had also set up explosive devices to bring the tunnels down. When I had returned at the Federation's request, we had barely survived. They would use the same fail-safe.

When we captured Lesley Barnes, we'd marched in wearing Federation uniforms like we owned the place. It wouldn't work again.

"We go in tonight," I said.

King, Nokita, Alden, and Eagle sat in a circle with me. "We slip in after midnight," I continued. "Twenty

Warriors should do it. There won't be enough room for a larger force. Our main troops should attack an hour after we get in or immediately if we're spotted."

King looked at me, and I knew I wouldn't like what he said.

"We need a night to watch their guard activity."

No, I didn't like it.

"The longer we stay here with this large of a force, the greater chance we're seen," I said. "If that happens, we won't have surprise on our side, and Barnes will slip through our fingers again."

"Our main force can move a few miles away," King said stubbornly.

Why did I argue when a little bird in my head said he was right?

"Vote," I said.

I lifted my hand in favor of his plan and King winked at me. Waiting was the hardest part and I was sick of it.

That evening, King and I took watch together. We'd found a good spot where we could see the camp and the surrounding area, so no one snuck up on us. We were too close to the enemy for speech and simply watched and waited.

It went quiet at eleven and not much stirred after that. I played scenarios in my head that would give us the best advantage but mostly I was bored. The

Federation guard changed at 2 a.m., and at 3, Eagle and Nokita came to relieve us.

I slept in King's arms. When I opened my eyes, the sun was higher than I expected. King was still out, and I lightly ran my hands over one of his braids. It wasn't as long as when I first met him because we cut our hair in order to look like Federation soldiers when we took Mrs. Barnes. King's hand flew up and captured mine, bringing me in close so he could kiss me. It wasn't much of a kiss because of our fangs, but it still gave me the warm fuzzies.

"I'll grab food," I told him. "I have an idea to get into the tunnel."

We ate our breakfast quickly. Nokita and Alden wandered over.

"Where's Eagle?" I asked.

"He's on watch. He'll be off in another hour."

"Okay," I said. "We'll meet as soon as he returns. He can sleep afterward." I zeroed in on Nokita. "Bring Desmond with you for the meeting."

When they left, I stretched each part of my body and then sat for ten minutes of meditation beneath a large tree. I'd used disassembling and reassembling my rifle as a way to clear my mind. Now I used Nikayla. In my head, I lay back on the bed, pillows propped behind me while she nursed. I could almost smell her. She opened her eyes and stared at me while she fed. Trust and love showed in her gaze, and I couldn't look away. I slowly counted her fingers and toes because it's something prewar parents did. I thought of my mother. She would have loved Nikayla. I remembered my mom's arms around me when I scraped my knee learning to ride a bike. When I stopped crying, she told me a story about learning to ride her bike.

"My older sister would ride at breakneck speed, and I couldn't keep up because I had training wheels. After I learned to ride without them, she snuck away so I couldn't follow."

"What happened to your sister?" I'd asked.

"She died many years ago. I still think about her. The pain of losing her is still bad, but life continues, and you need to take each precious step you're given."

Thinking about my mom was still hard. Her and my father had hidden the fact that I was Shadow. It bothered me that I couldn't ask them why. They loved me like I love Nikayla. They had their reasons, but I would like to have answers.

"Marinah?"

My eyes snapped open.

"You need to eat before the meeting," King said, handing me food.

Our freshly prepared meals had run out, and now we were stuck with MREs. Yum, my favorite, not!

Nokita walked up with Desmond. The young man's entire persona was different. He no longer looked like the same angry kid he'd been two weeks before. With the children he and his sister took care of, he felt useful. Then he was thrown in with Shadow Warriors on an island that was well-run and needed little from him. But he was a born fighter, and it's where he excelled. My question was could he remain calm and act like someone he wasn't? We were about to find out.

After Alden and Eagle joined us, I laid out the plan.

"I can do it," Desmond said. A creepy grin formed on his lips.

"Then we're set."

We waited in our hiding spot while Desmond did his thing. We were still covered in mud, but we'd caked more on him. We added a few rips to his clothes, and he took off one shoe.

"Help, help," he cried, running into the camp.

"Halt," one of the guards yelled and pointed a rifle at him.

"They're chasing me," he sobbed.

"Who's chasing you?" the man demanded.

"Hellhounds. They killed my father. Help, please," he went to his knees, almost kissing the guard's shoes.

A female guard squatted by his side and placed her hand on his back. She spoke low, and we couldn't hear her. Desmond threw his arms around her neck and cried. There may have been real tears. As far as acting went, it was a little over the top if you knew the kid but the soldiers appeared sold.

"He's good," King whispered.

"Too good," I replied.

My mate shrugged.

The woman stood Desmond up, and he began talking. He turned and pointed behind him then waved his hands before grabbing onto the woman again.

"And we thought fighting was his specialty," said Eagle.

Within five minutes, they led him into the entrance of the tunnel without having searched him. A group of ten soldiers formed and took off in the direction Desmond had pointed. Nokita would see they didn't return.

We waited thirty minutes before Nokita took care of the problem and came back. "Anything?" he asked.

"Not yet. His best chance will be at night."

It seemed like this entire mission was hurry up and wait.

CHAPTER FORTY-FIVE

Marinah

A LITTLE AFTER 2 a.m., Desmond crawled into our makeshift camp. He held his finger to his lips because he knew as well as I did that noise traveled in the stillness.

"I found another way into the tunnels," he whispered. "I couldn't get through the main exits because there were a lot of guards. There's a small door with only two guards outside of it down a narrow hallway."

"What happened when you were inside?" I whispered back.

"They fed me and found me a bed. Suckers." He chuckled quietly.

"How did you get out?"

"The guards are stupid and they were half asleep. I was worried I couldn't kill them both before one of them sounded an alarm. They heard a noise and went to see what it was. That's when I got my chance."

He was sneaky and smart. The kid was going places, though I didn't think he should go with us.

He noticed my face in the moonlight. "I did the most dangerous part. You can't leave me out of the fight." Anger flashed in his voice.

He was right. He deserved to go, but he was so damned young, and I was terrified something would happen to him. I nodded, and his shoulders relaxed.

Our Warriors would circle the two main entrances and attack if it were necessary. They were warned that the tunnels might explode if President Barnes escaped. They also knew Barnes would sacrifice his men to kill us. King, Nokita, Desmond, and I were going after Mr. and Mrs. Barnes. Alden would lead the Warriors. Eagle would set up his sniper rifle and cause havoc if it were needed.

The two guards were asleep when we found them. We slit their throats. Desmond showed us a small trap door that would be a tight squeeze. One of us had just given birth and was carrying a few extra pounds. My stretchy Warrior pants were tighter and proved it. I silently growled over what would happen if my ass got stuck.

I made it with King's help and had a nice scrape on my upper hip to prove it.

I stood slowly and gazed into the darkness though my Warrior eyesight helped me see. It smelled of damp earth and stagnant air. Something buried inside me triggered. My stomach clenched, and an unwelcome knot tightened my gut. I had spent years in tunnels. Every breath I took had been recycled. Death bit at my heels inside those small spaces. For two years, I was one step away from red stripe duty.

Apprehension pricked the edges of my mind. It was a sensation I hadn't felt so acutely since King came into my life. Or I guess, I came into his.

"Ready?" King asked.

He touched my face, then released me. His presence was an anchor. I nodded, unable to trust my voice just yet. Some part of me wanted to scream no. Tunnels were where I had been weak.

I took the first step. The dirt floor was soft and squishy beneath my bare Warrior feet. The air immediately grew heavier. The only sound was the echo of my too-loud breathing. King realized something was wrong and squeezed my hand.

This was stupid. Where the hell was the fear coming from? Hell, I hadn't thought twice about entering the tunnel when we captured Lesley Barnes. It hadn't been dark, though. Then it hit me.

Nikayla.

I had so much to live for and I wanted to see my daughter again.

Fuck you, Ms. Beast. You should be controlling this, I said internally.

Kill, she whispered back.

That's not helping. I called on Nova. Nothing.

I inhaled slowly. I was a Shadow Warrior, and I would do this. My daughter would rest in my arms again. I squared my hairy shoulders.

A steady drip of unseen water surrounded us. No sun. No sky. Only walls. *No*, I was falling back into the disastrous hole of fear. Ms. Beast stirred, and a low growl grew in my chest. She remembered the fear because she was part of me, but she was not afraid. If she whispered, "sissy," I wouldn't have been surprised.

I stopped walking and turned my head back toward King. "Barnes is here," I whispered. "I can smell him." His scent and the need for revenge were my guiding force. Fuck my memories. I needed to kill the president and his wife.

"What the fuck?" a man yelled when he almost ran into me.

I grabbed him around the throat, and he made a gurgling sound.

We froze. Did his shout go unnoticed?

The blare of an alarm filled the tunnel.

"Get Desmond," I told King over the noise.

Desmond was pulled forward so we could hear each other.

"How far are we from the president's quarters?"

"Don't know," he said. "I didn't get anywhere near him, but there was a hallway with guards stationed at the entrance."

That had to be it.

"How far?"

"Fifty yards, maybe."

I started running.

We turned a corner, and bullets exploded, causing me to pull back. King placed a dagger in my hand. I had my own, but he must have had his out. We were at a T junction.

"Backup," I yelled over the sound of gunfire and the alarm.

I took three steps back and launched myself into a low slide, crossing to the other side, and released the dagger at the midway point. Someone cried out, and the gunshots stopped for a moment. King flung himself around the corner and barreled toward the men. Another gunshot sounded. I was right behind him, and Desmond behind me, stupid kid.

King killed two of the men, and I grabbed one and twisted his head until I heard the vertebrae snap. Desmond stabbed another, and Nokita finished him off.

The alarm stopped, and the tunnel lit up. I squinted into the flood of light.

"Are you hit?" I asked King.

"Yes, shoulder, not serious. We're doing this."

At the end of the long, straight tunnel, a group of soldiers appeared from another intersecting shaft. They moved in the opposite direction from us. In the middle of their formation, I saw Lesley Barnes in a white nightdress. Two soldiers followed, and then President Barnes came into view.

My vision went red, and I started running.

King stayed close behind me. More gunfire rang out. I didn't care. A bullet entered my side, and I barely felt it.

The soldiers went through a metal door and tried to close it, but I was too close and threw my weight against it.

"Push," a man yelled from the other side.

They didn't stand a chance. I shoved with my Shadow Warrior strength, and they flew backwards. I barreled inside a room that was maybe twenty by twenty. The soldiers had landed on their asses and were trying to gain their feet. I didn't concern myself with them. A scream and a grunt sounded behind me. King took them out.

I grabbed a soldier standing between me and the president and flung him into Barnes. Lesley headed to another door. A guard was trying to push her through. Strangely, she stopped and turned toward me. She held a gun in her hands. I charged the president.

King launched himself at Lesley, knocking her away from the door. She twisted and fired at King point-blank.

Fuck.

More gunfire exploded, and I saw Nokita leap over a table and take down two soldiers with the spread of his arms.

I grabbed Barnes around the throat and spun so he was between me and the last two soldiers. They turned and ran through the door. A moment later, they backed into the room, their hands in the air.

Lesley was on the floor, her back to the wall, the white gown around her, and the gun aimed at King, who had fallen. A circle of blood spread beneath him. He wasn't moving.

"This time I'll shoot him in the head. He won't recover from that," Lesley said.

Her eyes told me she was going to do it anyway. She glanced quickly at the exit door and smiled.

"Ace, I'm so glad you're joining us. Stay there while I explain a few things."

I stared at the bipedal creature before me. He had massive, clawed hands and thick skin that looked almost armor-plated but with short charcoal grey hair. His back was hunched and his body was very different from his Warrior form. The head was distinctly canine, similar to a hellhound, but something more. His open jaws revealed long fangs that extended past his upper and lower lips. The inside of his mouth and his tongue were deep red. His eyes seemed to glow. A thick, spiky mane erupted from his neck and shoulders. A prominent, lighter-colored ridge ran down the center of his forehead and snout. The broad, muscular chest was covered by fur, and the long, dark claws were larger than mine.

Oh Ace, my heart cried.

The president whimpered.

"Shut up, you stupid fool," Lesley yelled at him.

"She's going to kill me," he croaked.

"No, she's not," his wife said. She turned the gun and fired again.

I felt the impact but the bullet didn't pass through the president's chest. She was using hollow points. I almost laughed.

His body went limp, but I kept him as a shield.

"He was nothing more than a simple-minded dimwit," Lesley yelled. "I had to put up with him for years. I ruined your little plan to kill him, didn't I?"

Lesley Barnes was insane.

She laughed. "I did everything. Each scientific discovery was mine. The entire plan was mine starting on day one. He took the credit and received all the glory while I was forced to stay in the background. The fools actually named him president."

Saliva dribbled from the side of her mouth.

"You warped the formaldehyde?" I asked calmly, wanting answers. One of King's finger's twitched.

"Me, you bitch. It was all me." She laughed again. "Men are too stupid. They think with their dicks and only see the small picture. I envisioned the destruction of the entire damned world. I'm the genius and they wouldn't listen to me. I even had to fix my husband's stupid mistakes. The hellhounds got out of hand because of him. He needed the Shadow Warriors to fix the fucking problem he created. I wanted to kill all of you from the beginning. You were far too dangerous, but again, the idiot wouldn't listen to me." She was panting now, trying to get it all out so I could see the genius she claimed. "Then your worthless father took over the Shadow Warriors. He had a soft spot for them. Or I thought he did. It turned out, his daughter *was* one." Her laugh turned into a cackling sound that sent shivers down my spine.

My mind raced with questions. "What about the electromagnetic pulses?" This had bothered me for years.

"What about them?" I could almost see the wheels in her brain turning. "Oh," she laughed again. "You thought they were connected to the hellhounds.

You're as big of a fool as your father. Hellhounds and electromagnetic pulses have no connection. We used thermonuclear fusion deep beneath the earth's outer crust to throw the government off our scent. That was my idea, too. I would go into more detail, but you're too stupid to understand." She glanced at Ace, who remained still, then looked back at me. "The U.S. government had lost all credibility in this country and abroad. We were a laughingstock, and the administration left me no choice. While the men in charge picked their noses, I did what had to be done. I am the brains behind the Federation."

Evil leaked from her pores. Because of her, millions of people died. I didn't care if she was clinically insane or completely sane. She would be next.

"Do you really have a cure for the hellhound serum?" she asked snidely.

"Yes," I lied. "But you'll never get it." I wanted her to die thinking that she would turn into one of the monsters she created. I couldn't think of a more fitting punishment.

"I'm not sure I believe you," she scoffed, "but even if you do, hellhounds are only the beginning. I'm making a new breed of monster." She gestured toward Ace. "He's my crowning glory. His kind will be under my control, and just think, you brought Shadow Warriors to my doorstep."

Her gaze dropped to my side where I'd been shot. I could feel the blood running freely. "You and your monster are going to be mine. She glanced at King. Or maybe he's dead already." She smiled again.

Ace shifted slightly toward Lesley. I was waiting for him to attack me. Nokita stayed back. I didn't see Desmond.

"Isn't he a work of art," Lesley said, turning and smiling at Ace for a second.

When her attention came back to me, he took another small step in her direction. It seemed odd.

"I'll kill her," Desmond yelled from beneath one of the tables. He held a gun leveled at Lesley. He was six feet away, closest to the thing Ace had become.

"Protect me," Lesley yelled at Ace.

The creature turned its head in my direction and stared at me for two seconds. Then he lunged at Lesley and grabbed the gun from her hand. His other hand circled her throat. Her eyes grew large, but she could only squeak. He kept squeezing and dug his claws into her neck. He pulled sharply, and her head came off in his hand. Blood sprayed across the walls in all directions saturating her gown.

Before I could move, he looked at me, brought the gun to his head, and fired.

My brain was having trouble keeping up.

He fell on top of Lesley, but he wasn't dead. His eyes stared into mine. His low, growly voice filled the room. "I can't control it. Take my head."

I stared at him, understanding he wanted me to kill him. He'd saved our lives, and this is what he asked. I stood frozen.

King materialized in front of Ace and severed his neck with a powerful swipe of claws. For just a second, before Ace died, his eyes showed relief.

King fell again and landed face-first. He didn't move. I dropped to my knees. The Barnes were dead, and I didn't care. My hand slid through King's blood. I grabbed him and turned him over. He'd taken a bullet to the chest. Blood pumped from the wound with every shallow breath he took. A rasping scream filled the room.

It was mine.

CHAPTER FORTY-SIX

Ruth

WE WAITED IN THE tunnels. Some Shadow Women held children, some entertained them. One group sang funny songs, and a smile escaped me a time or two.

Mostly, I waited for an attack. I looked at Julia and saw the same look in her eyes. We couldn't trust the Shadow Women to defend us. We stood between life and death for the children.

I had watched hellhounds tear my father apart. My mother and I barely escaped. I wouldn't run again. Maylen asked me to take her head if she died. I knew I could do it. If I'd been injected with the hellhound shit, I would want the same thing. I couldn't remember the little girl I had been once. Death and war were what I remembered. The kids on my team hadn't had it as bad but they had all lost someone. We were tired of being insignificant and a liability.

My friend Che sat against the stone wall, holding a small sword. Che's father and then his stepfather were killed by the monsters. He was too young to battle hellhounds on his own. I was too, but I now had a team standing with me, and we would kill the enemy.

Waiting was the hardest part. It was something Marinah told me and she'd been right. I was worried about my mother and glanced over at my baby brother, held by a Shadow Woman. He slept peacefully and had no idea what we were facing.

Julia and I were becoming friends. She didn't see me as a child. I was only a year younger than her. I knew part of her story, but she wouldn't talk about most of it. Her brother, Desmond, had gone with Marinah. She was worried about him. Desmond fascinated me. He seemed older than he was. I hoped he would be okay but I knew that there was always a chance he wouldn't return.

Suddenly, the walls shook, and small rocks and dust rained down from above.

"The tunnel has been breached," a Shadow Woman said loudly.

I jumped my feet. The women grabbed children and placed them in the far corner establishing a defensive wall around them. Maylin had injected them with the serum that hopefully would protect them from a hellhound bite or scratch. No one knew if it would work because they didn't shift to Warrior. They had no claws or teeth and I had no idea how they would protect the children. If they couldn't fight, they were only good for babysitting. My mind snapped back to the present as the sound of scraping claws and muffled growls filled the tunnel. A few children cried, but I wasn't afraid.

I'd watched the hellhounds kill too many people. One day it would happen to me. I wanted to die fighting. Togg placed his hand on my back.

"Like we've trained," he said.

I nodded, then looked toward the entrance.

The first two grotesque shapes materialized. Togg, in his Warrior form, leapt in front of me and attacked the hounds. Julia and I spread further apart. The other kids on our team did the same. Togg killed the first two hounds and grabbed at two more, but one broke free.

Julia struck first, and I came in from the other side. Its claw almost got me, but I was too quick. Our group fought just as we had trained. It was my strike that ended its life. There was no time to cheer because another broke past Togg. No, two.

A Shadow Woman landed on one. I was shocked because she attacked with a blade. I hadn't realized any of them were armed. I thrust my sword into the side of the hellhound in front of me, pulled back, and another one of our team came in low and stabbed its gut. Che took the next swipe. He was supposed to be behind the line of Shadow Women, but I should have known he would fight.

He stayed in close and didn't pull back. I grabbed his shirt and jerked him away. Then it was my turn again. We took the hound down.

I was breathing hard as I looked for another. Togg clamped a hound in his jaws and tore its head off. That was pretty cool. I would never have teeth or claws, but I had a bloody sword in my hand, and that was cool, too.

I glanced behind me and saw the Shadow Women facing the entrance, each with a knife in their hands. Two of them were injured by hellhounds, but it didn't look serious, at least if the serum worked.

"What do we do?" I yelled at Togg.

"The hounds made it through, and that means the guards are dead. We need to block the entrance so the hounds can't get as close."

Our team followed Togg. Yes, he was bossy, but he never treated me like a child. I wasn't that old yet, but there was no time to be young when people all around me died.

The door separating the tunnel from daylight was torn off its hinges and lay a few feet away.

"Explosives," Togg explained quietly.

That meant there were human soldiers somewhere. They had sent the hellhounds in.

My back straightened. The soldiers would know that children were down here, and they didn't care.

"What do we do?" I whispered to Togg.

"We wait. If we go outside, they'll take us out. Move closer to the walls and stick to the shadows."

We followed his direction. It seemed like forever before a man stuck his head in and then pulled back out of sight.

"Block the tunnel again, and we'll let the hellhounds finish them," a soldier said.

Togg sprang forward and burst outside. The sounds the soldiers made were horrible. Julia was in front of me. She was the only one with a gun, and a shot rang in my ears. A soldier fell. I ran forward and brought my sword down on his neck. It took four strikes to take off his head.

Togg fell back with a soldier in his grasp. Several shots rang out, and Togg's body jerked. I stabbed my sword into the soldier's side. Togg rolled over and released the man.

Julia fired again, and the soldier stopped fighting. The smoke from the gunfire wrapped around us. Several of our team ran forward and looked outside. Someone yelled, "Clear."

"Guard the entrance," Julia shouted at them.

I dropped to my knees by Togg.

"I'll be okay," he said.

I wasn't sure what to do. He didn't sound okay, and blood was seeping past his hands and claws where he held his stomach. His head fell back.

"Togg?"

"I'm good," he said softly.

He wasn't good.

"Did you get scratched or bitten?" he asked me.

"No, we're okay."

"You're a hell of a fighter. I'm glad I was able to help you train. It's been an honor."

"Togg," I all but shouted.

I pressed my fingers over his and shoved my weight down to stop the bleeding.

"Honor," he said again, but this time much softer.

Maylin dropped on her knees beside me. I'd forgotten about her. She could fix him. She worked with Axel all the time.

She peeled back our hands to examine the wound. She looked up at me and shook her head. When I looked down, I could see his intestines and so much blood.

I took Togg's hand in mine and rubbed my other one over his fingers.

"It's been my honor," I whispered to him.

He looked up at me, and his jaws pulled back. He grinned showing all his teeth. His eyes glazed over with the grin in place.

Chapter Forty-Seven

Marinah

AFTER FIGHTING WITH AXEL over the fact that the gunshot wound in my side was nothing, I gave into his glare and lay on a damned cot beside King.

Axel had performed his usual miracle and removed the bullet from King's chest. He'd had to suction air from the chest cavity due to a collapsed lung. Another bullet was removed from his shoulder. King was breathing comfortably, his body healing.

Now it was my turn, and Axel grumbled the entire time.

"Here's the thing," he said. "If you die from a wound I can't fix, King will kill me. If he dies, you will kill me. I'm stuck between two crazy people with a death wish. What's a doctor to do?"

I rolled my eyes.

He decided it was a good time to dig for the bullet. I grimaced and glared.

"Got the sucker," he said with a smile.

"You enjoy dishing out pain," I said while trying to breathe.

"The wound had almost closed over. That's why it hurts so much. But, if I thought making these procedures more painful would make you stop, I would have no problem hurting you needlessly."

"You're all heart."

"Marinah."

My head whipped around. King was watching me.

"The Barnes?" he asked.

"Dead."

"Good."

"Casualties?"

"We lost fifteen Shadow Warriors. One of the tunnel entrances exploded and took out half of them."

King closed his eyes.

"You almost lost one more," Axel said. "Your chest wound was a millimeter from your heart."

"I have the best doctor in the whole damned world. Why would something like a little bullet worry me?" King asked with a smile in his voice.

"The two of you were made for each other."

I reached my hand to King's, and he squeezed my fingers. "Finally, something we can agree on," I said.

****

King

I watched the fourth aircraft fly off with Warriors onboard, heading back to the island. Desmond, who had a few bruises but was otherwise unhurt, was on the plane. Marinah and I would leave in a few hours.

Terry and his group didn't return. Marinah sent out a team to look for them. But there was no trace of anyone including the commanders. All they found were the disabled vehicles. If Terry and his men died, they were now hellhounds. It saddened Marinah but there were no do overs.

Red stripes had laid down their weapons after our first attack on the tunnels. Several had died in the explosion that killed the Warriors. They hadn't known about the explosives but it didn't matter. They had decided not to support the president and small groups of them had been slipping away every week. Even without the war against the Shadow Warriors, the Federation was losing ground.

Marinah's guard, minus me, systematically killed hellhounds they found in more semi-trucks. The red stripes helped. Nokita said some were their relatives.

Axel guarded the tent to make me lay on a cot while all the work was done. Marinah and her team located Lesley Barnes' files. They also found cases of light pink serum that changed humans into hellhounds. Marinah stood by and watched everything burn.

I'd seen the thing Ace had become. If he thought he could control himself, he wouldn't have wanted to die. He would receive a heroes funeral.

If there was a hell, Lesley and her husband resided there with their secrets.

We received news from the island several hours ago. Nikayla was safe, along with the other children.

Marinah wasn't the only one who longed to hold our daughter.

Twelve hours later...

We stepped off the plane.

Endura and Amissa stood watching us, Amissa holding a tiny bundle. Marinah had Nikayla in her arms a few seconds later. She hugged her to her chest until Nikayla began to fuss.

"We have a car waiting," said Endura.

"She's grown," Marinah said in wonder. She glanced up at me. "Look how big she is." Marinah's eyes held a touch of sadness with the overwhelming joy.

We had been away for four days.

Nikayla was wrapped in a lightweight cotton blanket, and honestly, I couldn't tell if she'd grown a quarter inch, but I grinned and took a slow, deep breath. Marinah was holding our child, and I could finally relax. I looked around.

"Where is Beck?" I asked.

"With Missy," Amissa said. "She was injured in the battle. She lost three fingers, but she will survive."

Axel walked over and peered at Nikayla. "She has grown," he said. "We'll need to weigh her."

"Give me a day," Marinah scolded. "You will not pry her from my arms for the next twenty-four hours."

He smiled and ran his finger over the top of Nikayla's head. "Twenty-four hours it is."

We finally made it to our room. Marinah fed Nikayla while resting back in my arms on the bed. We took turns holding Nikayla while the other one showered. Now we sat in bed admiring our child and neither of us could stop smiling.

We'd heard about Togg. In all, one-hundred-twenty-two Warriors died, and a little over two hundred humans. That included those aboard our submarine. There would be a week of funerals and time to mourn. For now, we celebrated life and our family.

Change loomed before us but we would have time to discuss our future later.

Chapter Forty-Eight

Marinah

"I'M PUTTING HER IN her bed," I told King.

He looked surprised but released me from his embrace. I laid Nikayla in her crib and walked back to the bed. I scooped Callie up and placed her on the cushion she seldom used that resided in the corner of the room. She didn't seem happy, but I ignored her sharp cry of hostility.

King's eyebrows rose.

I whipped my shirt over my head and slid out of my pants. I straddled King and looked down into his eyes. He tried to say something, but I placed a finger on his lips.

"Shh," I said. "I've healed. Being a Shadow Warrior has amazing benefits."

I leaned down and kissed him. King's arms went around me, and he rolled so he was on top. He stood quickly and divested himself from his clothes while I watched.

His chest wound was merely a small pucker of skin. I didn't give it more than a passing glance because his muscled chest and powerful arms held my attention. He slid into the bed and kissed me again.

We explored each other's bodies like it was the first time. My hands traveled over every inch of taut skin I could reach. The feel of him sent an electrical current clear to my soul. One of King's hands ran from my thigh, over my waist, and to one breast. A pearl of milk came from my nipple when he gently squeezed. He leaned down and licked the drop.

"You taste delicious," he said.

I rubbed my lower half against his erection. "I promise I feel better than I taste," I moaned.

He moved over me, his powerful body hard with desire. Usually, we spent time on foreplay, but it had been so long, and I needed him inside me. Slowly, pushing deep, he entered me. I stared into my mate's eyes. His warmth was quickly turning to a scalding heat that continued to rage.

I lifted my hips, and he started a slow rhythm. I sank my fingers into his hair, and my head went back. He kissed my neck and groaned as our bodies danced to the rhythm within us.

Slow was good but fast was better. I rolled us so I was on top again and showed him exactly what I wanted. My hands went to his chest, and I lowered myself.

"Try to keep up," I whispered.

I ground against him again and again, his hard length filling me. Our breathing grew ragged as each thrust took us deeper into bliss. I continued riding him until I lost control. He flipped us again and ground into me. My orgasm went on and on. Finally, he joined me and groaned my name.

I lay in his arms, my fingers playing with the hair on his chest.

"I no longer feel my Nova," I said.

"Did you need her during the fight?"

"No."

King slipped to my side and looked at me. His finger came out and rubbed across my lips.

"Such a wicked grin," he said.

"You are once more the leader of the Shadow Warriors."

He huffed out a laugh. "God forbid," he said. "What if there is no leader of the Shadow Warriors? We separate from the others and live out the remainder of our lives in peace. I like that idea."

"It does have a nice ring to it. As the short-term king, you'll need to tell Beck. The poor man may never recover."

King laughed. "I'll make you a deal. What if we tell him together, we can both see him lose his shit one last time?"

"I love you," I said.

King pulled me closer and whispered in my ear. "I love you."

EPILOGUE

Marinah

Three years later...

I F WISHES WERE HORSES, we would operate a horse ranch, and that's exactly what happened. Our plan to ditch the Shadow Warriors was a pipedream. They followed us. Well, most of them. Nokita and Caleb stayed on the island with their mates. We visited them every six months so we could catch up, and our children could play together. Rodrigo was now in charge of the island and doing a damned fine job.

A year after we settled in the U.S., Landan stepped down as governor of the outposts to enjoy more time with his growing family. In the election, Missy, Beck's mate, was named the new governor and resided over twenty communities. The loss of her fingers and part of one hand, never slowed her down.

Beck married her in a large ceremony six months after the last battle with the Federation. Missy was our hero for killing Knet. Her legend continued to grow, and it brought more people into her territory. Now Beck ran interference for her and became her problem, though I doubt she minded.

Our dream of a world without war wasn't what we thought it would be. There were oftentimes rumblings that someone was trying to form a new government and overthrow Missy. They could easily start communities of their own and form a government. Many had. But there were still those who sought power and domination over everyone.

Beck had enough Shadow Warriors and humans to put the talk down quickly. He'd formed a large militia, and they took care of business when it was needed. No one wanted a president or king. Hopefully, it would stay that way.

Mail was a problem in the U.S., and it gave us the idea for the horse ranch. King loved horses, which was something I hadn't known about him.

Alden, Eagle, and Axel came with us, which meant Garret came, too. They had a medical outreach program that needed horses. Their home base was a small property a mile from ours. They took on two additional orphaned children and had one of the largest families in the community.

Alden and Yamila had not worked out and he had yet to find a mate. He lived in our bunkhouse along with other Shadow Warriors who didn't want their own property.

Eagle and Julia became an item a year ago after she turned eighteen. Eagle was nine years older than her and it took a bit of doing to bring him in line. He wanted her to have more time to grow up. Julia put a stop to his stupidity. They had just moved into their own place.

Our herd of horses had grown substantially, and we provided what the new mail service needed. Letter writing was back in style. We saw automobiles occasionally, but they were older models that needed constant work. Horses were the general mode of transportation.

Hellhounds were still a problem, though on a smaller scale. We never found an antidote for the insidious injections spearheaded by Lesley Barnes. Maybe one day. The hounds were still attracted to technology. The upside was it kept the male carriers busy.

Desmond and Julia came with us and fit perfectly within our new lifestyle. Ruth lived two hours away, but she spent more time at our place than with her busy parents. Her little brother exasperated her endlessly because he could do no wrong in his parents' eyes, or so Ruth complained. She and Desmond hunted hellhounds together whenever she was here. Her crush was becoming more obvious each day, but Desmond ignored it and treated her like a sister. In a few years, he wouldn't stand a chance.

"Mommy," Nikayla said, running up to me, her curls all over the place and no longer in the band I'd secured them with earlier. She had a smudge of dirt on her face, mud-caked hands, and her coveralls, which were all she would wear, had more than a smudge or two. From experience, I knew her cherub face, that made you want to squeeze her tight, was deceiving.

I leaned over and tickled her sides until she giggled.

"Mommy, stop, I need to show you something." Her excitement was contagious, regardless of what was on the other end of it.

I hefted my pregnant body up from the chair. This time, Axel wasn't putting up with my crap. He swore if I rode a motorcycle or horse, he would lock me away until the baby was born. King backed him and kept a constant eye on me.

I still trained with my sword daily, but I had slowed down and didn't take the same risks I had when we were at war. Ms. Beast was in heaven, and her whispers of "baby" every ten minutes were getting old.

I followed Nikayla to our largest barn, her small hand tugging mine.

"Look," Nikayla said. "Daddy says he can be mine when he's old enough to ride."

I'd heard one of our mares had a foal the night before, and eventually I planned to check on mom and baby. She was one of our best mares. The foal was a beautiful dark bay with a classic star on his forehead and the long, wobbly legs of a newborn. The colt was the son of our largest stud and looked just like his father. The stallion was hell on wheels, and King was the only person who could stay in the saddle when he acted up. Nikayla would be five when the colt was old enough to ride. King would be sorry he made that promise.

"He's small now, but he's going to grow really big," I told my stubborn daughter.

She placed her hands on her hips and glared at me, seeing through my efforts. "Daddy said," she insisted. "I've already named him Starfire."

King and I would be having our talk sooner rather than later.

"Here you are, Nikayla," the man in question said as he entered the barn.

"Daddy," she squealed and ran to him. King picked her up and twirled around once before setting her down. "I named him Starfire, and mommy thinks he'll grow too big for me, but I'm growing too, and he's mine. You said he was."

King looked at me and grinned before turning back to his exasperated daughter. "He'll take work, and you'll need to learn a bunch about caring for a horse, but I keep my word." He covered his heart with his hand, and I growled. He had the utter nerve to wink at me.

"Amy made a batch of cookies, and she's waiting for you to taste test."

Nikayla didn't look back as she ran from the barn. She was capable of calming an entire room if she wanted to. She could also cause chaos, which seemed to be the stage she was in right now. No terrible twos. Her terrorizing ability came at three.

King held his hands up before I got started on the lecture he deserved.

"He'll be gelded in six months. If he's not a good mount, I'll break the news to her. I felt she needed to learn about raising a horse from the beginning, and he'll be a good bit of work for her."

"She's three." I glared.

"Going on thirteen." He smiled and walked toward me. His arms circled most of me. "How are you feeling?"

"Like a whale."

He laughed and shook his head. "A very beautiful whale."

"You think that makes me feel better?"

He leaned in and kissed me. It wasn't just a peck; it was a full-blown, "let's fool around" kiss. He scooped me up and carried me to a clean pile of hay at the back of the barn.

"What are you doing?" I asked.

"I'm hoping to make out with my wife."

"Your very pregnant wife."

He kissed me again, and I reciprocated because, hell, he was damned sexy, and I craved him even more with my hormones on overdrive. I knew it wouldn't go far because people walked in and out of the barn all the time.

Someone cleared their throat a few minutes later, and we broke apart.

"There's a fence down in the north pasture, and I wanted to know if you were planning to help, but I'll grab Alden," Desmond said with a disgusted look on his face.

This wasn't the first time he caught us in the hay.

King stood and helped me up. I pulled hay from my hair and dusted myself off.

"I'll be right there," King said. "Give me a minute."

Desmond turned and walked out.

"I promise, the horse will be perfect for her," King said.

"You'll keep that promise," I told him. "Go play cowboy, and I'll see you this afternoon."

He walked away with a chuckle. I moved to the stall and took a closer look at mom and baby. Callie walked over and circled my legs, begging to be picked up. Of course, I obliged.

I absentmindedly rubbed her head.

Our lives had changed so much.

Amy, our cook, was the soldier I'd saved on the island. She sometimes went hellhound hunting, but mostly, she ran the house, kept our supplies up to date, and managed the bunkhouse.

My Nova hadn't materialized in over three years. Cosway thought it was because of the meditation and my ability to control my rage. I thought it was because of Nikayla. Something happened deep inside me when she was born. I was completely vegetarian again and fully at peace. If anyone on the ranch wanted meat, they hunted it and kept it out of my sight.

Cosway had helped us start the ranch. She lived in a small apartment above one of the barns. She disappeared at regular intervals and came back with an assortment of animals who became part of the family.

Amissa and Endura visited often. The Shadow Women had formed their own community and were in Missy's territory, too. They would be helping us after the baby's birth. They had also helped me translate my great-grandmother's journal, along with the texts. Combining the men's and women's texts, we filled in most of the missing pieces. The home planet did not have a good history, and we were determined not to repeat their mistakes. My Grandmother Veda's insights were interwoven with sections of her mother's journal, which I hadn't understood until we pieced it together. Both these women inspired me to write my own journal.

Amissa had visited the day before and told me King and I were having a boy. She also told me his name.

The mare walked over for a nose rub, and I lifted my hand from Callie's head and gave her what she wanted. Like Nikayla, the name spoke to me. I let Callie down and placed my hand on my stomach.

"Your name is Samuel," I said softly, and smiled.

Baby, Ms. Beast agreed.

The End.

Thank you for reading Marinah and the Apocalypse! I have another post-apocalypse, paranormal novel titled Blood Promise. It's not a series but you will enjoy. Visit wickedstorytelling.com to learn more about me and my book.

Thank you,

Holly

About Holly

Holly S Roberts is an award-winning author which includes appearing on the USA TODAY list multiple times and selling more than one million books worldwide. Her career as a homicide and sex crimes detective kept her in the romance genre for a decade because she needed happy endings. After years of therapy and speaking publicly on matters close to her heart, she turned her pen to dark survival thrillers with kickass women that encapsulate her unique perspective. Max, her Rottweiler, is never far from her side because he listens when she has plot problems and offers rare insights when encouraged with cookies.

www.ingramcontent.com/pod-product-compliance
Lightning Source LLC
Chambersburg PA
CBHW070236200726
48293CB00005B/1648